# THE OTHER SIDE OF SILENCE

# Ted Allbeury

# THE OTHER SIDE OF SILENCE

CHARLES SCRIBNER'S SONS
NEW YORK

Copyright © 1981 Ted Allbeury

Library of Congress Cataloging in Publication Data

Allbeury, Ted.
    The other side of silence.

    I. Title.
PR6051.L52085   1981   823′.914   81-9119
ISBN 0-684-17309-3                AACR2

1 3 5 7 9 11 13 15 17 19 F/C 20 18 16 14 12 10 8 6 4 2

Printed in the United States of America.

Things fall apart; the centre cannot hold;
Mere anarchy is loosed upon the world,
The blood-dimmed tide is loosed, and everywhere
The ceremony of innocence is drowned;
The best lack all conviction, while the worst
Are full of passionate intensity.

Surely some revelation is at hand;
Surely the Second Coming is at hand . . .
. . . . . . . . . . .

And what rough beast, its hour come round at last,
Slouches towards Bethlehem to be born?

> *'The Second Coming'*, W. B. Yeats

# 1

The snow lay thick on the steps and the snowflakes driven by the wind looked black in the headlights of the cars. There had been no snow when he went inside although the clouds had hung black and ominous over the square. But there was no point in complaining about snow in Moscow in November.

He turned round to look back at the lights in the building. The KGB man standing in the entrance hall was still watching him. He turned up his coat collar and looked up at the sky. The Red Flag still fluttered on its pole in the yellow light from the floodlight at the corner of the roof. Despite his irritation he recognized that the blood-red flag with its hammer and sickle was romantic. It had a beauty and majesty that was undeniable. It gave him the same feeling he got when they sang 'Land of Hope and Glory' at the last night of the Proms. You didn't need to agree with what it represented. It just moved your heart and made you think for a moment of mankind in general. Number 4 Old Square was the offices of the Central Committee of the Communist Party of the Soviet Union. Not to be confused with the building next door which housed the Moscow Regional and Moscow City Committees of the Communist Party.

They were so stupid with their po-faces and their suspicious eyes. All he had asked for was a ball-park figure for Party members as a percentage of the total population. But after three different officials and an hour and a half of waffling they had blandly stuck to their story that they didn't know. He pointed out that Brezhnev himself had announced in public only a year ago that it was six per cent. All he wanted to know was if the figure had altered. Why should he be interested in such information, they asked? They had waved aside his journalist's accreditation pass, but a surge of bloody-mindedness had kept him pressing for an answer. He knew well enough that he only had to telephone Baskakov at Novosty and he'd get the figure to three decimal places. But like any good journalist he had thought it was better to go to the primary source.

They were their own worst enemies with foreign pressmen but that was their worry. He only had another couple of months to go in Moscow and there had already been hints from Bracken House that his next assignment might be Washington.

He brushed the snowflakes from his eyelashes and with his head bent he walked into the driving snow. He had been walking for several minutes before he realized that a man was walking alongside him. He glanced sideways at him and briefly noticed the lined face and the lack-lustre eyes before he bent his head again. He had just realized that he vaguely remembered the face when the man spoke. In English.

'Don't you remember me, Tom?'

He had just turned the corner into Nikitnikor Lane and he stopped to look at the man's face again. The man was half-smiling, that cynical set of the mouth that had almost become a trademark. The man took his arm and said quietly, 'Let's keep walking, we can shelter in the church.'

The Church of the Georgian Icon of the Mother of God had survived intact since it was built in 1658. One of those Russian fairy-tale buildings that generations of masons and architects had trimmed and ornamented until it had become a kind of history of Moscow architecture, period laid on period. He had done a freelance piece on it two years before, for the *Architects Journal*.

As they approached the church Farrow saw that despite the cold and the snow one of the massive doors stood half-open, casting an orange swath of light across the soft folds of snow that covered the church steps. And there was the smell of wood-smoke and incense as they walked inside.

The church was empty apart from an old *babushka* in black who was kneeling at the foot of the altar steps. When she coughed the harsh sound echoed eerily in the shadows of the vaulted roof.

Farrow waited as the man gazed slowly around the church and then followed him to the row of wooden chairs on the right-hand side of the church. Only as he sat down did the man take off his fur hat and turn to look at Farrow with searching, wary eyes. Farrow tried to work out how long it had been since he had last seen him. It would have been at the press conference at his mother's flat in Draycott Gardens. He guessed it must be almost twenty-five years ago.

'It's been a long time, Tom. Over twenty years.'

'Nearer twenty-five. How are you?'

The man smiled. 'Older but not wiser, I guess.'

'I heard that you were refusing to see journalists these days.'

'It got a bit tiresome. I had to draw the line somewhere.'

'I've just been to the Central Committee offices.'

'So I understand.'

'You knew?'

'I'd heard that you'd asked for an interview.'

'Why haven't you been able to get over to them that they're their own worst enemies?'

'What did you ask them?'

'The percentage of Party members to the whole population.'

'Why didn't you phone Tass or Novosty, they'd have told you?'

'I wanted it from the horse's mouth. What the hell harm can it do?'

9

'You could be writing a piece claiming that the low percentage indicates lack of support for the Party.'

'Oh, for God's sake we all know that it's bloody difficult to become a Party member.'

'The average Britisher doesn't know that.'

'It's been said and written often enough.'

The man smiled. 'I saw a piece in the *Telegraph* a few months back about a survey in East Anglia that showed that only two per cent of those questioned could name the Foreign Secretary or the Home Secretary. They aren't going to remember a piece in the *Guardian* about the structure of politics in the Soviet Union. Do you really want to know the percentage?'

'Of course.'

'It's six point two five per cent.'

'Does that include *Komsomols?*'

'No. They don't always get Party cards.' He smiled. 'Don't quote me as your source. Check with Novosty.'

'What are *you* doing out in the cold, cold snow? I should have thought you'd be at the Bolshoi in your best bib and tucker.'

'I wanted to see you.'

'You could have phoned me for God's sake.'

'I could have. I didn't want to.'

'I'm bound to report to the Embassy that I've talked with you otherwise I'll end up in the Scrubs one night under suspicion.'

'Suspicion of what?'

He laughed. 'Either defecting or writing another biography about you.'

'I want you to give somebody a message for me.'

'Why don't you phone them or write to them.' Farrow's reluctance showed all too clearly on his face. 'I heard that letters do come through from you from time to time.'

'This is a personal message. A confidential message.'

10

'Who to?'

'A man named Padmore. Arthur Padmore.'

'Who's he?'

'A prof at one of the colleges at Oxford.'

'I thought you were a Cambridge man.'

'I was. Still am I suppose.'

'What college is it?'

'St Anthony's.'

Farrow smiled. 'Ho, ho. What was Arthur Padmore? MI5 or MI6?'

'MI6'

'And what's the message?'

The wary, observant eyes looked at Farrow's face. 'Tell him I want to come back.'

Farrow swallowed slowly. 'You're kidding.'

'I'm not. I'm serious. Very serious.'

'They'd sling you in the Tower the moment you landed at Heathrow.'

The man shook his head slowly. 'They wouldn't, Tom. Anyway, just tell Padmore that I want to come back.'

'Why don't you contact the embassy?'

'You know better than that, Tom.'

'Do I get an exclusive on this?'

The worn face creased into a smile. 'It would be you in the Tower if you breathed a word about it. I've got to ask you not to tell anybody about this. Not your paper, not your wife or your girl-friend. Nobody but Padmore.'

'Who said anything about girl-friends?'

The blue eyes smiled but they were several shades colder.

'I'm thinking of the pretty one. The one in the flat in Islington. The one who looks like Britt Ekland. Mary Cooper, aged twenty, a tele-ad girl on the *Daily Mail*.'

'Jesus wept. Where did you pick that up?'

'Don't worry, my friend. We all do it. Just remember that

11

old Royal Navy toast – "To sweethearts and wives, may they never meet".'

'When do you want me to contact Padmore?'

'As soon as you can.'

'But I can't just swan off to London like that. I'm not due leave until Christmas.'

'Book a flight out for tomorrow. I'll give you a reason to go.'

'What is it?'

'You promise that you'll tell nobody but Padmore?'

'Yes. If that's what you want.'

'It is.'

'What's my excuse then?'

'It's not an excuse, it's a reason. On Friday afternoon or early evening the Special Branch will be arresting a Russian from the Trade Mission at Highgate on charges of spying. He'll be picked up at the entrance to Sloane Street underground station. His photograph and a reasonable amount of background material are in an envelope in my pocket. You'll be the only newspaper man who even knows his name. Is that enough?'

'Yes of course.' He looked at the man's face. 'Why do you want to go back, Kim?'

Philby sighed and half-smiled. 'Maybe I'd like to see the Australians at Lords just once more.'

He stood up. 'The envelope's on the floor. Bend down and pick it up after I've gone.'

'How can Padmore contact you?'

'He'll know how.'

'Cheers.'

'*Da svedanya.*'

Farrow saw a taxi with its green light on at the corner of Ulitsa Kirova and was back at his one-room apartment just before eight o'clock. Still in his wet coat and damp shoes he phoned the Intourist Service Bureau for a flight to

London. They would call him back in an hour, the girl said.

He draped his coat on a chair in front of the radiator, stuffed his shoes with an old copy of the *Financial Times*, and then headed for the bathroom.

As he lay soaking in the bath he went over in his mind what both of them had said. In a way it was a journalist's dream. To be the only man who knew that Kim Philby wanted to come back. He could make a fortune. Auction the story maybe. But of course Philby would deny ever having met him. That was probably why he had made it the furtive meeting in the street. Then there was the obvious threat to tell his wife about Mary. Kathy would raise real hell. Probably divorce him. If Philby knew all that, did it mean he'd used the KGB in London to find out? And if he had, that must mean that the KGB knew what Philby was up to. Of course he could have given them some other reason for wanting to know. The more he thought about it the less he liked it. But there would be no problems if he just passed the message to the Padmore chap. He would have his reward with the exclusive on the arrest of the Russian in London. It wasn't *Financial Times* material, but he could do a deal with the *Mail* or the *Express*. He could plead problems at home for his return for a few days. Two sexy days with Mary, a day at home, and then back to Moscow. Five hundred or a thousand better off into the bargain.

The long buzzes of the telephone roused him from the bath, and he wrapped a bath-towel round him as he dripped into the main room. It was Intourist. He was booked on an Aeroflot flight at noon the next day from Sheremetyevo. He could pay and pick up his ticket at the airport desk, or Intourist on Karl Marx Prospekt. Check-in time was 10.45 at the airport.

13

# 2

Powell stood looking out of the big windows across the river. The sky was a pale, wintry, blue-green, and the Thames was a heavy, leaden grey. The high tide was giving the small police launch a rough ride as it headed towards the South Bank jetty, and the traffic in Westminster Bridge Road already had its lights on although there was half an hour to go before the official lighting-up time.

He liked the new building. Not just for the view but for the facilities. There was no longer any need to cover half of Westminster to contact Central Records, Forensic, Signals, Cryptography and all the rest of them. They were all under one roof. But the three old boys hated it. They all preferred the ancient buildings that had housed the bits and pieces of SIS over the years.

Arthur Padmore was the first to arrive, nodding to him to save his breath as he took off his coat and eased the shiny black galoshes from his feet with the spike of his umbrella. He was a heavily built man with a full face that had obviously once been quite handsome. But the white hair and the way he wore it gave him an old-womanish look that took away from his dignity. He had alert blue eyes behind his gold-rimmed glasses, and he wore a Harris tweed two-piece suit that added to his bulk. He had an annoying habit of constantly touching his pockets one by one, patting them in search of items that he never found. Powell had heard that when Padmore had served in SIS during the war he had been nicknamed 'Fidget' and some of the old China hands still called him that to his face. He never seemed to take offence, but it would have been a mistake to see him as a mild old gentleman. He was far from that. He turned towards Powell, patting both of his jacket pockets.

'And how are you, my boy?'

'Fine, sir, thank you.'

'The others were notified, I assume?'

'Yes, sir. Mr Walker's already in the building and I had a call from Mr McNay to say that he was on his way.'

'Sir Ian in his office?'

'I think so.'

'I'll just have a couple of minutes with him. Call me out as soon as they're both here.'

He went off patting himself like one of Kojak's men checking for a hidden gun.

When it had first been formed in 1963 the small committee had met every two months; in 1970 it had been cut to quarterly meetings and since 1977 it had met at six-monthly intervals.

It was called the 'Milord' committee and consisted of only four men. Three of them were serving officers in SIS, and Padmore, the committee's chairman, had been SIS until he returned to his sinecure at St Anthony's. In addition to Powell, Patrick Walker and James McNay were the other two serving members.

John Powell was the officer responsible to the committee for the surveillance, as a minor and routine part of his normal duties in SIS.

When the committee had originally been formed it had only one responsibility. To establish, if it could, the identity of the person who had first put the finger on Kim Philby for the Russians. There had never been much doubt as to who the 'fourth man' was, and by the end of 1965 it was accepted that they had established his identity to everybody's satisfaction. Everybody except a judge and jury, that is. Not only would it have been impossible to prove, but it was taken for granted that a libel writ would be issued within the hour at any public hint of that man being suspect. The English laws of libel are more often used to protect the guilty than the innocent where subversion is the subject.

Even without the threat of libel the evaluation had concluded that merely to establish in court what they *could* actually prove would reveal far more than SIS were prepared to reveal to their enemies. And there was nothing much to prove anyway. He had never been involved himself. Somebody somewhere spotted the likely candidate and, depending on the man's background, somebody would make the first casual approach. And 'Milord' had been one of the Soviet spotters for the likes of Philby. The initial approach would have been ambiguous, but if the bait was taken the rest was routine. There would probably never be another contact between the spotter and his recruit. From that point a Russian professional would have taken over.

The man was no longer considered as merely a suspect. He *was* the man. They knew that. And he knew that they knew, and was faintly and arrogantly amused. But he was quick to respond when they moved too close. His suspected treason was known only to a handful of men, and he still had influence in high places. And used it. At Ascot, Royal Garden Parties, stately homes, exclusive clubs and expensive hotels there was always an observer. But there were always those wonderful English libel laws to be reached for by con men, crooks, and traitors. By now they knew that he must recognize them, but he never acknowledged that he did. A search of his house one weekend when he was staying with the outer circle of royalty had led to a solicitor's letter to the Home Secretary, who, in ignorance of what lay behind either the break-in or the letter, had responded as best he could. The solicitor had once been Solicitor-General in an earlier government of the Home Secretary's party. Referred to routinely as 'Milord' there were those, and they included

McNay, who felt that a .38 slug could save wasting a lot of time and the taxpayer's money.

John Powell had been in an orphanage on Tyneside when the other three had been scheming in World War II in the building at Broadway that purported to be an outpost of the Ministry of Labour, and he was untouched emotionally by the whole affair. He had been in Special Branch when Philby made for Moscow. Still in his early twenties, Powell hadn't known enough of the background to realize the enormity of what had happened. But the subsequent shake-up in SIS had seen him transferred overnight to the new organization. And among his new duties was the organization of the surveillance of the man suspected of being the NKVD's lookout in those distant days in the thirties, in Cambridge.

When both Walker and McNay had arrived Powell phoned Sir Ian Pouley's secretary, and Padmore came in a few minutes later, panting from the two flights of stairs.

Sitting himself at the head of the teak table he glanced with faint but unspoken irritation at the smoke from Walker's cigar. He nodded at both of them.

'Are we ready then, gentlemen?'

And without looking around he picked up Powell's five-page report and started reading it aloud. It was quite unnecessary, as the report had been circulated to all members of the committee in the previous week. Rumour had it that Arthur Padmore had once fancied his chance as a Shakespearian actor. He did have a deep, mellifluous voice but that, combined with a rather judicial air at meetings, only led to comments about pomposity trying to camouflage a plodding mind.

Powell looked at the other two as Padmore droned on. Patrick Walker had a private income, and Powell sometimes wondered what appeal SIS could have for a man with a luxury house in Chelsea and an eighty per cent shareholding in the largest independent brewery in the country. He was a

17

cultured, sophisticated man, amiable and charming; he carried his wealth and privilege lightly. Much the same age and build as Padmore he nevertheless looked at least ten years younger. His rather moonlike face was firm and unwrinkled and his eyes were always alert and clear. He had taken off his jacket, sitting with his chin on his hand. He wore a broad blue and white striped shirt and a pair of plain gold cuff links, and he half-smiled and winked at Powell as their chairman read on.

James McNay, who sat on the opposite side of the table, was definitely handsome. Tall and slim, his hair was still black, and his face, as he looked down at his copy of the report, was the face of a film star. A thirties film star, and his neatly-trimmed guardee moustache only emphasized his rather Latin good looks. But unlike the other two there was no amiability or charm about McNay. He was polite, formal, and he seldom smiled. A hard-liner on almost everything. He wore Marks and Spencer's clothing, including his suits, and he neither smoked nor drank. When Powell had first met him he thought that he must be a man with a secret sorrow. Long years of experience of McNay had convinced him that he was merely tough and efficient, and indifferent to what people thought of him. A man of sharp intelligence and an agile mind, he had apparently sometimes criticized Philby long before he was a suspect. The product of the old-boy network and his amiable charm had seemed to cut no ice with McNay. According to McNay, Philby represented unearned privilege, the arrogance of the upper classes and the phoney sophistication of the ambitious place-seeker. Those were still his openly expressed views.

There were times when it seemed to Powell that McNay's comments on Philby could almost equally well have been applied to Patrick Walker. Except that *his* charm was certainly genuine, and so was his sophistication. A large bear-like man whose self-assurance was tempered with a self-

18

deprecating humour that made it tolerable. He took his privileged background in his stride, as if it were much the same as any other man's. He hadn't been close to Philby, not even Burgess and Maclean had been close to Philby, but they had all four shared a wide circle of friends and acquaintances that had made their co-operation easy and relaxed. Walker had always maintained that Philby was no simple traitor. There was much more to it than mere treason. He listened, smiling amiably, to the bitter comments that others made on his one-time boss, and made the critics even more strident because of his obvious disbelief.

Padmore put the last sheet down on the table and looked across at Powell.

'Are there any new developments that should concern us, Mr Powell?'

'It's been pretty well the usual pattern, sir. But he's applied for various sums in foreign currency for overseas trips that have not taken place.'

'How much are we talking about?'

'Just over three thousand pounds.'

'What currencies?'

'Mainly pesetas, and a lesser amount in Deutsche Marks.'

'Has he infringed any Bank of England currency regulations?'

'Technically, yes. But there are several loopholes he could use as a defence.'

Padmore looked at the others.

'Does anybody feel like pursuing this point?'

McNay shrugged, and Walker shook his head.

'Anything else, Mr Powell?'

'The gardener we've got at his farm has developed lumbago. We're going to have difficulty getting another man to replace him.'

Padmore leaned his big head on one side and said, 'We'll

leave all that in your safe hands, Mr Powell. There are more important things to discuss this time.'

He had his academic's voice on, Powell noticed, and he spoke slowly and carefully as if his words were being delivered on a silver salver. Flicking imaginary dust from his sleeve Padmore seemed to savour having got their faintly bored attention. He looked up at them, his bushy eyebrows raised.

'Philby wants to come back, gentlemen. He sent a message through a journalist.'

There was a long silence. Powell could hear the urgent siren of a police car heading towards Waterloo Bridge. Then Walker said, 'Who was the journalist?'

'Tom Farrow.'

'Who's he with now?'

'The *Financial Times*.'

Walker laughed softly. 'How like Kim to pick the *FT*.'

Padmore looked at McNay, 'What's your reaction, James?'

McNay raised his eyebrows. 'You don't need to ask me, Arthur.'

Padmore turned to Walker, 'And you, Patrick? What's your reaction?'

'What exactly was the message?'

'Just that. That he wants to come back.'

'Any conditions. Any suggested deal?'

'Just the message.'

'Who was it to?'

'Me, personally. He gave Farrow my name.'

'How are we going to keep Farrow bottled up. Who's he talked to already?'

'Apparently Kim Philby has already done that by some means or other. Farrow hasn't told anybody and isn't intending to.'

'He could change his mind.'

'My impression was that he wouldn't talk under any circumstances.'

'Blackmail?' McNay asked.

'Who knows. Anything's possible in Moscow.' Padmore put his plump hands flat on the table, his fingers spread as if to hold it down.

'So what do we do, gentlemen?'

Powell saw McNay glance at Walker who looked away and made much of breaking off the long ash of his cigar in the ashtray. Then he turned to Padmore. 'Is he in trouble. Have we had any reports recently?'

Padmore shrugged. 'I looked at the embassy file on him. There doesn't seem to be anything special. Very few visitors. All Russian. Mainly KGB. He makes a couple of visits to Dzerdzhinski Square each week but he doesn't stay long.'

Walker smiled at Padmore. 'It could be a very interesting exercise, Arthur. Very interesting indeed.'

Padmore looked at Powell. 'What do you think, Mr Powell?'

'Has this eventuality never been discussed before?'

'Not so far as I know.'

'Has the Foreign Secretary been told?'

'No. Not yet. Apart from us, only Sir Ian knows. The message was specifically for me. He's asked us to make our recommendation.'

McNay banged his fist on the table. 'Give me one good reason why we should have him back.'

'We could put him on trial for one thing,' Powell said. 'We could find out why he wants to come back for another. And he might tell us a lot that we want to know.'

Powell's voice was calm and mollifying. But McNay was not going to be calmed so easily.

'I really thought we had heard the last of this saga. Surely it's better forgotten.'

Padmore looked at Walker, who didn't respond, and then he looked back at Powell.

'Could I ask you to leave the room for a few minutes, Mr Powell?'

Powell pushed back his chair and stood up.

'I'll be next door, sir.'

'Thank you. One of us will come in for you. I'd just like a little chat with my colleagues.'

Powell sat in the next office almost an hour before Walker came in. He half-smiled, but it was rather forced.

'Come back little Sheba. All is forgiven.'

There was an air of constraint or something odd as he took his place again at the table.

'Mr Powell. I felt it was unfair to involve you in our consideration of this problem. You have little knowledge of the background to all this. It was a long time ago. There are conflicting views on the whole episode of Philby. But just because of that, I felt that you had a valuable role to play. Nobody who didn't live in those times, and work in SIS, could possibly have any idea of the rights and wrongs of the Philby affair. You were not of those times but you have an open mind. We haven't. You have another advantage. You are a trained, experienced, and, if I might say so, respected officer in SIS. Putting all those facts together we want *you* to make the recommendation as to what our response should be. Talk to all of us. Ask anything you like. Check any records you think would help. Go and see Philby in Moscow. And then when you're ready tell us what you think.'

Despite his experience and seniority, Powell was flattered by their decision. But at the same time he felt cautious, or uneasy, he wasn't sure which. Why didn't they just decide for themselves? They had all at least known Philby. Why make a production out of it? But if that was what they wanted that's what they would get. One thing was for sure, it was going to be interesting.

'What staff can I have?' And Walker smiled to himself at Powell's defensive response.

'None. Facilities, yes. All the facilities you want, but you will not discuss, or even hint, to anyone else, what you are doing, or the approach from Philby.'

'What reason can I give for talking to people and calling for files?'

'Tell them that we're stepping up "Milord" and you're checking backgrounds.'

'What about my present assignments?'

'What are you doing at the moment apart from supervising the "Milord" surveillance.'

'I'm debriefing two defectors. A Czech and Pole.'

'I'll talk to Sir Ian and get you relieved of that.'

'Who do I report to?'

'This committee. Nothing formal. And nothing in writing. Just keep in touch.'

'Any time restriction?'

'Take as long as you want within reason.'

Padmore looked around the table. 'Are we agreed, gentlemen?'

Nobody spoke. Padmore waited for a few moments then he said, 'Is silence agreement or disagreement, gentlemen?'

Walker smiled. 'I think both James and I are both still a bit stunned by the news. The more I think about it the more impossible it seems. It's hard to think in rational terms about any of it. I've no objection to Powell doing what you suggested. But he'd have to be well briefed. It could be a trap of some sort.'

'What about you, James?'

'On one condition.'

'What's that?'

'That we agree now that whatever his deal is, we say no. String him along if you need to, but the answer is always going to be no.'

23

Walker half-smiled. 'He might be offering us the working drawings of SS-18s, James.'

'If he was guaranteeing the defection of the whole Politburo I'd still tell him to get stuffed.'

Padmore was used to such situations. Philosophy Fellows behaved much the same if they had a lay audience.

'Well we've all had our say. Mr Powell, I'll talk to Sir Ian so that you can get what help you need. Take your time. Talk to Mr Walker and Mr McNay. Form your own conclusions. I'd like you to come and have a chat with me sometime before you go off to Moscow.'

'Right, sir.'

Walker had stopped to talk with Padmore, and as McNay walked with him down the corridor Powell said, 'When would it be convenient to talk with you, Mr McNay?'

'Have lunch with me tomorrow. Twelve-thirty at the Caledonian Club. Ask for me at the desk.'

When John Powell asked the porter for McNay he was taken up the wide staircase, along a corridor and then shown into a room.

McNay was standing, looking out of one of the tall windows. When he turned he pointed to the table.

'We don't want interruptions so I got them to bring us some cold cuts. We can help ourselves.'

There was an open briefcase on the table alongside the big plates of salad and cold meats, and as soon as they were seated McNay said, 'You've read the books about Philby I expect. And his own book?'

'Yes. I'll re-read them, though.'

'They won't help you much.'

'Are they inaccurate?'

'Here and there. But there's more than just facts to Philby. You can read everything that's been written and you still won't know what it's all about. And of course Philby's own book was meant to make our security services look like fools.'

'Were they?'

'God, who knows? I was one of them, and I can never make my mind up.'

'What's your general opinion?'

'He was a traitor. I've no doubt about that. You'll find my opinion on the record long before he was officially suspect. He was ruthless. Hundreds of men died because of what he did. And he did it cold-bloodedly. Knowing that they would die. Always remember that. He didn't just betray secrets, he betrayed people.'

'You wouldn't let him come back?'

'No. I'd need a lot of convincing to change my mind about Philby. He was a traitor, and for me that's the end of it. Help yourself to the food, we can talk as we go.'

They both ate in silence for several minutes but Powell noticed that McNay was watching him intently.

'What are your own views, Johnny?'

Powell shrugged. 'I guess much the same as yours. The facts are there. What other conclusions are there to draw?'

'You'll hear other views than mine. From people who think that a boy from Westminster School who went to Trinity and belonged to the right clubs couldn't possibly be a traitor. Don't believe it, Philby was a traitor all right.'

'What makes you so sure?'

'Facts, laddie, facts.'

'Tell me some.'

'Look into the Albanian business. Look at Otto John in Lisbon. Look at Volkov. They'll do for a start. He sent men to their deaths because some bastard in Moscow thought something *might* be to their disadvantage. And friend Philby wished 'em luck. Shook their hands. Knowing that they were going to certain death because he had arranged it himself.'

25

'What was he like as a man?'

'They'll tell you what a charmer he was and what a hard-working officer he was. Forget it. He was a shit, a twenty-four carat shit. They have to say their piece because he was one of them. Well-off, university, part of the old-boy network, a drunk. He was the kind they recruited. The kind they were sure that they could trust. The public-school boy, the Cambridge man who knew the right people and belonged to the right clubs. He was like them. Half of them *still* don't believe he was a traitor.'

'What do they believe?'

'They're like our friend Walker. There's some explanation, they say. There is. He was an out-and-out bastard. For months after he'd defected there were people like Walker hinting that maybe it was the Russians who'd been fooled. Maybe we'd planted him on them, and he was a hero not a defector. He'd got an OBE and they protested when it was withdrawn.'

'Did you have much to do with him?'

'Off and on. He had his finger in every pie. Made it look like he was the tireless, never-sleeping organizer. If there's a problem Philby can solve it. And they believed it. Made him a senior officer of SIS. How stupid can you be?'

'But surely it was *his* skill in deceiving them that made him successful rather than their stupidity?'

'Rubbish. He'd been a Commie at Cambridge. He mixed with Communist Party members. His wife was a Viennese Communist. Not secretly but openly. An active official. D'you think I'd have lasted five minutes if my wife had been a Communist Party official?'

'Did they know that?'

'Yes. It was on his bloody "P" file. It wasn't a secret.'

'So why did they leave him in the service?'

'I've told you. He was like them. A gentleman. Being a Communist was just a boyish prank like scrumping apples.'

'People have said that he was very successful against the Germans. Do you think that's true?'

McNay sat there, pulling a roll apart as if it were Philby himself. It was a couple of minutes before he spoke.

'In a way. In a way. But he wasn't doing it for us. He was doing it for the Soviets. He was helping *them* win, not us.'

'Is there anything good about him that you can remember?'

'You must be joking, laddie.' And McNay stood up. 'If you want to see me again just phone me. And remember this. Whatever that bastard wants it won't be for our good. It'll be for himself. And if you gave him everything he asked for he wouldn't be grateful. He'd see it as his due.'

Powell was at the door when he turned to look at McNay. 'You said that there was something in Philby's autobiography that was very revealing. What was it?'

McNay looked away, towards the windows, his tongue probing his teeth as he thought. Eventually he turned to look at Powell. 'Read it twice, laddie. Read it the first time as yourself. Then read it the second time as if you were head of KGB. If you don't spot it, ask me again.'

# 3

The small boy looked up at the blue sky and watched the seagulls as they circled over the promenade, then over the beach and out to the edge of the ebbing tide. He walked behind his parents, his skinny legs trying to take the same strides as his father.

His father, a balding, bearded man, walked with a small man's swagger, beating time against his leg with his yellowing panama hat as he strode briskly along.

The small boy was seven and he was glad that at last his father had decided what school he should go to. They were now on their way back to Eastbourne station and the rented house in London. Their luggage had gone on ahead in the charge of his grandmother.

He sometimes wondered if his father didn't prefer his grandmother to his mother. He had said so once to his mother as she was fixing the tortoiseshell comb in her hair. She had turned to look at him, her blue eyes on his face. He had thought for a moment that she was going to be cross but she had turned back to the mirror and had said nothing.

They had travelled third class on the train and he thought he knew why. His father was away for most of the time. Living rough in tents with the Arabs. He spoke Arabic and explored the deserts for the Saudi kings. He was King Ibn Saud's adviser. His father had shown him pictures of the king and his family with his father standing alongside him.

He was staring out of the carriage window when his mother touched his knee.

28

'You'll like Aldro, Kim. You'll meet nice boys there I'm sure.'

'Yes, Mother.'

His father looked at him from behind The Times.

'I'm expecting a lot of effort from you, my boy. You know what I want?'

'Yes, Father.'

'What is it that I want?'

'That I go to Westminster, Father.'

'As a King's Scholar. Nothing less. You'll be following in my footsteps.'

'Yes, Father.'

The boy had a vision of his father's footsteps in the desert sand. His father had shown him the maps that he had drawn himself. Every camel trail, every feature of the almost featureless terrain was marked and plotted. His father was always at his most amiable and expansive as he talked of Arabia and the tribes. He sensed that his father was an important man. He wondered sometimes if he wasn't also a hero, although he wasn't sure exactly what a hero was. Important men listened to what he said. Not only Arabs but Englishmen. Politicians and statesmen. Men from the oil companies who talked with American accents.

The small boy tried never to let the thought settle in his mind that he liked it best when his father was away. But his mother seemed a different woman in those long months. Laughing, teasing him, relaxed and happy. It was comfortable and safe with his mother and his sisters. He was their hero then.

The boy looked out of the carriage window as the train rattled slowly on its way towards Haywards Heath and London. The smoke from the engine billowed from time to time in a sulphurous cloud alongside the carriage. Above his father's seat was a photograph in a brass frame of the Kyle of Lochalsh. There was a mirror over his mother and op-

29

posite him a photograph of fishing boats on the beach at Hastings.

His eyes went back to the hedges and fields. There were pools of bluebells at the edges of the woods and clusters of late primroses on the embankment. A small boy and a girl sat on a fence, waving as the train rattled by. And across the fields he saw the Sussex oasts and the fat sheep with their lambs grazing in blossoming apple orchards. At a level-crossing there was a group of soldiers in hospital blue. Heads bandaged, tunics loose on their shoulders to accommodate arms in slings. And a few drooping on crutches, puffing at cigarettes as they waited for the train to pass. It was May 1919.

# 4

Powell walked to Patrick Walker's house in Tite Street. It was a handsome three storeyed house with a white exterior. An ancient wistaria threaded its way from one corner up to the top window frames to curve along the white-painted wooden boards that protected the gutters.

Walker answered the door himself, but Powell saw a maid hovering in the background. A genuine, old-fashioned maid wearing a black dress and a white apron. Walker himself was wearing a khaki, woollen army officer's shirt and a pair of cavalry twill trousers.

There were portraits of what he thought must be Walker ancestors on the wall of the stairway, which was wide with a wrought-iron balustrade painted white. On the landing large indoor plants were ranged on the terrazzo floor. Monsteras, ficus, philodendron and edible figs. Walker led him through to a large well-lit sitting room. One wall was lined with books and on the opposite wall was a portable colour TV on a white shelf, flanked by a modern hi-fi system. A small fountain played in a Bryant water garden and he saw the golden glint of a fish between two lily pads.

Four leather club-armchairs were set round a low, glass-topped coffee table and Walker pointed to one of them and waited until Powell had settled before he sat himself. There were two glasses and a misted bottle of white wine, and Walker poured them each a glass.

Walker sat back, relaxed, in his chair. He beamed as he said, 'And how did you get on with Jimmy McNay?'

'I don't really know. I think perhaps I learned more about him than I did about Philby.'

'Oh. Tell me more.'

'He seems to see Philby as unmistakably a villain. I felt he was very prejudiced against that type of man.'

Walker smiled. 'Why do you think he is prejudiced. What causes it?'

'I guess he's prejudiced about people who went to university and came from upper-middle-class backgrounds. A class thing.'

Walker laughed. 'I shouldn't think so. Jimmy McNay got a good degree at Aberdeen. His family have been iron-founders ever since iron was discovered. His elder brother is a bishop, and his sister is married to the Lord-lieutenant of one of the midland counties. So I wouldn't say it was a class prejudice.'

'You surprise me. You really do.'

'Maybe that's a good thing. Helps *you* to avoid prejudices too early in the game.'

'The world at large sees Philby as a traitor; do *you* think Philby was a traitor?'

Walker fished behind him in his armchair and dragged out a moth-eaten teddy-bear. Glancing at it for a moment he put it gently on the coffee table.

'Sally's I think.' He closed his eyes for a moment and when he opened them he said, 'Yes, I suppose he was. The difference between me and McNay is that I feel there's more to it than that.'

'Why?'

'My God, that would take weeks to explain. Years maybe. Let me try. Most people agree that whatever he did it wasn't for money or any material reward. They would probably agree that it was ideological, political if you like. His father was an eccentric. Agin all authority. Kim was like him in many ways. A loner, almost an anarchist, and if that's the

32

way you think then it's a damn sight easier to admire a government that you don't live under than the one you're actually stuck with. There were a lot of people in those days who saw a new light for the world in Moscow. Well-known people, some of them still around who'd prefer not to be reminded of it today.'

'Was he a likable man?'

Walker shrugged. 'If you forget what he did, that he was a traitor, yes he was likable. Nobody ever got close to him. Not even his women. Obviously as a double-agent he couldn't afford to have people close to him. But he was good company and a good brain.'

'You liked him?'

'I'm afraid I did.'

'And now?'

'What do you mean?'

'Do you still like him?'

'I wouldn't cut him dead if we met in the street if that's what you mean.'

'Are there any other reasons why you think that there was more than just treason. What else could there be?'

'God knows. But there was so much that went unexplained. You could be an admirer of the Soviets without being a traitor. What made him go that far? And once he was a real suspect why did we give him so much rope? He was named in the Commons as the "third man" by an MP. He was interrogated by our people. Competent people. He was found a job as a journalist. He hung around Beirut for years. He could have been arrested or killed, but nothing happened. Our people are not as stupid as they're made out to be, you know that. So why was it all made so easy?'

'Perhaps they saw it as the least embarrassing way of getting rid of the problem?'

'No. That won't wash. People who ought to know better have suggested that before. Its effect on our relationship with the Americans, the CIA and the Nuclear Agency people was catastrophic. They've never really trusted us since then. It was bad enough what he had done, but for him to slip out to Moscow under our noses was too much. They even wondered if there wasn't some cunning British game going on. The double-agent who'd been turned into a triple-agent. There was even talk that Moscow was beginning to wonder which side he was on.'

'D'you think he *could* have been a triple-agent?'

'I doubt it. There was too much that he didn't like about this country for that. And neither he nor SIS would have thought going to Moscow was a good idea if he was playing that sort of game. I'd say that sort of talk was probably started by our people just to keep Moscow on the hop.'

'Do you think that there is anybody who really knows the whole story about Philby?'

'You mean from start to finish?'

'Yes.'

'No. I suppose there are perhaps half a dozen people who, if you knew who they were, could put together their pieces of the jigsaw and be pretty near the truth.'

'Why hasn't anyone done it?'

'For several reasons. First of all nobody knows who the half dozen people are. They don't realize it themselves. Secondly, at least two of them are in baulk. "Milord" is one, and Kim's KGB controller is another. One of the things that is going to concern you is not just *why* he wants to come back, and don't forget it may just be a ploy, but do his KGB friends know what he's up to and approve it.'

'How would *you* tackle this assignment?'

Walker shook his head, smiling. 'I wouldn't even try. I'm too much part of those old days. Old Padmore's no fool, you know. He didn't suggest you for this operation for your beautiful blue eyes. He knew that anyone from the old days would be useless. Not just that we're all prejudiced one way

34

or another, but we've all been over the ground too many times. We analyse what we know in the context of those days. Those who rather liked him, people like me, put his treason down to him being converted to Communism. But there are no real grounds for thinking that. He'd got a sharp analytical mind so why should he have fallen for that crap? Most of the early Moscow-worshippers changed their minds when they saw what they were really up to. So why not Kim? But we hang on to that theory because there seems to be no other motivation. It wasn't money. It was unlikely to be blackmail. Maybe it was power. Who knows? Maybe you'll be the one to find out.'

'And how would you recommend that I find out? Where do I look?'

Walker sat silently, his chin on his ample chest, the fingers of his right hand doing slow arpeggios on the arm of the chair. Eventually he drew a slow, deep breath and turned to look at Powell.

'He was almost certainly recruited in 1933. Before then he was openly Communist. He made no secret of it. But about the end of 1933 he was covering up his tracks and talking like a convinced right-winger. Or at least pro-establishment. As an avowed Communist he would have been no use to the KGB. But you've got to remember that in 1933 Hitler was only just in power. Nobody saw him as a danger, least of all as the man who would start another world war.

'So what did the KGB expect from Kim at that stage? Nobody knew that he would end up in intelligence, let alone as a top man. Put aside any question of treason and no man could have planned Kim Philby's career even if he was only motivated by ambition. He would have no idea of even the existence of MI5 and MI6. A vague intelligence service in the background perhaps, but nothing more. So what did the Soviets expect him to do? It was always the Soviets' view that there would be no war with Germany. You're going to have to start at square one. Back to the start of the war. See what was going on on all sides. Us, the Germans, and the Russians. Read the books, talk to people, absorb the atmosphere. And you'll be able to look at our friend in Moscow with a fresh eye. That's what it needs. A fresh eye.'

Sir Ian Pouley had been the head of SIS for too long to be either as wary or as agitated as his committee chairman had been by the message from Moscow. He had agreed with Padmore's recommendation without inquiring too closely about the details. It could be no more than a little tactical exercise by the KGB, or it could be real. Either way it didn't warrant too much in time or resources. It was part of the routine and had to be dealt with.

Strangely enough his mind had gone back to Philby that same evening. He was at a formal dinner at Grosvenor House with his wife, and it reminded him of a photograph of Philby that he had seen way back on the files. Philby and one of his wives at a dinner of the Anglo-German Fellowship in the nineteen-thirties. It must have been just before Philby went to Spain. If *he* were doing the check on Philby that is where he would concentrate. It was there that a few years later Philby negotiated with Otto John and then sold them all down the river. A waitress leaned over his shoulder with a pink-coloured ice cream and he brought his mind back to the present proceedings.

# 5

John Powell was a couple of months short of forty-four. A stocky, well-built man with pale blue eyes and the pink skin that often goes with light-red hair. He was pleasant looking without being in any way handsome. His small eyes, neat nose, and his reddish moustache gave him the air of a perky bull-terrier. Ready to fight, but with his mouth always on the edge of a friendly grin. His torso, shoulders and arms were solidly muscled, and his lightweight clothes seemed barely able to contain the faintly aggressive body. And despite the frequent nearness to a smile his eyes were shrewd, and when you looked carefully, hard. He seemed the kind of man who would wear Harris tweed sports jackets with leather elbow patches. But he never did.

He had been left well wrapped-up in a woman's cardigan, and in a cardboard box, on the steps of the police station in Berwick-on-Tweed. A cheerful baby, the station sergeant had estimated that he was almost two weeks old; and the next day the Salvation Army had taken him over. It was they who gave him his names. Powell after a well-known northern comedian of that name who also had red hair, and John after the station sergeant who had discovered him.

The orphanage just outside Sunderland had been his home until he was eighteen. Despite the Salvation Army's usual efficiency in tracing missing relatives they had never been able to trace either of his parents. He had been bright enough to win a place at the local grammar school. Good at games, and of an apparently calm temperament, he had been no problem to the staff at the orphanage and was seen as one of their successes; sound in mind and limb. It was a fair enough assessment on their part because they would have needed to have had the time to be much closer to the small boy to have perceived the separate fantasy world that he escaped to when he was alone.

He was sure that he was a Scot. His red hair and the place where he had been found were almost enough; but apart from that he *felt* that he was a Scot. And the parents in his dream-world were Scots. There was a song he had heard, sung by Harry Lauder, called 'I love a lassie', and the last line said that the girl was – 'Mary, my Scots bluebell'. And for him, Mary the Scots bluebell was his mother, and he was sure that it was she who had given him the red hair, the blue eyes, and the flushed pink colouring of his skin. He imagined his father as an officer, an officer in the Black Watch or maybe the Gordon Highlanders. Something romantic and a bit swashbuckling. When he thought of him his father was always standing at the top of a hill, one foot on a small mound, in full dress uniform, and his mother, who was very young, was on a swing, in an orchard, laughing, in a pale pink dress with a frill round the hem of the skirt. His thoughts never went beyond the two dream figures. They had no lives, no background, just those eternal poses. Sometimes, when he was low, he wondered what the reasons could have been that caused him to be abandoned; lurching from one alternative to another, but always he would shake his head to blot out the thoughts.

There was still a tendency in those days for staff in charge of male orphans to edge them towards a life in the services or the police, and John Powell had eventually been recruited by the Metropolitan Police as a cadet on probation.

If you are an orphan you are used to discipline, and you have only small expectations from life itself; and a life in the police, which could seem irksome to others, seemed like

freedom itself to the likes of John Powell. He was a sergeant
by the time he had been transferred to Special Branch.

When he was moved into SIS five years later, he had had
to work his passage, like other new boys, in an atmosphere
of general suspicion. After Philby, and Burgess and Maclean, morale was low, and nobody was completely trusted.
Even hard work and enthusiasm had become suspect. But in
those five years he learned the essence and techniques of his
new world, and gradually he became part of that inner core
of SIS whose purpose is not espionage but counter-
intelligence, the penetration of other intelligence organizations. Even those of friendly states. Because history had
shown so recently that today's ally can become tomorrow's
enemy. Oil, food, territory, trade, and the lust for power
motivated friends as well as foes. Expediency was the watch-
word of diplomacy, and the end could always be shown to
have justified the means. SIS were the means.

When Sir Ian Pouley became head of SIS he had looked
for the crusaders. Those men who did their work, *enflammé
d'enthusiasme*. And he moved them to the sidelines. He was
at one with Talleyrand. Crusaders were all too often zealots,
and Philby had been both. Pouley wanted middle-of-the-
road men. Men who didn't inhale. Men who could look at
religions, political creeds, races, nations and events as they
really were, assess their effect on others, and finally assess
their effect on the interests of the UK. He saw John Powell
as such a man, and tested him from time to time. He
found him, despite the red hair and the bull-terrier face,
to be a man whose mind was subtle and perceptive, who
dealt in analysis rather than opinion. Judgement values
were applied, but they were the tools of analysis not the
forerunners.

In 1970 Powell had been promoted, and until 1975 had
been the officer responsible for first the Middle East, and
then the whole of the eastern side of Africa from Egypt to

the Republic of South Africa. Then for three years he had been one of the officers responsible for the evaluation and debriefing of all defectors from the Warsaw Pact countries, including the Soviet Union. His membership of the 'Milord' committee was one of the routine items that had been tacked on to his schedule. Apart from controlling the surveillance and evaluating the routine reports it took little of his time or thoughts.

Technically, his flat was in Belgravia, but spiritually and architecturally it was in Pimlico. It was the two upper floors of a Victorian family house in the muddle of streets behind Victoria Station. The estate agent had described it as a maisonette. And he lived there with the second eldest daughter of Sir Arthur Tracy.

Vanessa Harper was twenty-eight, and had frequently been referred to by the gossip columnists, in her society days, as 'the blonde bombshell'; which was more a tribute to her father's wealth than an accurate description of her appearance. Blonde she certainly was, but she was no more than averagely pretty. In her twenties she had been typical of most of the so-called 'swingers' to be seen shopping in Portobello Road; but a marriage, a child, and a divorce had left her with a resentment against fate that showed in her petulant mouth and her too frequently raised eyebrows. Her relationship with her family was tenuous, and her former husband had custody of their only child. She had lived with John Powell for almost two years.

If John Powell had been asked why he had chosen Vanessa Harper as his girl-friend he would probably have rubbed his neat nose as he thought about it and then suggested that it was because he found her attractive and intelligent. It would have been only part of the truth. There were other reasons, but he would not have wanted to acknowledge them. He only acknowledged them subconsciously even to himself. He would not have wanted to admit that being unwanted by his parents had made him lean towards lame ducks in his personal relationships. He had a strong but subconscious urge to do unto others what had not been done unto him. Under the tough exterior John Powell had a need to love those who needed love, even if that love was never returned. In his private life he didn't apply the realistic criteria that he applied to his work. But he had never told her what he did. She seemed to accept without curiosity that he worked at the Foreign Office in some nebulous and mediocre capacity. He had had half a dozen such relationships but none of them had lasted as long as this one.

Powell reached for the phone as it continued to ring, and gave his extension number.

'One nine four seven.'

'Walker here, Powell . . . I was thinking about what I said to you about going back to square one. Thinking about it I realized that there's a lot of square ones. I suggest you look at the records on Gehlen and Otto John as well as Philby. There'll be some clues lying around in those areas. If you look hard enough.'

'Thanks. Any others?'

'Not that I can think of, but don't forget old Padmore. He knows more than he lets on.'

'OK. Thanks.' And he slowly replaced the receiver.

Powell loosened his tie as he leaned back in his chair. He remembered skimming through Gehlen's main file when he first came to SIS. It was basic reading even for experienced operators. He remembered Otto John too; he'd been some sort of defector to East Germany. He made a note to check where the journalist was who had passed on Philby's message.

She was sitting on the stool at her dressing table, leaning forward to look in the mirror as she patted some liquid from a bottle on to her cheeks. He watched her, smiling, from where he lay in the bed, a paperback book in one hand.

'I thought you were rather rude to Mommie tonight.'

'I don't remember that. What did I say?'

'You said "rubbish" to something she said.'

He laughed softly. 'I remember. But it *was* rubbish.'

'I don't think so.'

'I said you looked pretty, and she said it's more important for a girl to look smart than pretty.'

'I know. I was there.'

'*Would* you rather be smart than pretty?'

'Oh for heaven's sake. You know what she means.'

'Of course I do. It's just a kind of snobbery.'

'How do you make that out?'

'What she means is that there are pretty girls serving in Woolworths, but in her book they don't count because they don't wear Hermes scarves, and can't tell a fish-knife from an avocado spoon.'

'Now *you're* talking rubbish.'

'What do you want to do tomorrow?'

'I asked Cynthia and Bobby round for drinks mid-day and maybe we could go on to the Connaught for lunch.'

'OK. So long as you don't complain again if I have the steak and kidney pie.'

She turned, smiling, to look at him. 'When are you going to grow up?'

'When you get into bed.'

She turned back to the mirror. 'Who was the tall guy with the wavy hair you were talking to?'

'Jake somebody or other. I think he fancied you and was trying to find out if we were married.'

'Why, what did he say?'

'He said that he'd heard you were rather a funsy girl.'

'And what did you say?'

'Practically nothing. He sounded a real creep. Only a creep would use a word like funsy.'

'I rather like creeps in a way.'

'I know. I thought you'd got over it though.'

She slid, laughing softly, into the bed beside him.

# 6

He looked across at Tom Farrow, and wondered why journalists always look more like down and outs, when they so much wanted everyone to see them as the fourth estate. They always seemed on the defensive. They were aggressive enough when *they* were putting the questions, but when they were questioned about themselves they quoted the 'confidentiality of sources'.

'How many people knew that you were going to the Party headquarters, Tom?'

'Nobody except the officials there. I'd made an appointment.'

'How long before?'

'About ten that morning. The appointment was for five o'clock.'

'And it was just before seven when you left?'

'Roughly.'

'When had you last spoken to him?'

'About six months ago. He was sitting behind me at the Bolshoi. I hadn't noticed him but he tapped me on the shoulder in the interval.'

'What did he say?'

'Just said hello, and how did I like Moscow.'

'How long before that since you saw him?'

'Not since the press conference he gave after Macmillan had cleared him in the Commons.'

'Was he alone at the Bolshoi?'

'No. He was with his girl-friend. And they were in a party.'

'Who were the others. Were they KGB?'

'I wouldn't know. All Russians look like KGB to me. They were senior officials whoever they were.'

'Did you feel your meeting with him this last time was an accident or deliberate?'

Farrow grinned. 'You know bloody well it must have been deliberate. He wouldn't pass a message like that on the spur of the moment.'

'Did anyone follow you?'

'I didn't see anyone, but I didn't really look. I was surprised.'

'Did you think he was serious?'

'He was serious enough about me delivering the message. Only you chaps can decide whether he is serious about coming back.'

'Why are you so sure that he was serious about the message being delivered?'

Powell saw the flicker of fear or anxiety in Farrow's eyes before he answered.

'He was very specific. Very ... pressing.'

Powell leaned back in his chair and ostentatiously pushed his note-pad and pencil to one side.

'I heard on the grapevine that it was you who tipped off the *Mail* about Special Branch arresting Rakov. Did you?'

'I gave them a hint. Yes.'

'Must have been more than a hint for eight hundred quid.'

'Maybe.'

'Was that what Philby gave you for delivering the message?'

'Maybe.'

He wasn't going to talk, and Powell didn't want to get him in a corner. Not at this stage anyway. The decision to arrest Rakov had been taken two weeks before they actually arrested him. It *could* have leaked back to Philby. But his informant must have passed it to him via the London end of the KGB. And in that case why didn't the KGB smuggle Rakov out as soon as they knew he was for the chop. And as they hadn't done that, maybe they hadn't been tipped off, and Philby's source was direct from Special Branch or MI5.

'How did he look?'

'Much the same as ever. A few more lines and creases maybe.'

'Who was the girl-friend at the Bolshoi?'

'The pretty one. Nina. I've not heard her full name. She lives with him.'

'Did he look ill?'

'No. Older, but fit enough.'

'What was he wearing?'

'A dark sort of coat with a fur collar and the standard fur hat. That's all I noticed.'

'Did you leave the church together?'

'No. He left first. I stayed behind.'

'You didn't make any attempt to follow him and see where he went when he left?'

'Not bloody likely. It shook me; all I wanted was to get away. And following KGB officers in Moscow gets you straight in the Lubyanka.'

'Who did you tell about this?'

'Nobody. I phoned Padmore from Heathrow, and he told me to go and see him before I contacted my office. He read me the Riot Act about what would happen if I talked about it.'

'What about your editor?'

'I haven't told him. Nor anybody else.'

'Did Padmore make you sign the piece of paper?'

'Of course.'

'How long are you due to stay in Moscow?'

'A couple more months. Maybe a little longer.'

'When do you go back?'

'Next week.'

'D'you want a story?'

'Exclusive?'

'Of course.'

'Can I quote a source.'

'Sure. "A usually reliable source".'

Farrow smiled. 'OK. What's the story?'

'One of our diplomats reports seeing Philby two days ago in Syria with two KGB agents who were identified.'

Farrow shook his head, smiling. 'I'm not printing teasers for the benefit of the Foreign Office. You know me better than that.'

'It's not a teaser. It's fact. You can see that section of our man's report if you want.'

'OK. Show me.'

Powell opened the top drawer of his desk and pulled out two typed sheets that were stapled together. Glancing at them he folded the sheets carefully, twice, and then pushed them towards Farrow, a hand on each side of the paper. Farrow read the exposed section carefully, and Powell could see his lips moving as he tried to memorize the exact words. Eventually he looked up at Powell.

'Any corroboration from elsewhere?'

'Not so far.'

'Thanks.' He stood up. 'If there's anything I can do to help let me know.'

'Thank you, Tom. I will.'

Arthur Padmore asked him to go down to Oxford when he telephoned. Pressure of work and all that. But Powell guessed that it was the mountain making the position clear to Mahommed.

The porter at the college gate was expecting him, and led him to the professor's house through the gardens. Padmore himself answered the door and he was waved inside with unusual friendliness. Padmore obviously wanted to make clear that away from the committee he could be quite avuncular to his juniors. When they were sitting together Padmore wasted no time.

'How have you been getting on?'

'It's hard to say, sir. I've been absorbing material rather than evaluating it.'

'Quite so. Very wise of you if I may say so. And Walker and McNay, have they been helpful?'

'I think so. I shall know more when I've spoken to Philby. At the moment none of it makes much sense.'

'Oh. Tell me more.'

'I can't see why he should want to come back here or what he expects the reaction to be.'

'Feelings would be mixed, of course.'

'But he would be tried as a self-confessed traitor.'

'It would be very difficult to do that. Suspicion is one thing, evidence to satisfy a court is another. We had to work that out a long time ago.'

'His own book?'

'Have you read it?'

'Yes.'

'At no place does he admit that he was a traitor. And he could claim that it was written under duress.'

'He's an officer in the KGB. The British government admitted in 1963 that he had been a Soviet agent since 1946. He's been awarded the "Order of the Red Banner".'

Padmore shook his head slowly. 'All meaningless in court. We went over it all at the time with a fine-tooth comb. The Attorney-General said that he would have to instruct the Director of Public Prosecutions not to go ahead if we tried to bring a case on that evidence.'

'Why did SIS still use him after they knew? Why did they use their influence to get him employed by the *Economist* and the *Observer*?'

'I wasn't privy to those decisions I'm afraid.'

Powell looked steadily at Padmore who looked back at him unblinking. Powell knew that he was facing one of those hurdles that had been put up years ago. He would be wasting his time if he didn't try to jump it.

'Can I be frank, Mr Padmore?'

'I should imagine you well could be, Mr Powell.'

Powell recognized the grammatical nicety directed towards him, and the formality of the 'mister', but he pressed on.

'What did *you* think of Philby?'

'He was intelligent, and hard-working, and he had unreliable friends, but who hasn't? When he was a young man he had a young man's enthusiasms. And as so often happens they were misplaced. On occasions he let those old enthusiasms over-ride his better judgement.'

'You don't feel he was a traitor?'

'It depends on what you call a traitor.'

'A man who gives or sells his country's secrets to its enemies.'

'Are you referring to the Soviets?'

'Of course.'

'They were our allies most of the time that Philby was working for SIS. Our enemies were the Nazis.'

Padmore's mouth was set in a thin line of determination, and his eyebrows were raised quizzically as if to query what more there might be that could be asked.

'Why do you think he wants to come back, sir?'

Padmore relaxed visibly.

'He'll be sixty-eight next January. He must be bored and lonely.' He shrugged. 'I suppose he wants to die in his own country.'

Powell had not seen any indication of such sentimentality in Philby's record but he suspected that he would get nothing more from the older man. He asked one last question.

'Would you welcome his return, sir?'

For a moment there was confusion in Padmore's watery eyes.

'I think I would. Yes. I think I would. Perhaps "welcome" is going a bit too far.'

'Why would you have him back?'

'For the same reason I gave when they asked me about him before they first took him on in Section D.'

'What reason was that, Mr Padmore?'

'I knew his people. There was nothing wrong there. There's nothing wrong with *him* either. Others misled him.'

On the train back to London Powell felt his first real doubts. He was being put in a race with lead weights on his feet. He was going to get comment and opinion but nothing more. He was being used but he wasn't sure why, or even who was using him. Only a fanatic like McNay saw the facts as they really were and the others seemed blinded by those same things that had blinded them from the start. He was used to the old-boy networks but not in these sort of circumstances. He was amazed at Padmore's piece about "knowing his people". Long ago he had heard a story where Padmore had turned down a possible recruit because he had dirty fingernails. He had assumed at the time that it was a joke. Maybe it wasn't.

'Is this the whisky daddy gave you?' She held the glass up, quizzing it with one eye half closed.

'Yep.'

'It's ghastly.'

'It's Glen Grant. The best there is, a malt, but you shouldn't put water in it. Maybe you should stick to gin.'

'I thought you said I drank too much gin.'

He closed the leather case, tucking in the cuff of a shirt before he buckled the straps. She was always a bit tetchy before he went on a trip.

'Where did you say you were off to this time?'

'I told you. Warsaw.'

'And what's the embassy been up to there? Using too much carbon-paper or slipping vodka into the diplomatic bag?'

'Something like that,' he said quietly, and turned to look at her. 'You've got enough cash for the week haven't you?'

'Yes. Oodles.'

But he knew his lady and noticed the tears at the edges of her eyes.

'When I come back, how about we go up to see young Lydia?'

She wiped her eyes with the backs of her hands, sniffed, and stood up. She stood close to him, her hands on his jacket lapels. Putting her head on his shoulder she said softly, 'I don't know how I'd survive without you, Johnny. You're my rock of ages.'

'You give me a lot too, sweetie.'

She looked at him quickly. 'Do I? What do I give you?'

'Someone to care for, someone to talk to, someone to be with.'

The grey eyes looked at his face. It wasn't the answer she had hoped for. But in some ways it was good enough. She kissed him gently on the mouth.

# 7

*The rocks they sat on were hot against the boy's legs and as he looked to where his father pointed, the air itself shimmered with heat, distorting the perpendicular columns and casting a mauve, blue sheen on the mosaics.*

*'The Moors made this the centre of art and philosophy. They built this mosque in Cordoba in the eighth century. The Arabs swept through Spain right through to southern France. All this . . .' He swept his arm in a wide arc. '. . . every bit of it is Arab. In those days they were the scientists, the astronomers, the mathematicians, the artists. Never forget that, Kim. They aren't just Bedouin roaming the deserts.'*

*'Is that why you like them so much?'*

*'It's part of the reason. They've been badly treated by our people. They were given promises during the war that we've never kept. Promises of independence.'*

*'Why didn't we keep the promises?'*

*'Our people never intended to keep them, Kim. They just used the Arabs. Never, never trust politicians. They'll lie, and deceive, and intrigue, for their own ends.'*

*'What do you do in Jiddah?'*

*'Advise the King.'*

*'Does he pay you for that?'*

*'He gives me trading rights. To import and export, and negotiate oil concessions on his behalf.'*

*'Why don't we live there with you?'*

*'Your mother doesn't wish it. She's quite right. It's very rough and primitive. It's a country for men not women.'*

*'Do you think I'd like it?'*

'We'll have to see. All in good time.'

He took out his leather wallet and showed the boy the photograph. He had seen it before but he had only glanced at it.

'Is that the king standing by you?'

'That's the king.'

'And this?'

'That's his brother, the prince.'

'And this lady?'

His finger pointed at a girl. She was dressed in a white jelab, the hood pushed back from her face.

'That's a slave-girl.'

'And the two children?'

'They are her children.'

'What are their names?'

'The tall one is Khalid and the other one is Faris.'

The boy looked intently at the sepia photograph. He wondered what it would be like if your mother was a slave-girl. What did slave-girls do. None of them was smiling and the strong light left their eyes as no more than black shadows. Even the king and the prince looked straight at the camera, serious and sharp featured like the vultures at the zoo.

He handed the photograph back to his father. 'Where are we going next?'

'To Granada. Then it's back to London. And Westminster for you.'

'Will you be staying in London?'

'No. I'll be going back to Jiddah.'

'Do you miss the family?'

The old man's brown eyes looked at the boy.

'Never be dependent on anybody, Kim. Just you remember that. It's a weakness in a man. Stand on your own two feet. Go your own way. Don't be a sheep, be a man. If you need other people, even one, then you're never free.'

'Yes, Father.'

*And without knowing it Kim Philby had seen for the first time a photograph of his two half-brothers. The sons of St John Philby and Umm Fahd, one of the two girls given to the eccentric Englishman by his royal master.*

# 8

The immigration officer at Sheremetyevo took his passport
to one of the small offices beyond the barrier and another
officer took over to check the passports of the other passen-
gers. Powell leaned against the empty desk and waited. It
was fifteen minutes before the Russian came back. He
handed over the passport and waved Powell through to
where the embassy chauffeur was waiting for him.

In the car he opened his passport in the darkness and
touched the page that showed his photograph. Both pages
felt damp. It had obviously been in a copier.

It was a Sunday night, and November. The gaunt blocks
of workers' flats that lined the route into Moscow looked
grim and forbidding, and only the thin layer of snow relieved the sombre landscape.

At the embassy Jerry Cole, whose ostensible post was Assistant Military Attaché, was waiting for him. He was shown
to a small ante-room and afterwards they had a drink
together. He had already had the routine briefing in London
which laid down that the embassy had to be considered as
insecure. There was a room within a room where top secret
matters could be discussed, filtered and protected electro-
nically, but Cole suggested that they wrap up and walk down
towards the bridge.

'What's going on, Johnny?'

'You passed on the message?'

'Yes. I've fixed a meeting for you tomorrow.'

'Where?'

'I've put you in at the Rossiya in Red Square. The

55

meeting is at the fountain in the GUM Store tomorrow afternoon at three. It's just the other side of the square. I'll point
it out when I take you to the hotel.'

'Was there any problem?'

'No. You'd almost have thought that he was waiting for a
message, expecting one.'

'Does the embassy keep tabs on him?'

'No. Not apart from me that is. I'm not exactly made
welcome at the embassy myself. They don't want to know
what I get up to. They'd rather not know. His Excellency
made that clear the day I arrived. Here on sufferance. Don't
involve embassy staff. Not lift a finger if I end up in the
Lubyanka. The usual crap you get from ambassadors and
heads of missions.'

'Who does Philby mix with apart from the Russians?'

'Practically nobody. He might contact a journalist if he
wants a letter posted in the UK. They know the drill. We
have a look, seal 'em up and they go on their way. You
always get copies and a report for your committee files.'

'Can I use your radio if I need to?'

'Provided you've got a grade one code clearance, you
can.'

'What code are you using?'

'Good old-fashioned one-time pads.'

'Will it be dark at three o'clock tomorrow afternoon?'

'You bet. The bulletin tonight said heavy snow expected
during the night.'

'How far is it to the hotel?'

'I'll take you in the car. About ten or fifteen minutes.'

They were about a hundred yards past the Lenin Library
when they turned back towards the embassy.

Half an hour later they were crossing the Kalinin Bridge,
the Comecon skyscraper ablaze with light, then the Ok-
tyabr Cinema was on their left as they headed up Prospekt
Kalinina. The Kremlin domes and towers were floodlit, and

56

one bright white beam was on the Red Flag that fluttered above the cupola of the Council of Ministers building. Five minutes later they were at the Rossiya.

It took almost twenty minutes to go through the registration formalities. His room was on the fourteenth floor. With accommodation for 6000 guests service tended to be slow, and it was midnight by the time they had finished their meal at the self-service restaurant on the tenth floor.

After Cole had left, Powell took the elevator down to the ground floor and walked outside. The snow that had been forecast was already falling. The cold air was raw on his chest as he breathed, and when he was halfway to St Basil's he stopped and turned back. He felt slightly depressed. Moscow was an awe-inspiring city, and to him it already had a grim, threatening air. He was used to strange cities but Moscow was different. There was no feeling of welcome despite its eagerness to attract tourists. It was Birmingham or Pittsburgh on Sunday night, and it wasn't even Sunday. No wonder Philby wanted to come back. All the privileges the KGB could give him wouldn't make up for the all-pervading stifling hand of bureaucracy.

He slept uneasily until eight the next morning. He gave his room-key to the *dezhurnaya* at her table in the corridor and found his way to the restaurant where they had eaten the previous evening. They served a standard breakfast but he put aside the yoghurt, ate the soft-boiled egg, and drank the bitter coffee that wouldn't relent even with four spoonfuls of sugar.

From the foyer he looked out. The snow was thick on the ground. Several inches had fallen in the night but a wintry sun shone faintly in the pale green sky. He turned back to the service desk and asked for a copy of *The Times* before he remembered that even in London they couldn't have provided one. The girl offered him a two-day-old copy of the *Morning Star* which he took rather than give offence. In desperation he read it, in the coffee-room, and although it was two days old there was nothing in it that he had read in any other British newspaper on that day. Policemen had brutalized workers demonstrating for a living wage. Mrs Thatcher was threatening the Soviet Union, and unemployment was the highest in Western Europe. A provocative deal had been done with the lackeys of capitalism in China, to assemble combine-harvesters in Peking. And in Northern Ireland troops and police continued to maintain a reign of terror against the freedom fighters and the civilian population. A fascist judge in the High Court had threatened peace-loving pickets with imprisonment unless they abandoned their struggle against their capitalist employers.

The day dragged slowly by until it was time for him to leave. He set out early to give himself time to find the GUM building and the fountain.

The wide arcades were far more crowded than he had expected, mainly by Russians rather than foreigners. Halfway down the main arcade he came to the fountain. There were twenty or thirty people sitting on the wooden benches that encircled it, or leaning with their parcels on the octagonal surround of the fountain itself. He walked round the fountain twice before he recognized Philby. He was wearing a cap with ear muffs and was reading a paper. There was no space to sit beside him. A woman with a baby on her lap sat on one side and a sailor on the other. He circled the fountain again, slowly, and just before he got to him Philby folded his paper and stood up. As the wary eyes looked at him, for a moment he was disconcerted. They were very shrewd eyes, and the face was harder than he had expected. Older too. The photographs were out of date.

He felt Philby's gloved hand on his arm. 'Keep walking,' Philby said. They walked together in silence, threading their way through the groups of shoppers until they were back at the entrance. It was beginning to snow, but there was no wind even across the wide expanse of Red Square. The snow fell softly and steadily, and somewhere in the distance a clock chimed the half-hour as they walked across the Square. They seemed to be heading for a big building with ornate arches and old-fashioned spires. Suddenly Philby stopped, holding Powell's arm, looking at his face. He half turned and stretched out his arm, sweeping it in a wide arc.

'Tell me what you feel about all this. You've not seen it before.'

He pointed towards the Kremlin walls and then the cathedral of St Basil the Blessed.

'I don't see it as you do.'

'What does that mean?'

'I've always seen it on films and TV. Full of tanks and rockets and goose-stepping soldiers.'

There were flakes of snow on Philby's face and anger in his eyes.

'You don't feel in any way impressed by its history or its beauty?'

'Of course I do. But I feel scared as well. There's more feeling here of Stalin than Pushkin.'

Philby's eyes lit up for a moment and he almost smiled before he turned and walked on.

Philby led the way up the steps of the History Museum and a few moments later they were sitting together on a bench in front of the sledge which Napoleon had used during the retreat of 1812. Philby sat with his cap in his hand, his hand resting on his knee. And with his free hand he unbuttoned his coat, brushing the snow from his shoulders before he turned to face Powell.

'What's their reply?'

'My visit is the reply so far. I'm sure you'll understand that they want to know a lot more before they give you a yes or no.'

'Sir Ian was told?'

'Of course.'

'And he sent you?'

'No. It was dealt with at another level.'

Philby's eyes were half closed in disbelief. 'I don't believe it.'

'You don't believe what?'

'That Sir Ian would leave it to others lower down to decide.'

'But you must know, Mr Philby, that whatever the level anybody would want to know why you wish to come back. It's been a long time, and you haven't made it easy for yourself.'

Philby's eyes seemed to be focused on something far away and his tongue probed slowly at the corner of his mouth. He sighed deeply, and then turned to look at Powell. There were tears in Philby's eyes.

'Why are they playing games, Powell? Just tell me that.'

'I don't think they are. They're just being cautious in case *you're* playing games.'

There was a long silence and then Philby said, 'Ask me what you want to know.'

'Why do you want to come back?'

'I'm sixty-seven, Mr Powell. I'm tired.'

'Is anyone watching us now, Mr Philby?'

Philby smiled. A slow amused smile.

'You'd better call me Kim. No, nobody's watching us.'

'So far as you know.'

'OK.'

'Are there any other reasons?'

'Of course there are. A lifetime of reasons.'

'Don't you think that maybe it's a few years too late?'

'Why?' Philby looked genuinely surprised.

'Too many people remember too many things. Even those who like you don't understand why you did it.'

'Which of them likes me?'

Powell ignored the question.

'Why did you do it, Kim?'

'Do what?'

'Go over to the Soviets?'

'It's a long story. Others could tell you better than I could.'

'Who?'

'Have you got time to come to my place?'

'If you want me to.'

'Yes. Let's go.'

Philby waved to a taxi with a green light on its windscreen, and when it stopped he said something in Russian and opened the door for Powell to get in.

It was a journey of only a few minutes and the taxi stopped outside a modern block of flats. A uniformed soldier in the foyer stood to attention as Philby walked over to the lifts. After pressing the button he stood with his eyes closed until the lift doors slid open.

There was a large sitting room, one whole wall lined with books from top to bottom. A radio, a turntable, and about thirty records. At the far end of the room was a table with six chairs, and near the window where they were standing was a coffee table with four leather armchairs around it.

Philby took off his coat, put out his hand for Powell's coat and put them both on one of the armchairs. He sat down and pointed to the chair opposite. He was breathing heavily and he looked around the room before he started speaking, as if somebody might be there with them. When he turned back towards Powell he shrugged and shook his head as if he were explaining something away.

'Did they send any message?'

'No. I was asked to make contact with you and find out why you want to come back.'

'They must know why I want to come back.'

'I don't think they do.'

'Can I ask who instructed you?'

Powell saw the tension as Philby's hands gripped the arms of his chair.

'Arthur Padmore himself.'

Philby smiled and seemed to relax.

'What else do you want to know?'

'I want to know more about you.'

Philby half-smiled. 'I'm sure you already know everything there is to know. The files, and the good men and true.'

'I'd rather hear from you. Neither the records nor the gossip make sense.'

'In what way?'

'All of them, for or against, say that you're highly intelligent, a rational thinker, that many undergraduates of your generation felt that the Soviet Union might be the new Utopia. Most of them soon changed their minds when they found out what was really going on in Russia. So why not you? Why did you work for the Russians? And go on working for them?'

'Do you see my war-time activities against the Nazis as working for the Russians?'

Powell's blue eyes looked at Philby's face. And there was a pause before he spoke.

'You're giving me smart answers, Philby.' He shook his head. 'They won't wash with me. I'm not the right generation for that. We'd be wasting our time if we went on like this. If you're going to stay on the defensive I might as well head back for London.'

'What were you doing in 1932?'

'Nothing. I wasn't born until 1935.'

'So how can you understand what it was like in those days?'

'I can't. But I don't need to. All I want to know is why you *really* want to come back. And when you've told me I need to assess whether you're telling me the truth, and what your alternative motives might be. Whatever your reasons it won't be easy. You've got a lot of explaining to do.'

Philby shook his head. 'Padmore will already know why I want to come back. There are others who know too. I don't know why we have to go through this charade.'

'My orders come from Padmore. If he knows the reasons then he obviously isn't convinced that they're valid.' He paused and then said, 'Yet.'

'And you expect me to give you my life story before you weigh me in the balance.'

'It's an exaggerated way of putting it. But yes.'

'I could just go to Sheremetyevo and get on the next plane to London.'

'I doubt if your KGB friends would like that.'

Philby looked at Powell's face, contempt in his eyes for long moments, and then he relaxed, leaning back in his chair, stretching out his legs in front of him. It was several minutes before he spoke.

'How long have you been in the firm?'

'A long time. Years.'

'You realize they're playing games with both of us?'

'Tell me.'

'There are things that some of them know that they're never going to tell you. And there are things that I can't tell you either. And if they haven't told you, then you'd need to know far more than you ever can, for me to convince you.'

'About what?'

'About all of it. What happened from 1931 onwards.'

'You could tell me.'

'I couldn't. And if I could, then you would want to check it all out. That would take too long.'

'Just tell me the truth about why you want to go back.'

There was anger in Philby's eyes as he looked at Powell, and he said slowly, 'Why are those bastards playing games?

63

They know why I want to go back. Ask Pouley. Ask Fredericks. They're making a fool of you and they're trying to make a fool of me. You tell them that if they won't do it quietly then I'll do it my way.'

'Do the KGB know that you want to leave?'

'Oh for Christ's sake. Work it out for yourself.'

'That'll take time, Kim. But if that's what you want . . .'

Philby slumped back in his chair, his chin resting in his hand as he sat thinking. He sighed deeply as he looked back at Powell.

'There are things I can't say right now, and the things I *can* say won't convince you. I don't blame you. How could you know? You weren't around in those days. Gehlen's just a name to you, so is Otto John. But you'd better tell London that one way or another I'm coming back.' He paused and then went on. 'And if I'm left to do it my way then, by God, what's gone before will look like . . .' He shook his head. 'No don't say that.' His eyes were on Powell's face. 'Try and work it out for me yourself, there's a good chap.'

'Is there any real urgency to this. Are you in any danger?'

Philby smiled and shook his head. 'No. I'm not in danger. The urgency is my age. I want some peace.'

'Don't you get that here?'

Philby put his head on one side, thinking. 'In a way I do. It's like spending a long holiday with distant relations. It's fine for a time, but you look forward to going back.'

'Can I ask you one more question?'

'Of course.'

'Were you, are you, a triple-agent?'

Powell had watched Philby's face carefully. Looking for a clue. Ridicule, anger, or some easy lie. He didn't expect the answer he got.

Philby said softly, 'I honestly don't know. I never did know. It was the same for me then as it is for you now.'

'Do you have many friends in Moscow?'

Philby shrugged. 'It depends what you call friends. There are two or three people I like who like me.'

'Would you miss them if you went back to England?'

'Not so that it mattered.'

'I was told you had a girl-friend. What about her?'

'I've no obligations there. They'll look after her when I've gone.'

'Have you any other reason for wanting to go back apart from . . .' he shrugged, '. . . homesickness?'

'No. Just Auld Lang Syne. I'm not planning subversion or working for the Soviets. Apart from anything else I'm too tired to play games. I've had enough of all that.'

'Are you disillusioned about Communism?'

Philby smiled his knowing smile. 'That implies that at some stage I was deluded. I never was. What I believed then, I believe now.'

'But if you believe in Communism why don't you prefer to stay in Moscow?'

Philby shook his head as if he was impatient at having to explain once again. Irritated by Powell's inability to grasp an obvious truth.

'My coming back isn't anything to do with Communism or politics or whose side I was on. It's nothing to do with whether I was a traitor or a patriot. Can't you understand that?'

Powell shook his head. 'I'm sorry, but I can't, you'll have to explain.'

'Do you like England yourself?'

'Yes.'

'Why?'

Powell shrugged. 'I suppose I could put up some rational reasons. Tolerance, freedom, and all that. But I doubt if they would be real. I just like it. It's where I belong.'

'That's all it is for me. Habit, what I understand without thinking, the place where I grew up.'

65

'You told Farrow you wanted to watch the Australians at Lords. There's nothing in your records that shows an interest in cricket.'

Philby gave a short laugh. 'I've never seen the Australians play, and I've never been to Lords. I'm not that interested in cricket. I can barely remember even the basic rules. For me cricket is summer, village greens, and the last night of the Proms. The Boat Race, apple blossom, country trains and . . .' he shrugged '. . . nothing much more than that. I'm not sure it's even any of those things. They're just symbols.'

'What would you do in England?'

'Nothing. If they'd let me. Just read, be there. I'd keep out of the way.'

'It wouldn't be that easy. You might be recognized.'

'Would you have recognized me?'

'I'm not sure. Who recruited you for the Soviets?'

'You know that as well as I do. You've been working on it.'

'How did you know that?'

Philby smiled. 'I'm a KGB officer.'

'How did they know?'

Philby slowly shook his head. 'I'm not trading information if that's what you want. Did they make that a condition?'

'No. It hasn't gone nearly far enough to consider conditions. Those would come later if they gave a positive response.'

'Meantime?'

'Meantime I came to Moscow to talk to you.'

'It must all be on file by now. What else is there you need to know?'

'It isn't all on file. That's just the words, I'd like to hear the music.'

For the first time since they had met Philby looked at him with real interest. His eyes searched Powell's face as if there might be some clue to his intentions in the pale blue eyes. Eventually he said quietly, 'That could take quite a bit of time.'

'I've got nothing else to do until the decision is made.'

'Talking to me won't really help you. You know that. You won't know if I'm speaking the truth.'

'I've been deciding whether people were telling lies or the truth for a long time now. I'll get a pretty good idea.'

'When are you planning to go back?'

'Tomorrow morning. I'm already booked on.'

'That doesn't give you much time to decide one way or another.'

'It does. I'm taking it step by step. As soon as I'm getting a negative feeling I shall stop. Until then I shall go on taking the steps.'

'Have I given you negative feelings today?'

Powell saw Philby's hooded eyes watching him; they were intent but not alert. He was reluctant by training to give an answer, but he knew that Philby needed an answer. Despite his air of assurance he was on edge. It could be because some convoluted KGB game hung on his success, or it could be because he desperately wanted to come back just for the reasons he had given.

'No,' he said. 'I've got no negative feelings from talking to you today.'

'What have you learned?'

'The shape of a man, the sound of his voice, his own words not the words of others.' Powell stood up. 'Could you fix me a taxi back to the hotel?'

'Of course.'

Philby walked to the telephone on the shelf by the door and dialled six numbers. While Philby was talking Powell leaned across and switched on a second radio that stood on a small table under the window. Somebody was talking about the songs in *Evita*. It was the BBC's World Service. In

English. He switched off the set. It was a sign. Maybe no more than a sign of thoroughness from a man used to covering every angle of a double life. But it was a sign.

When Philby hung up he turned and said, 'It will be here in three or four minutes. I'll walk down with you.'

'I can see myself out. Don't bother.'

'You wouldn't get out unless I was with you.'

They looked at each other silently for several moments. Powell absorbing the significance of what had been said, and Philby a mixture of arrogance and unease. It was Philby who broke the silence.

'You don't need to go through the embassy if you want to contact me again. You can write to me at PO Box 9497 Moscow. Or you can phone me here. Moscow 155–50–03. Do you want to write it down?'

Powell reached in his jacket for his diary and repeated the two numbers as he wrote them out. He looked at Philby.

'Do you want a code?'

'No. Just discretion.'

Philby was silent as they went down in the lift and as they crossed the entrance hall the guard stood to attention and Philby nodded to him.

The taxi was already there. Philby stood on the steps of the block of flats and as the taxi moved off Powell was aware of the pale face watching as he left.

# 9

The 'Milord' committee met informally to discuss Powell's report. It took up three A4 pages and had been circulated to the three of them two days before the meeting.

None of them looked very amiable and only Walker nodded to Powell as Padmore settled himself at the head of the table. Padmore wasted no time. He waved Powell's report in one hand as he spoke.

'I don't think much of this, Mr Powell. No recommendation. Nothing decisive in the whole report. Are you holding something back?'

The sheer effrontery of the comment after the way they had waffled away at the interviews took him by surprise. Enough for him to show his resentment.

'No, Mr Padmore, I'm holding nothing back. My impression is that everybody else is though.'

'What does that mean exactly?'

'It means that everyone I've spoken to so far has dodged the issues. On the one hand he's a traitor but on the other he's a gentleman.'

'And what do you conclude from that?'

'I conclude that Philby is a gentleman traitor and maybe something went on in those days that everybody would rather forget.'

Padmore turned irritably towards McNay.

'What's your opinion, James?'

'My opinion's the same as it always was. There'll always be plenty of people to put in a good word for Philby and maybe Powell is right.'

'Right in what way?'

'Maybe something did go on in those days that a lot of people would prefer to sweep under the carpet. For me he was a traitor and we're wasting Powell's time and our own. Obviously even the Russians don't trust him, so why the hell should we?'

'What makes you think they don't trust him?'

McNay smiled. It was almost a sneer.

'You've read what Otto John said after he came back?'

Padmore snorted. 'My God, *he* was a traitor if ever there was one.'

Walker leaned forward. 'What was your impression about Kim, Mr Powell?'

'I've said what I think in my report.'

'Perhaps you could bring yourself to repeat it.' It was Padmore who spoke.

The sarcasm in Padmore's voice was undisguised. Powell looked straight at him.

'I think he wants to come back, and I think he expected to come back without any trouble. And I think he can't understand why we're going through this ritual.'

Walker looked at the tip of his cigar as he spoke.

'Any other impressions?'

'Yes. I'm quite sure that Philby will seriously consider carrying out his threat to come back his own way if we don't agree.'

McNay's rasping voice interrupted Padmore as he was about to speak.

'In your report you suggest that Philby said that there were things he couldn't say. What d'you reckon all that was about?'

'I didn't suggest that, Mr McNay. I reported what he actually said. I gave near enough his own words.'

'And what did he mean?'

'I don't know.'

'What do you *think* he meant, damn it?'

Powell looked slowly round the table at each one of them. Then he said slowly, 'I've no idea what he meant, but I suspect that I'm the only person in this room who doesn't know what he meant.'

Padmore flung himself back in his chair with impatience or annoyance, it was hard to tell which. He sighed theatrically, fiddled with Powell's report and then leaned forward again, his arms on the table. He looked directly at Powell.

'Mr Powell, I think perhaps we are all beginning to miss the point. We accepted right from the start that none of us old hands from the days when Philby was an officer in SIS could put aside his knowledge of those days and assess the present situation satisfactorily. I think that in trying to avoid passing on those prejudices to you we have maybe clouded the position for you even more. That was stupid. There is a simple issue at stake here. Should we or should we not agree to the request of Kim Philby to return to the United Kingdom. Now . . .' He clasped his hands. '. . . Now. How do we resolve the problem? I suggest . . .' He waved one hand towards the others. '. . . Subject to what my colleagues may have to say, that we leave you to deal with this problem in your own way. Forget our views, go back to the primary sources. Satisfy yourself. Report to us only when you have arrived at your own opinion.'

'I'd like to ask to be taken off this assignment, sir.'

Padmore threw up his hands and flopped back in his chair. Patrick Walker looked across at Powell.

'This assignment did not come from this committee, Johnny. It came from the top. We can all understand your feelings. It shouldn't take long. You can refer to any of us if you wish, otherwise go your own way.'

'And in the end what happens? Whichever way I recommend, however carefully I go into it, the committee, or Sir Ian, or somebody else, can just ignore my advice.'

'Oh no.' Padmore's voice was urgent and harsh. 'We will abide by your recommendation whatever it might be.'

'Can I have that in writing?'

There was no hesitation. Padmore said, 'Certainly. Before I go back tonight if you so wish.'

'Yes, I'd like that, sir.'

Padmore turned to Walker. 'Patrick, would you draw up something appropriate and I'll sign it.'

'Certainly, Arthur.'

Half an hour later, after the others had gone, Walker handed the brief note over to Powell. He read it carefully and then put it in his pocket. He was alone with Walker.

Walker shifted in his chair at the other side of the table.

'Would you say I'm a twicer, Johnny?'

'No.'

'Then don't take that note. Put it in my safe. I'll give it to you any time you want it. Night or day. It's a dangerous piece of paper to lose.'

'Fair enough. Give me an official receipt for an unspecified document signed by Padmore, today's date.'

'OK.'

Walker reached down the table for one of the official note-pads, wrote a few lines and handed over the note as he stood up. Powell glanced at the note and stood up too.

'He gave you good advice, Johnny. Don't ignore it just because you're angry.'

'What advice do you mean?'

'Ignore our views. Go back to primary sources. Be a historian.'

'The trouble is that what everybody says makes sense. Until you put it together. Then it doesn't seem possible that you are all talking about the same man or the same events.'

'Maybe we're not, my friend. Maybe we're not.'

Powell stood with one hand on the door knob as he turned towards Walker.

'I noticed of course that Padmore didn't deny that I was the only one in the room who didn't know what Philby meant when he said there were things that he couldn't say.'

'Maybe his mind was on other things.'

'Do *you* think that was why?'

Walker looked at him. For a brief moment there was sympathy in his eyes.

'I guess not, Johnny.'

'So what is it you all know that I don't?'

Walker leaned his head against the door-frame, looking down as he thought. When his head came up he shrugged. 'It's a problem of semantics. We don't *know* anything that you don't know, or couldn't find out. We just have our suspicions, our own explanations for why it doesn't all hang together. You'll be the same in the end.'

'I have my suspicions now.'

Walker held up his hand. 'Don't tell me. I don't want to know.' He looked at Powell's face. 'You've got more chance of finding out the truth than the rest of us ever had. But you'll have to turn over a lot of stones before you find the worms.'

'How far back do I go and when?'

Walker looked towards the window and without looking back at Powell he said, 'Cambridge 1931, Vienna 1933, Section D 1940, Madrid 1944.' He shrugged. 'I could go on all night. Then there's Gehlen and Otto John.' He turned back to look at Powell and said very softly, 'If my suspicions are correct you'd better get a move on.'

# 10

He had noticed the handful of people as he came out of the bookshop and he turned to look where they were looking. It was February, and a cold thin fog hung in the air so that at first he had thought they were looking at the two mounted policemen on their horses. But then he saw them, and heard the ragged clatter of their boots as they walked down the centre of the street.

They marched in silence, no singing, no talking, their faces white; the white of dirty, unbaked pastry, their eyes half closed with exhaustion and hopelessness. He had never seen men like them before. Their clothes were torn and patched, and their breath hung in clouds, their mouths open and their nostrils pinched. There were damp placards on rough sticks that said simply – 'Give us work' and as they filed past, a few gaudy, much-embroidered trades-union banners fluttered in the centre of the column.

He and the others at Trinity had talked about the unemployed, but none of them had imagined them as being like this. They looked like ghosts. They were men at the end of their tether, beaten men, asking not for more dole or sympathy. All they asked for was work.

There was a ragged cheer from the people watching, but none of the marchers turned his head. Something held him there watching them pass by. It was half an hour before they had all filed past. He remembered one of the placards. He wasn't sure where Jarrow was. He vaguely recalled that it was somewhere in Yorkshire, a town where they built ships.

*As he walked slowly back to Trinity he felt hot despite the cold wind. Hot with anger at a government and an establishment that could let these men and their families starve. No wonder they were said to have turned the Prime Minister's picture to the wall. Ramsay MacDonald, their hero, the Labour Party's hero who had seen his party routed, with 46 seats to the opposition's 497, and then accepted the premiership of the coalition from the King. Cornford and Haden-Guest were right. Socialism had been betrayed, and now there was only Communism to save the world from total disaster. He remembered his own words when he had campaigned for Labour in the election. 'My friends, the heart of England does not beat in stately homes and castles. It beats in the factories and on the farms.' It was utterly banal, sickeningly trite, and terribly true. It wasn't enough though. It was time for new thinking. You couldn't just keep bandaging one open wound after another. They'd have to throw the old system away and start again.*

*The shrewd eyes looked across at the young man stirring his coffee.*

*'But it's the same all over the world, Kim. Nobody's building ships anymore. You can't create shipbuilding orders out of thin air.'*

*'It wasn't market forces, Rupert. It was deliberate. It was policy.'*

*'Who says?'*

*'I went back that night to the drill hall and talked to one of them. The leader of the men on the march. He told me what had happened.'*

*'What's his name?'*

*'David Riley.'*

*'An Irishman. They're always at the root of all industrial troubles.'*

*'That's ridiculous. He's a Councillor, a responsible man.*

He's lived there all his life. The march was backed by Conservatives as well as Labour. There's over seventy per cent unemployment in Jarrow. The Town Council sent an official deputation to the House of Commons. They were interviewed by Walter Runciman. D'you know what he said? ..."Jarrow must work out its own solution." How could a man say that?'

The older man smiled. 'And what would your solution have been?'

'Socialism. Social Democracy. A whole new perspective. Caring about the losers. Putting the capitalist bullies down.'

'State intervention?'

'Yes.'

'That always leads to loss of personal freedom.'

'Better that than millions of men thrown on the scrapheap.'

'That's what Hitler is doing in Germany.'

'Never. That's just a group of hooligans after power.'

'That's special pleading, Kim. He's finding work for the unemployed, and giving the Germans back their national pride.'

'There are better ways. There must be.'

'Such as?'

'What the Soviet Union is doing.'

Rupert Mark laughed. 'So you're advocating red revolution in England?'

'A revolution in thinking anyway.'

'What are you going to do after you've finished here?'

'I want to have a few months in Europe.'

'Where?'

'I haven't decided.'

'Have a look at Vienna. That's going to be where the real struggle starts. The struggle for Europe. Or maybe the world.'

Kim Philby shook his head. 'You sound like a very high-class tour operator. Luxury tour to see the end of civilization.'

Rupert Mark smiled and stood up. 'It's time we were turning in. Breakfast's at nine.'

'How have you done so well so quickly, Rupert?'

The man brushed an imaginary speck from his elegant suit. 'I just got to know people. They've been terribly helpful.'

Later, after Philby had gone to bed, the man dialled a local number. A Cambridge number. And when he heard the familiar voice at the other end he said, 'I agree.' And hung up. A degree in English and Eng. Lit. from Warsaw University, and five years in England had left only the faintest, attractive, trace of an accent. The English accepted it without doubt as French and if your name had originally been Markovich and you'd been born in Lodz it was quite an achievement.

The thick cotton wool snow had been beaten down where they had been lying and the afternoon sun shone through the trunks of the tall, dark pines that cast their blue shadows along the smooth folds and hammocks of snow.

She was smiling up at him as she buttoned her bodice, her face rosy red and her eyes sparkling. As he reached out a hand to pull her up she took it and said, 'That was the first time you'd ever done it, wasn't it?'

He half-smiled. 'A gentleman never tells, Litzi. It's one of the tests.'

Laughing, she brushed the snow from the back of her skirt and then took his hand.

'Will you come to the meeting with me tonight?'

'I promised to see the English couple.'

'Do you think they might help?'

He shrugged. 'God knows. Maybe it was just all talk.'

'What was their name again?'

77

'Gaitskell.'

'What a funny name.'

'I think she'll be more use than he will, I think she'll help with the refugees.'

She slid her arm round his waist as they stumbled through the snow to the road. His motorcycle still leaned against the tree stump where they had left it. He unlocked the padlock and slid the chain from the spokes of the wheel. It took a couple of kicks before it would start, then, with the girl on the pillion, he headed back towards Vienna.

When he eventually turned into the cobbles of Latschkagasse she thumped him on the back and he stopped.

'What is it?'

'We don't live here anymore, dummkopf.'

He laughed, turned the motorcycle and headed for their new home.

Until two weeks before he had been just a lodger at her father's house. Israel Kohlman was a Polish Jew who had moved to Austria before World War 1. Used to his daughter's passionate, impulsive behaviour he had raised no objections when they had eventually moved out to live together in two dingy rooms. Married briefly at eighteen she was no longer Alice Kohlman but Alice Friedman, divorced, and much impressed by the young Englishman in front of her on the motorbike. She found him handsome and charming, and almost puritanical. Slightly shocked by her drinking, and her readiness to live with him, nevertheless he seemed to share her views on politics. He had quickly absorbed the politics of Vienna, the strikes, the police violence and the battles in the streets as the city was abused by first one political group and then another. He cared about working people, and although his German was poor he quickly made friends with her Socialist friends in the Karl Marx Hof and the Goethe Hof, the blocks of workers' flats that were Vienna's pride.

She had long left Socialism behind. For her it was a dying creed, and only Communism would save Austria now. But the young man still had his doubts. He was English and he didn't really understand. She reckoned that he would learn fast in Vienna.

It was three weeks later that he really began to learn the lesson. He was lying on the old-fashioned iron bed reading a German phrase-book, mildly irritated by the dull banging next door. Litzi had gone to one of her secret meetings to plan the uprising. The perennial uprising that would never happen. He half-smiled to himself. Maybe it was better to dream than sink back into lethargy, and the few rusty rifles in the sewers probably gave the dream some faint semblance of reality.

He looked up smiling as she burst into the room. All female Communists seemed to burst into rooms.

And then he saw her face. White and stricken, her mouth distorted and as she fought to get her breath, panting, she said, 'Why didn't you come?'

'Where?'

'Can't you hear it? The guns.'

He swung his feet to the floor, looking at her.

'I thought it was the people next door. What is it, Litzi? Tell me.'

'The bastards are shooting the workers. Killing them.'

'Who? Who's killing the workers?'

'The Heimwehr and the police. The Palace of Justice is on fire.'

'Was this the solidarity march against the killing of the child?'

'Yes.'

'Sit down.'

He patted the bed beside him and reluctantly she sat down. He took her hand in his.

79

'They'll have to decide now. They'll have to fight back.'

'They're going to call a general strike.'

He sighed. 'That will be useless. It will finish them.'

'What else can they do?'

'They can dig up those guns and fight back.'

She turned her head to look at his face.

'They won't, Kim. They haven't got the guts. They're Socialists and they only understand strikes. Strikes and protest marches, and then you go home for dry bread and acorn tea.' She looked at him and said softly, 'Help us, Kim. Help us before it's too late.'

'How can I help?'

'Join us. Help us to plan.'

'Plan what?'

'Plan a resistance. An underground.'

'It's the Socialists who need the help, Litzi. Your people have got Moscow. The Socialists have nobody.'

'Then make them join us. They'll listen to you.'

He smiled. 'Why the hell should they listen to me?'

'You're English and you care. You're one of us really. You just don't want to admit it.'

'Who's that ugly Hungarian?'

'Gabor Péter.'

'Let me talk to him.'

But by the time it was dark that night eighty-five civilians had already been killed. The general strike had been called for the next day, and in three days, faced with government violence and terrorism, it collapsed.

By the end of the year Litzi and Kim were deep in the game of hide-and-seek that helped smuggle refugees from the Nazis over the German border to shelter in Vienna. There were pass-words and secret meetings, and the distribution of anti-government tracts, but more time and effort was spent

80

*in begging cast-off clothing and accommodation for the
refugees than on politics.*

*At the turn of the year the Austrian Nazis began to come
out into the open, and the Heimwehr, the home-grown para-
military units under the handsome Prince Starhemberg, used
the Nazi terrorists as an excuse for settling their final ac-
counting with the Socialists.*

*In desperation the Socialists used their solitary, tradi-
tional weapon. A general strike. The signal for the start of
the strike would be that the trams would stop.*

*In the next forty-eight hours Chancellor Dollfuss struck
back. The Socialist Party was banned, and police moved in
on Party offices and factories. Barbed wire ringed the inner
city and the workers fled to their homes. Nobody knew
whether the strike was still on. Nobody gave them orders.
They were left to their own devices. Men and women
searched in vain in gardens and sewers for their hidden
arms. Groups of workers retreated in fear to the only shelter
they knew, the big blocks of workers' flats. Those visionary
buildings that even the outside world had praised and
admired, with their swimming pools and playgrounds, and
their promise for the future.*

*So on those blocks, packed with their usual families and
those who had run there in fear and desperation, the government poured artillery fire. Litzi and Kim Philby had stood
with the silent crowds, watching in disbelief as the shells
pounded the walls to rubble. And when white flags were
hastily thrust through the shattered windows the Heimwehr
and the police swarmed into the buildings. Smashing furniture, ripping mattresses in the search for arms, killing and
beating as they went. By the end of the day there were 300
dead and 800 wounded. And a silence fell on the city that
could be heard all over Europe.*

*In the following days the police hunted down every politi-
cal suspect on their long lists. Socialists, Communists, union*

*officials, activists of any left-wing group. Litzi Friedman was on their list, and as an underground Communist she was a high priority arrest.*

*Eleven days after the shelling of the workers' flats Litzi Friedman became the wife of Harold Adrian Russell Philby, aged twenty-two, 'Student, without religious faith', in a brief ceremony at Vienna Town Hall. Litzi Philby was now a British citizen.*

# 11

McNay sat well back to avoid the bar of pale sunshine that fell across his desk from the window. John Powell sat opposite him on a straight-backed chair that had obviously been smuggled over when SIS had moved from its old quarters at Queen Anne's Gate. It creaked each time he moved, and was singularly uncomfortable. But McNay wouldn't worry about such social niceties, he was seldom long in London. His area was Hong Kong and Australasia, and his target country was Red China. As McNay finished signing his letters Powell tried to imagine the inscrutable Scot in his dealings with the inscrutable Chinese who his people would have to use as his line-crossers. Then McNay closed the box and pushed it to one side, putting the cap on his pen and tucking it into his inside pocket.

'Now, Mr Powell, what can I do for you?'

'Were you in SIS when Philby was recruited?'

'Yes. I came in about six months before he did.'

'What had he done after he left Cambridge?'

McNay leaned back in his chair and closed his eyes in thought. Powell looked at the tanned face. The straight, thin nose, the bushy eyebrows and the rather sensual mouth. McNay's eyes opened and he looked across at Powell. They were unusual eyes for a man. Dark brown, the irises almost as dark as the pupils. They were melting eyes, a woman's eyes. Powell guessed that women would find them devastating.

'He had some sort of sabbatical in Vienna. Improving his German or some such excuse. He married his first wife. She

83

was a Jewess and a Communist. He was there about a year. He came back in 1934 and worked on some magazine. It put together reviews from other sources. It must have been about that time that the Soviets recruited him. There was no more Communist talk from Philby. He joined the Anglo-German Fellowship, a pro-Nazi organization. And he edited their magazine. He visited Berlin several times and had talks with Ribbentrop's people and Goebbels' office. Then he went to Spain as a freelance journalist. After a few months he became *The Times* correspondent reporting on Franco's side. Was awarded some Franco medal or other. He was *The Times* correspondent in France until Dunkirk, and it was then he was recruited into SIS.'

'Who recruited him?'

'Burgess got him in. They knew one another at Cambridge.'

'But Burgess wouldn't have had the authority to take him on. Who actually said "yes"?'

'I'd say it was a combined decision. He had the usual preliminary interview at St Ermin's. Then several further interviews. I was at one or two of them myself.'

'Were you for or against?'

McNay smiled. 'I was for.'

'Why?'

'Because he didn't seem all that keen to join. I've always had the theory that the eager beavers are dangerous. Philby seemed aloof. He was working for *The Times* and said that he wasn't sure that he wanted a change. There should be reports of the various interviews in the files.'

'There should be, but there aren't.'

McNay raised his eyebrows. 'Nothing at all?'

'Absolutely nothing. Not even a note on the index to say that material has been removed.'

'What about Burgess and Maclean's recruitment reports?'

'They're still on file.'

McNay shrugged. 'Very strange.'

'What made Philby change his mind?'

'God knows. Probably Burgess.'

'Tell me about Burgess.'

'What part?'

'His background.'

'His father died when he was eight or nine, he was a Royal Navy commander. His mother married again, a wealthy man, Colonel Basset. Burgess went to Eton and then Dartmouth. He had some medical problem. His eyes, I think. He was sent back to Eton. Won the Gladstone Scholarship and went up to Trinity. Handsome, arrogant, talented, debauched. That's about it.'

'When do you think Philby was recruited by the Soviets?'

'I'd guess he was looked at in Vienna. That was 1934. And I'd say that he was working for them by the time he went to Spain.'

'Why then? I thought he was working for *The Times*?'

'He was already in Spain as a freelance when *The Times* hired him. Before that he was broke. So where did the money come from? How did he finance the trip?'

'What did the Soviets want him for?'

'I imagine that it was useful to have information from the Franco side, and I'd guess they were setting him up for MI5 to spot him as a useful recruit.'

'And who recruited him for the Soviets?'

'I'm sure he was looked over by "Milord". And I'm sure that it was "Milord" who had already spotted Burgess and Maclean. At that stage I should think that Burgess was the man who mattered. 'I'd say too that Philby got his Soviet funds through Burgess.'

'What was "Milord" doing at the time?'

'Teaching science at Cambridge. The details will be on your files.'

'When did you first suspect Philby yourself?'

'I was suspicious first in 1945 when I heard about the Volkov affair. That stank of Philby. And I was *sure* in 1949 when my people went into the trap in Albania.'

'Did you say so at the time?'

'Too bloody true. I raised hell about it and I put in a separate report in 1952 when Milmo questioned him.'

'What happened?'

'The old-boy network started working. I nearly got the push myself. I got a call from one of the nationals offering me a foreign correspondent's job. And I knew where that suggestion would have come from.'

'Who?'

'I don't mean one person. There were a couple of dozen busy protecting Philby.'

'Have you thought any more about why he wants to come back?'

'I've got my suspicions.'

'What are they?'

McNay shook his head. 'No thank you, my friend. The network's still there. I'd like to retire gracefully in a couple of years' time. I've already put in a few extra years.'

As Powell walked to his car he realized that both Walker and McNay had said they had their suspicions about why Philby wanted to come back. They had both actually used the word 'suspicion', and they had both been reluctant to pursue the matter any further.

He drove the car to the underground garage and the sergeant filled the tank. The shortage of petrol was beginning to bite, and the SIS petrol was still four-star. Dyed blue for identification. He drove straight to the Connaught where he had arranged to meet her. Her parents had taken a suite there for the weekend.

'You know, Johnny, there's something about men with freckles. Makes them look like boys all their lives. Kind of sexy.'

Lady Tracy was in one of her Nancy Cunard moods. The thin face heavily made-up, the big grey eyes that were her sole claim to beauty surreptitiously watching the reaction of the others as she leaned forward to look at Powell. He was used to it. She quite liked him, but when she was in her 'salon' mood she liked to make clear to the assembly that he was not there by right, he was there because of her daughter. One of Van's strays. He smiled back at her.

'I'm afraid they can be deceptive, Lady Tracy. Like big grey eyes.'

'You're a naughty boy, Johnny.'

She reached for the brandy. There was no question of ladies retiring at Lady Tracy's dinner parties. They sat with the men, and drank brandy if they so chose. She looked around the table.

'Johnny's not long back from Warsaw you know. He's something important at the FO. Aren't you, Johnny?'

Powell smiled amiably. 'I just carry the bags, ma'am.'

'What do you really do? Tell us.'

Sir Arthur stood up. 'It's time we should be moving, sweetie. It's a punctual start, and it will be difficult to park near the theatre.'

Powell and Vanessa had not been invited to join the theatre party. There was a limit to her mother's acceptance of her daughter's life. The divorce had been bad enough, and Powell was not the kind of man she had in mind as her daughter's second husband. One mistake could be excused as no more than youthful foolishness, but two would be inexcusable. To Lady Tracy divorce was for the middle classes. The well-off may make incompatible marriages, but they came to an arrangement. Divorce was unmistakably vulgar. Vanessa's divorce had been bad enough, but marrying an abandoned bastard was definitely not on. Especially as he made no secret of his background.

Powell and the girl took a taxi back to the flat, and as they sat silently, Powell wondered if Sir Arthur knew something. Several times the old bitch had probed about his job and on each occasion Sir Arthur had seemed to divert her. It could be just coincidence. But it was worth remembering. Sir Arthur moved in government circles and had always been more amiable than his wife towards him. Maybe he had heard that his status was not quite so humble as it seemed.

Back in the flat he poured them both a drink and sat watching her as she looked at herself in the mirror. When she sat down and had taken a gulp of her drink he said, 'Would you like to go up and see her tomorrow?'

'How did you know that was what I was thinking about?'

He smiled. 'Would you like to?'

'Ralph probably wouldn't agree.'

'I'll phone him now and ask him if you want.'

'Why am I such a coward?'

'You're not a coward. It's just easier for me. I'm not emotionally involved. I'm an outsider.'

'Would you?'

'Of course.'

He stood up and walked into the hall. She heard him talking but couldn't hear what he said. He came back after a few minutes and plumped down in his chair.

'All fixed. I'll pick her up at twelve, we'll have lunch at the Woolsack and then take her down to the river.'

Her eyes were on his face. 'He wouldn't let me pick her up? Not even with you?'

'Ignore it. He's a weak man, Vannie. He needs to hurt when he can.'

'He always seemed pretty tough to me.'

He smiled. 'He's not tough, sweetie. You don't need to

88

hurt people if you're tough. He's more or less normal I'd say. Spiteful rather than tough.'

'Do you think she remembers me?'

'Of course she does. She saw you only a couple of months ago.'

'I love her, Johnny. But I hate seeing her.'

'You don't. It hurts. It reminds you of things, and it's tough when she has to go back. But you have to take all that for her sake.'

'She'd be so much better off with me.'

He looked at his drink and said nothing.

'Don't you think she would, Johnny?'

'I think Ralph cares for her. She's got the same nannie she's always had. She would certainly be better off if you were there too, but I don't think she'll come to any harm. He's well-off, and he can provide all she needs.'

'He was a pig to me.'

'He didn't know how to cope with you, honey. I expect he tried to understand but couldn't make it. My guess is that he cared for you quite a lot. He's very Brit, and that doesn't help. And your mother didn't help either.'

'She was on his side, even during all the palaver of the divorce.'

'He was a social catch, sweetie. And you were throwing him back into the sea. For her you just go on being the dutiful wife for the sake of being married to a rich man. And his parents count in your mother's circle. She'd sacrifice a lot to keep all that going without rocking the boat.'

'She sacrificed me all right.'

'Not really, Van. You dealt them all very good cards and they played them.'

'If you had been married to me would you have kept Lydia and prevented me from seeing her?'

He smiled. 'If I'd married you there wouldn't have been a divorce. Not while our child was young anyway. If you did

things I found outrageous I might have kept you at arm's
length but I'd have kept us together. I might have threatened
you, but nothing more.'

'Do you think that way because you were an orphan?'

'Maybe. I don't know.'

'You know, when you're away I think about you such a
lot.'

'Tell me.'

'Whenever we talk about anything you play it straight
down the middle. You don't work out what answers might
suit you best. You say exactly what you think. You don't
grind an axe.'

He laughed softly. 'It wouldn't be much use to you if we
played games.'

'But everybody does.'

'They *don't*. I don't.'

'You don't tell me the truth about your job.'

'Tell me more.'

'You aren't the kind of man who carries bags or does a
humble job. So why not tell me?'

'I had to sign a piece of paper that I wouldn't talk about
it.'

'Are you a spy?'

'There ain't no such thing outside TV and films.'

She saw the blue eyes and the bull-terrier smile, and despite her low spirits she smiled back.

'Thanks for fixing for me to see Lydia.'

'We'll have a nice day, don't you worry.'

# 12

He walked slowly down Fasanenstrasse from the
Kurfürstendamm and he deliberately didn't look up at the
window until he was almost at Foto Lange. Then he looked.
A quick glance. The window was open and the geranium was
on the balcony. Otto John looked both ways before he
crossed the street.

At street level Foto Lange's window display in war time
was little more than big enlargements of portraits and land-
scapes with the Leitz label in the corner of each photograph,
cardboard displays for Agfa, and a shelf display of second-
hand bits and pieces.

He waited until the solitary customer had been served,
nodded to the man behind the counter and walked through
the hanging curtains.

It was the fourth meeting he had attended, and so far as he
was concerned, it would be the last unless they showed signs
of actually doing something. It was time they decided one
way or the other. If it wasn't for his brother Hans he might
have left them to their own devices. There was no doubt that
they had courage, but they were so often indecisive, and that
could be fatal. They had been talking and planning for a
year already, and that was too long. Like the words that
Shakespeare had put in his plotter's mouth – 'If it were
done when 'tis done, then 'twere well if it were done
quickly'.

He knocked on the door, the three spaced-out knocks that
always embarrassed him because it seemed like school-boy
play-acting. When it was opened he saw that only von

91

*Stauffenberg was there. And that surely must mean that the decision had been taken to go ahead.*

*As they went over the frontier the big Junkers Ju52 banked slowly for the last leg to Lisbon. The lights inside the plane were so dim that it was impossible to read, but now that they were in Spanish airspace he put his finger against the taut, cotton, window curtain and made a gap so that he could look out. There were no signs of war, there were lights tracing the main roads, and clusters of lights that marked small towns and villages. Franco was playing a subtle game with both sides. Despite Hitler's pressure he had kept Spain neutral; nevertheless he was happy to allow the Abwehr to operate openly wherever they wanted; and if German watchers from the cliffs at Algeciras could note the details of the Allied ships turning to Gibraltar then that could pay off the debt for the Luftwaffe's help in the Civil War. The British had offered him nothing. All the same, his eyes were just as blind to the Allied prisoners who escaped and came over the Pyrenees from Perpignan.*

*Dr Otto John was a lawyer. Legal adviser to Lufthansa and thirty-five years old. A mild looking man, an unlikely conspirator. He would have been disturbed by such a description. He saw himself as no more than an adviser to the group of anti-Nazis. Much as he was to Lufthansa. But he would have admitted to being an anti-Nazi. As he sat there he was aware that his hands were trembling as he was given a cup of coffee. And his stomach churned violently no matter how he arranged his body in the seat. He was used to giving advice, but he wasn't used to implementing it. He was a man of conviction but not of action.*

*For months he had been urging them to make up their minds. Not about the main issue. That was already decided. But the approach to the British; that was where they always hesitated. His brother Hans, von Stauffenberg, Beck and von*

*Witzleben. They all said that it was crossing the line from being resisters to being traitors. His advice was that in Nazi law there was no such line. If they were one, then they were equally the other.*

*What happened after they had done it? You couldn't just draw a line and say 'the war stops now'. The war would go on. Life would go on. Unless the Allies said, 'OK. Now it's different. Now we'll talk.' And they had all agreed that it would be better if they said it before rather than after.*

*Again and again he'd gone over in his mind how to present their case. There had been meetings he had attended when he had been bored, and his mind had wandered as they went over the plan for the hundredth time. Had there been some vital point that he had missed where he would have no sensible answer for the British? Maybe they would feel it was a plant, a move to make them show their hands. To see if they really meant it when they said 'unbedingungslos Kapitulation' – unconditional surrender.*

*In the next few days nothing would matter except this one vital thing. If they said 'no' it would still go ahead. But the prize would be smaller, and the lives still to be lost would be in the hundreds of thousands. He took a deep breath as he felt the acrid taste of bile at the back of his mouth.*

*Between his feet was the thick, black, leather briefcase with the letter that would establish his credentials. It was an innocuous looking letter. Signed by Admiral Canaris, it introduced Herr Dr John as the Lufthansa legal adviser, and asked the Lisbon Abwehr Stelle to extend to him any assistance he required to fulfil his duties in Lisbon. If he was questioned by any other German authority as to what help he might need from the Abwehr he would indicate that the airline was concerned with the legal complications of travellers from neutral countries being refused entry facilities in Berlin as undesirable aliens. Could the Abwehr provide a black-list that could be applied by Lufthansa desk staff in*

Madrid and Lisbon airports, and cut down the diplomatic problems in Berlin?

The actual official object of his journey was to advise Lufthansa Lisbon on the inter-government freight contract for carrying mail between the two countries.

Then the aircraft was wallowing in the thermals on the approach path to Lisbon airport, and fifteen minutes later they had landed.


Otto John had spent the morning at the Lufthansa offices and then lunched with the Commercial Attaché from the embassy. By mid-afternoon he was on his own. He walked casually down to the Estacão do Rossio, across to the far side to where the three telephone kiosks stood side by side.

He dialled the number he'd been given and turned to face the square as the number rang. He couldn't see anyone watching him. When the embassy operator answered he asked for Mr Bailey. It was a quiet voice that came on the line. The arrangements had worked and he was obviously expected. The meeting was arranged for that evening. Seven o'clock at the bridge. His contact would be carrying a copy of that day's Frankfurter Allgemeine.

Back at the hotel he lay on the bed, his eyes closed, he was tired, but far from sleep. He had negotiated with Englishmen before the war about landing rights at Croydon. They hadn't been quick to make up their minds but he felt that that was because he had been young and inexperienced. They probably sensed his need to go back with a successful deal. It had taken some years of negotiating before he realized that waiting was just part of the game. But this time he felt the same as the first time. He needed to go back with a deal. Or at least an understanding.

It seemed a long time to six o'clock, and by then he was dressed and had shaved again. He checked the street map one last time.

He walked slowly down to the bridge and stood watching the anglers on the bank. They were casting far out, maybe twenty metres, with slow expert casts that sent the lightly leaded floats smoothly and silently into the slow cross-currents of the Tagus.

At five to seven he moved to the bridge itself, leaning on the parapet, still watching the anglers and trying desperately not to look at his watch. He was irritated when a girl stood alongside him, leaning forward to look down at the river. It was several seconds before he saw the newspaper that she had placed on the parapet. Its title clear despite her hand. It was the Frankfurter Allgemeine. He had taken for granted that the contact would be a man. She turned to look at his face and said softly in English, 'There's a white Mercedes just past the other end of this bridge. It's on this side of the road. I'll be waiting for you there in five minutes. OK?'

'Where are you taking me?'

'Don't worry. It's all OK.'

Then she had gone. Taking the newspaper with her. He fought back the inclination to look around and see if anyone was watching.

He saw the girl in the driving seat as he approached the car and she leaned over and opened the rear door. As he slid clumsily on to the back seat she said sharply. 'Lie down. Keep out of sight.'

Ten minutes later she told him that he could sit up. The road on either side was flat and empty. Rocks, sand, and clumps of brown grasses came right up to the edge of the metalled road, and a few minutes later he saw a signpost that said 'Estoril 7km'. Then he saw another car parked at the edge of the road just ahead of them. The girl jammed on the brakes and they pulled up in a cloud of dust. The girl turned in her seat to look at him. 'You change cars here. Just get into that car and the driver will take you to your meeting place.'

'How do I . . .'

'I can't answer questions. I just do what I'm told. You must do the same. It's for your protection.'

She spoke English with an accent. It wasn't German and it didn't seem Spanish or Portuguese. For a moment he hesitated and then he got out. It was even hotter outside the car and the day's heat shimmered over the sandy landscape as he walked to the other car. It was a Lancia, a black Aprillia, its rear door already half open. As he ducked inside he saw that the driver was another girl. Dark-haired, pretty, but unsmiling. As he swung the door to she started the engine and turned the car so that they were going back the way he had come. The other car passed them without acknowledgement heading towards Estoril.

They passed the signpost, then a couple of villas, and beyond them was a plantation of orange trees just beginning to blossom, and the Lancia turned between two white stone gateposts, bouncing up a rutted pathway towards a long single-storeyed building with a clay-tiled roof. There was bougainvillaea over the arched doorway and jacaranda trees lined the driveway.

When the car stopped the girl said, in German, 'Go in the villa. There's somebody waiting for you. The door is open. Just walk inside.'

He was hardly out of the car before it drove off and turned out of sight round the far corner of the building.

As the girl had said, the big wooden door was open and he walked inside. Despite the sunshine outside, the big room was cool and dark, and it took a few moments for his eyes to become acclimatized to the dim light. He could make out the shapes of heavy local furniture, armchairs, a long crudely carved dining table, a coffee table, a long sideboard with a glint of bottles and glasses, and then two soft wall-lights came on and he saw a man standing at the archway that led to another room. He was of medium height wearing a well-worn light-weight suit. He had a glass in his left hand and the drink looked like whisky.

'Good evening, Herr Doktor John. I'm sorry about the complicated arrangements but your countrymen are quite efficient in these parts. We couldn't take any risks.'

Otto John nodded without speaking, and the man waved his drink towards the inner room.

'Come in here and we can talk.'

The inner room was a small study. A photograph of President Salazar hung side by side over the fireplace with a photograph of the Pope. Both side walls were lined with shelves of books. A big Italian Phonola radio and a record-player were on a small table alongside a brass-studded leather armchair. There were four other armchairs in a small circle and the man pointed at one of them.

'Let's talk before we eat. A drink?'

'A sherry if you've got one.'

'Of course.'

When the man came back with the bottle and a glass he said, 'I've never met a German before who liked sherry.'

Otto John raised his eyebrows but didn't reply. His mind was on his business and he had no capacity for small talk that could interfere with the train of his argument.

'May I ask who I'm talking to?'

'What name were you given?'

'I was told that I would be negotiating with a Mr Freeman.'

'That was just a contact name. I've come from London especially to meet you.'

'Are you political or military?'

The man smiled. Otto John wasn't sure whether the smile was friendly or merely patronizing. 'Neither. I'm an intelligence officer.'

'It was your people here who were contacted by Canaris.'

'Yes.'

'What were you told?'

'That a Herr Otto John, a lawyer, wished to talk with a British representative on a top secret matter.'

'You must have some idea of my mission or you wouldn't have come specially from London.'

'I am responsible for intelligence operations in this area, Herr John. I have a suspicion that I know what you may want to discuss. But no hard facts. I take it that you are here to enlighten me.'

Otto John took a deep breath. 'There is a group ... an influential group ... who feel that it is time to negotiate a peace.'

He waited for a response but there was none.

'I represent that group, and wish to discuss the British attitude to such a ... such an attempt.'

'There have been such contacts before, Herr Doktor. Ever since the war started. Feelers through Sweden, through Lisbon and Madrid.'

'Those feelers were from the Nazis for their own ends. We are different.'

'Who is "we"?' Philby's voice was harsh and almost aggressive.

'Senior officers of the General Staff. Public figures. Anti-Nazis.'

'And what are you proposing?'

'We intend bringing Adolf Hitler to justice.'

'How?'

'We intend to execute him.'

'Assassinate him?'

'If you care to put it like that, yes.'

'And then?'

'And then the General Staff will take over. There is no love lost between them and the Party as you will already know.'

*Philby picked up his glass and leaned back. John felt that he was losing interest.*

'There have been several attempts on Hitler's life. They have all been unsuccessful. Why should yours succeed?'

'This is no amateur attempt, Herr Freeman. This is a well-planned operation by determined, experienced men. Men of moral courage as well as physical courage. Our plans go far beyond merely dealing with Herr Hitler.'

'Who would be the new head of state?'

'We intend a liberal monarchy under Prince Louis Ferdinand, son of the Crown Prince.' He hesitated and then corrected himself. 'The ex-Crown Prince.'

'What are you asking from us?'

'We ask for an undertaking ... or at least an understanding ... that when we have taken over, a peace, an armistice, can be negotiated immediately.'

'A peace with whom?'

'With you. The British.'

'What about the Americans?'

'The Americans too. Of course.'

'And the Russians?'

'We have no contact with the Russians.'

'Who is in your group?'

'I am not authorized to give names but I can assure you that they are of high rank and capable of carrying out our plan.'

'Is Canaris one of them?'

'He is informed.'

'So what you're asking is an undertaking that the British and American governments should negotiate a separate peace with a new German government? After Hitler's death.'

'Precisely.'

'When do you plan to start?'

'This year.'

99

'It's February, Herr Doktor. When exactly?'

'Hopefully in May. But perhaps in June.'

'That's a long waiting time. A dangerous time for you all.'

'We know that.'

'You realize that I can't possibly give you an immediate answer.'

'I understand. How long would you require?'

'At least a month. Maybe longer.'

'May I ask your personal impression?'

'You've got a considerable problem, Dr John. I feel that the British government would not wish to be seen as implicated in an assassination of a head of state. Not even an enemy head of state.'

'They would not be implicated. Only in the peace negotiations that followed.'

Philby sighed. 'Nobody would believe that. Your own people could gossip. People always do. But perhaps there are ways to avoid that.'

'What do you have in mind?'

'How many people will you report to about our conversation?'

'The main group. Six, seven people.'

'Would you agree to limiting your report to one person? I would do the same.'

Otto John sensed success in his mission. He tried to keep the excitement from his voice.

'I could guarantee that.'

'Who would it be on your side?'

Otto John hesitated for a moment and then said softly, 'Field-Marshal von Witzleben.'

'So our negotiations will be known only to him, to you, and to me.'

'And to your senior.'

'Of course.'

'Your senior's name is what?'

'I couldn't reveal that. He would not be known to your people anyway.'

'How will I contact you again?'

The knowing eyes looked across at Otto John.

'How often do you come here?'

'Perhaps three times a year. And the same to Madrid.'

'Can you come at short notice?'

'If it was sufficiently important. But not more than once.'

'Are you allowed to hold escudos in Germany?'

'Not as a citizen, but at Lufthansa we have all currencies passing through our accounts.'

'I suggest that you take five hundred escudos back with you. Your own money. You just forget to exchange it for Marks when you go back. When you want to contact me you put a personal advertisement in the Correo di Lisboa. In German. Let's say . . . "alles gute an Litzi von Heinzl". If I need to contact you I will have the same message put in the Frankfurter Allgemeine. And we put a date. A date of a suggested meeting. You come here for that day and we will contact you.'

'How will you know where I am?'

The man smiled. 'I shall know. Don't worry. Let me give you a meal before they take you back to Lisbon.'

'I'd rather get back. Somebody might be looking for me.'

Philby stood up and held out his hand. 'What happens if London doesn't agree to giving an undertaking?'

'Then we shall still go ahead. I expect that after Hitler is dead we should make an open offer of peace talks with the Allies.'

'Including the Soviets?'

'We have no contacts there. We should have difficulties on the Eastern Front.'

'Why?'

'No German government would ever trust Moscow.'

101

'What does that mean?'

John shook his head and shrugged. 'They were our allies once. We didn't trust them then. They are your allies now and I would think that London and Washington don't trust them any more than we do. Until the Russians have been beaten there will be no peace for any of us. But our first enemy is the Nazis. Agreed?'

'You're quite right, Herr Doktor. And I wish you every success. Let me get the driver.'

Philby was away for five minutes and then he came back. 'There will be only one car this time. It will drop you near the railway station just outside the church of São Roque. Walk around for a bit before you go back to the hotel. Look at the shops so that you've got something to talk about if anyone should ask you where you've been.'

John nodded. 'I hope to hear from you soon.'

'Not soon, my friend. That's most unlikely. But I'll see what I can do.'

'You have no doubts about our determination?'

'None at all. Now you must go.'

'Good luck to you in London.'

Philby half-smiled. 'And good luck to you in Berlin.'

The taxi dropped him just past Swiss Cottage station and he crossed the main road and turned into Fitzjohns Avenue. It was raining by the time he got to Wedderburn Road and he put up his umbrella for the last couple of hundred yards to the house.

The house stood back from the road, a typical Hampstead family house that had already been converted into four flats, including the basement. At the top of the steps he shook the rain from his umbrella, then turned and pressed the bell marked Rudi Stein. With a buzz the door clicked open and he walked into the tiled hallway.

There was no lift, and the flat was the topmost one, its

*door to the landing was solid mahogany, and the fittings were heavy Victorian brass. There was a Yale lock and another more complex lock, and he used a pair of keys from his coat pocket to let himself in.*

*He walked through to the big sitting room and the man sitting at the Bechstein grand turned briefly towards him, half-smiled and then went on playing.*

*Philby took off his coat, propped his wet umbrella in the fireplace and found himself a comfortable chair.*

*Then the pianist had finished. He turned on his stool and looked at his guest.*

*'Do you know that piece, Kim?'*

*His voice had a heavy accent. Not an attractive accent, the words were laboured and hard-edged.*

*'You know me, Sergei. I can hardly tell Beethoven from Fats Waller.'*

*The man smiled. 'You exaggerate. It was by a Frenchman. Erik Satie, and it's called "Gymnopédie number one". It would make nice theme music for a film. Yes?'*

*'If you say so. It would need some violins.'*

*'All film music needs some violins.'*

*Philby put his head on one side. 'Any problems, Sergei?'*

*'Of course. Is always problems.'*

*'What is it?'*

*The Russian shook his head. 'Is my problem. You tell me yours.'*

*'Mine's not a problem, comrade.'*

*'So tell me.'*

*'I had a meeting with a German in Lisbon. They plan to kill Hitler and negotiate a separate peace with the British and the Americans.'*

*'The bastards. What have your people said?'*

*Philby smiled. 'Nothing. I haven't told them.'*

*'What about the Germans?'*

*'I'm just stringing them along.'*

**103**

*The Russian slowly shook his head as he looked down at the carpet. Then he looked at Philby.*

*'Moscow has always feared this. It's Munich all over again. A separate peace deal leaving the Wehrmacht free to concentrate on us. My God. What a blood-bath.'*

*'It won't happen, Sergei.'*

*'You think you can control them?'*

*'I'm sure I can. Madrid and Lisbon are their only channels back to London. And I'm in charge of both.'*

*'What about Stockholm?'*

*'Possible. But these people have made contact with me. Why should they go elsewhere?'*

*'When they don't get results from you maybe.'*

*Philby smiled. 'But they will get results from me. I shall encourage them and promise them a deal. Nothing in writing of course, but I shall cheer them on. They might even kill Adolf. You never know.'*

*Stein sighed. 'So far there have been nineteen attempts. All unsuccessful. They sound like amateurs.' He paused and looked at Philby. 'Can you do anything about Gehlen?'*

*'In what way?'*

*'His organization are really getting through at all levels. We got hold of his version of our order of battle. It was far too good. We have seen three of his personal reports to Hitler and he takes a very optimistic view of German victory in the East, and that encourages Hitler and the General Staff. Gehlen is first class at bringing intelligence but his military judgement is amateur. Because his facts are constantly proved to be accurate Hitler is encouraged by his evaluations. They are totally misplaced but they encourage the Nazis to keep fighting.'*

*'In what way are his evaluations misplaced?'*

*'He talks in terms of space ... territory. The area they take. He doesn't realize that that's all they have won, or can win. Empty space. It looks good on a war map, but on the*

104

*ground it's fatal. The German army just gets sucked into that space and vanishes. They are losing on every Russian Front, I assure you; they are fighting on because they are military morons. Sooner or later they will realize this. We have got to make it sooner. We're bleeding to death even though we are winning.'*

*'Can you let me have photocopies of actual Gehlen documents. Two order-of-battle situation reports, and his personal evaluations that go with them?'*

*'It would take ten days, maybe fourteen. But yes, we can get them for you.'*

*'I want more than that, I want one of our top people to do an evaluation of the two evaluations. Praising the order of battle material, but tearing the evaluations to pieces. Don't overdo it. Just a cold harsh report that makes them look ridiculous.'*

*'What have you in mind?'*

*'I can feed it back into Berlin through my contacts.'*

*'Moscow won't let you feed it through our Swiss network.'*

*'I know. I don't need them.'*

The girl sat with her long legs bent under her, her head to one side, her chin cradled in the palm of her hand. She was neither beautiful nor pretty but her face had a gentleness, a calm, that emphasized her femininity. It was a loving face and a face that would induce love in others.

The man sitting in the armchair opposite the girl on the settee was only a few years older, but his face, although handsome, revealed nothing of his character. His eyes were wary and his demeanour was that of a man who was well used to plotting a safe way through the minefields of politics and power in the KGB. He didn't look at the girl as he spoke.

'How about sex. How often does he screw you?'

105

The girl looked down at her legs, brushed something non-existent from her black skirt, and then looked up at him.

'How old are you, Georgi?'

'Thirty-seven.'

'He's sixty-eight next birthday. Whatever it is it's not that.'

'So what do *you* think it is?'

She sighed deeply. 'I think it's just what he says. He's an old man, he wants to go back to where everything is familiar. He's homesick.'

'Oh, for God's sake. He's lived in Moscow now for sixteen years. He belongs here now. He's no background to go to in England.'

'He doesn't belong here, Georgi. He never did belong here. He's a dreamer, an idealist. You all pretend. He pretends too. None of you understands him. I don't think he understands himself.'

'And you think you do?'

'Don't smirk, Georgi. It's a most unattractive habit.'

'So answer my question.'

'Yes. I think I understand him. Not because I'm more intelligent or shrewder than you, but because I'm a woman.'

'Are you in love with him?'

She was silent for a few moments. 'No. But I care about him.'

'In what way?'

She shrugged. 'As if he were my child or maybe my father.'

'Why do you think he never belonged here?'

'It's so obvious, Georgi, do you really need me to explain?'

'Yes.'

She shook her head slowly in disbelief. 'He was disgusted with the politics of his own country, and at the same time angered by what the Nazis were doing. His political instincts

106

were to the left. He felt that Communism was the only hope. He fell in love with a system and a country that he knew nothing about. He was like a man whose friend arranges a blind date. They told him how beautiful she was in 1933 or thereabouts but he didn't meet her for thirty years. He sent her flowers from time to time in the shape of information and then in 1963 he comes over the border to Moscow and meets his lady. He knew that she wouldn't be like the photographs but he'd put a life's work into that love affair. And for the last sixteen years he's been a faithful husband. Out of duty, not love.'

'Why not love?'

She laughed softly. 'Why is it you can't see it, Georgi? Any of you. He fell in love with a manifesto but when he came here he had to live a day-to-day life. A strange language, strange people, strange place. Food, habits, everything was different. He fitted in as best he could. He was loyal, but that was with his mind. His heart was somewhere else. Not because he wanted it to be, but from habit and the years.'

'Why the hell did he come to Moscow then?'

She smiled, and despite her little homily, it was almost a smirk. 'He didn't come in any great hurry, did he? Not the first plane to Moscow after he was elbowed out of SIS.'

'What's all that mean?'

'It means he only came when he had no choice. When it was Moscow or the Tower of London.'

'Go on.'

'Don't you see? He despised his own country's politicians but at least he was used to them. And he stayed on in that life until he had no choice but to leave.'

'What does he dislike about Moscow?'

'Nothing that I know of. It just isn't where he belongs. He's like Solzhenitsyn and the other dissidents who went to America. They don't like what the Politburo do but they're

107

homesick for Mother Russia. They don't belong in Washington or wherever.'

'Is there anything he wants that would make him happy?'

'Yes.'

'What is it?' he said eagerly.

'He wants your people to love him enough to let him go back without making out that he's a traitor.'

'He must know that isn't possible. They may agree to let him go back but he won't go with a bunch of red roses from Dzerzhinski Square. He must know that.'

'Maybe he does. But maybe he hopes that what he has done for all those years might make him the exception.'

'Do you want to go with him?'

'He hasn't asked me to. I'm sure that isn't what he has in mind.'

'Would you go if it was necessary?'

'How could it be necessary?'

'If our people made it a condition of his going.'

'Why should they do that?'

'So that you can keep an eye on him. See that he doesn't play games.'

'He would never agree to that.'

'He may have no choice. It's the only solution I can think of which might make them agree. I'm not making much progress.'

She smiled. 'Are you trying very hard or looking over your shoulder?'

'I had orders to put his case and make a recommendation.'

She laughed softly. 'And you're trying to find out which way the cat will jump before you jump yourself?'

He stood up and reached for his coat and fur hat.

'Don't tell him what we have talked about, Nina.'

'Of course I will. He's more important to me than you are.'

'Just remember, my dear, you might well be here in Moscow long after he has gone. You'll always need our goodwill. You wouldn't be at home in one of those little frontier towns in Sinkiang Province.'

Her face stayed calm but her eyes were angry. She said softly, 'Don't give me that shit, Malik. They can send me to the Gulag but I'm not doing anything so that you or the others can frame Kim.'

'You stupid bitch. Why should we need to frame him?'

The bath itself was a sign of privilege. It was deep and over two metres long and the big taps were chrome plated.

He lay back in the warm water, his head resting against the rim of the bath, his knees bent and his eyes closed. His forehead was covered with beads of condensation from the steam and she sponged his shoulders gently. The sponge had been a gift from the KGB office in Vladivostok after a visit two years earlier.

Slowly and carefully she soaped and then sponged his inert body, as if he were a sleeping child. From time to time he sighed deeply and she looked at his face. He had given up the terrible bouts of drinking and for over a year had seemed to be content with a glass or two of wine. He liked the Yalta wine from Massandra. But over the last six months there had been bottles of whisky from GUM. His face was pallid but the only wrinkles were the smile wrinkles at the corner of his eyes. It wasn't the face of a man who was approaching seventy. It was a boy's face. She kissed him gently on one wet cheek but he didn't respond.

She turned and reached out, lifting each foot from the soapy water, massaging each swollen instep before she sponged it. Then she knelt there, the soft wet sponge heavy in her hand as she looked at his face.

'It's time to get out, Kim, the water's getting cold.'

He opened his eyes slowly and looked at her.

'Why do you bother with me?'

'You know why.'

'Tell me.'

'Because I like you. I care about you.'

'But why?'

'I don't know why. I just do.'

'Because they pay you. A little swallow from the KGB.'
She shook her head. 'No. For my own reasons.'

'Tell me your reasons.'

'They're women's reasons.'

'Tell me.'

'I care about you because you are often sad. Because you have to pretend so much. Pretend that you don't miss your children. Pretend that you aren't hurt when the people in Dzerzhinski Square ignore your advice. And pretend that you are sure that it was all worth the sacrifices that you've made.'

For a moment the glazed eyes looked at her face and then he said, 'You stupid bitch.'

# 13

At five o'clock on the morning of 20 July it was already warm, and through the open windows of the house in Wannsee von Stauffenberg could hear the shrill clamour of the dawn chorus. Thrushes and blackbirds dominating the finches and warblers, and from far away the vibrations of a woodpecker. There was a heat-mist already rising from the slope of the lawns where they bordered the pond, and as he looked from the window there was a faint flicker of summer lightning from behind the woods. But no thunder followed and he turned back towards his bed.

He expected to be back in Berlin that night and he really only needed the four buff-coloured files covering his special report to Hitler on the 'Volksgrenadier' divisions. But he pushed down the towel to the bottom of the brief case between the files. And then wrapped his spare service shirt round the bomb and slid the bundle down until it touched the folded towel.

The bomb had been made in the cellar of a building in London. In Petty France, almost in sight of Buckingham Palace. Once the glass capsule was broken the acid would eat away the wire, and that would allow the firing pin to hit the percussion cap. The thickness of the wire regulated the time before the explosion. The wire that had been fitted was very thin. There would be only ten minutes from breaking the capsule to the explosion.

Since he had left the War Office in Bendlerstrasse the previous evening Colonel von Stauffenberg had felt almost at peace after the tensions of the previous months. He had stopped the car on the way home to Wannsee and the driver had waited as he prayed in the church at Dahlem. And he had spent the rest of the evening quietly at home with his brother, Berthold. He had prayed again at the side of his bed, before he slept. The prayer in the church had been for his country and his countrymen, and the prayer at his bedside was for his friends and their families. Neither prayer touched on his own safety or even the success of his mission. Those were for Caesar, not God.

He closed the briefcase and looked at it, turning his head so that he looked with his good eye. It was a well-worn briefcase in a light tan-coloured leather that he rather disliked. It had two outer pockets side by side, each of which had small locks, and a broad leather strap, also with a lock, went right round the briefcase under the handle.

He looked at his watch. He had forty minutes before the car would come for him and he walked over to the side table, unscrewed the flask and poured himself a coffee. He sat on the edge of his bed, sipping the bitter ersatz drink. He put down the cup and reached in his pocket for the wad of cottonwool. Pushing up his eye-patch he dabbed the tears from the empty socket. It had been fifteen months since it had happened. One minute he was a whole man and then a minute later, after the Hurricane had come low over the sand-dunes and straffed his car, he was a man with one eye, no right hand or forearm, and only three fingers left on his other hand. He had only arrived in Tunisia a couple of months earlier.

His fellow conspirators were all equally odd in some way. Goerdeler, who would be the new Head of State, was stiff-necked and narrow minded. A man who wouldn't have a divorced person in his house. Trott zu Solz and von Moltke were the young idealists, so charming and so civilized, so gentle and yet so determined. And all those endless discussions about a monarchy. Von Witzleben a Field-

Marshal. Bonnhoeffer and Dohnanyi, already in the hands of the Gestapo. Not one of them was motivated by anything other than a need to expiate the deeds of the Nazis for the benefit of their countrymen. Not an office or power seeker among them. Pray God that their motives were enough.

The car arrived at 5.55 and his adjutant, Lieutenant Werner von Haeften, had brought along a friend, a naval lieutenant, just for company to the airfield at Rangsdorf. That meant that they wouldn't be able to go over the plans again together. There might be time at the other end but he supposed that it wasn't really necessary.

Von Stauffenberg was to make his report to Hitler at the situation meeting at 1 p.m. at the 'Wolf's Lair', Hitler's headquarters at Rastenburg. When the bomb exploded it would be up to Fellgiebel, the General in charge of Signals at the Führer's headquarters. He would phone Berlin to inform them and Operation Valkyrie would start. And Fellgiebel would put out of action all communication with Berlin except his single line.

They landed at Rastenburg at 10.15. Von Haeften went off to the junior officers' mess, carrying the other briefcase and the second bomb. Von Stauffenberg was invited to breakfast with Keitel's senior staff officer.

At 12 noon he reported to Field Marshal Keitel's office and Keitel had personally informed him that the conference had been brought forward to 12.30 due to the arrival of Mussolini who had just been rescued from captivity in the hands of the British by Otto Skorzeny and his men. The Führer wanted to welcome his erstwhile ally personally.

A few minutes before 12.30 he walked with Keitel across the compound. They had taken only a few strides when von Stauffenberg excused himself to go back for his belt and cap. And in the ante-room he bent over his open briefcase, took the small, metal prongs in his three fingers and broke the *glass capsule. In ten minutes the bomb would explode.*

Hitler wanted Heusinger's situation report first, and after placing his briefcase under the conference table von Stauffenberg whispered to Keitel that he needed to make a telephone call.

Von Stauffenberg was standing with Fellgiebel by the signals hut in the compound when, with a roar of smoke and flame the bomb exploded at 12.42. The end of the building was blown off as if it had been hit by an artillery shell. His staff car had its engine running and as he slid into the back seat von Haeften accelerated away. The inside perimeter was no problem but the SS sentry at the outer wire had already been alerted. Von Stauffenberg bluffed his way through. When it was examined later the guardroom logbook showed the entry 'Colonel von Stauffenberg passed through the guard-box at 12.44'.

On the road to the airfield von Haeften stopped the car, hurriedly dismantled the reserve bomb and flung it piece by piece into the bushes at the side of the road.

It was 3.45 before the Heinkel landed at Rangsdorf and von Stauffenberg raced to the nearest telephone.

The sentries at the Bendlerstrasse saluted von Stauffenberg as he hurried up the steps. The place seemed strangely calm and deserted. Even on the top floor where he found von Witzleben and General Beck and Gisevius they seemed to be in a dream. There had been no call from Fellgiebel and they seemed suspicious when he swore that Hitler was dead. There was no communication with Rastenburg but Olbricht had already phoned Paris and the other outlying units to inform them that Valkyrie was in operation.

Operation Valkyrie was ostensibly the General Staff plan to counter a civilian uprising started by foreign slave-workers, but the plotters had converted it to their plan for

114

taking over control. The tanks and men would already be on the move. Meanwhile the plotters waited in a kind of breathless limbo.

Then Colonel-General Olbricht had at last got through to Field Marshal Keitel at Rastenburg: Keitel told him that there had been an explosion, but Hitler was alive and virtually unharmed. He would be speaking on the radio that evening and meanwhile troops and SS and Gestapo were closing in on the plotters. Olbricht hung up slowly, sat for a few moments in cold, stunned silence and then walked through from his office to the others. When he announced Keitel's news von Stauffenberg swore that Keitel was lying. And lied himself. Swearing that he had seen Hitler's dead body.

Back at Rastenburg there was confusion and recrimination. Admiral Doenitz attacked Goering for his inefficiency, and the enraged Goering turned on Ribbentrop. Hitler himself shouted them both down, raving at the top of his voice as the rain lashed down noisily on the windows. Goebbels was still in Berlin, giving the urgent desperate orders to Major Otto Romer to surround the Bendlerstrasse and arrest the plotters whose names they now had. The prime target was von Stauffenberg.

Von Stauffenberg, Olbricht, Lieut. von Haeften were already dead before Hans Fritsche, Hitler's radio spokesman, was announcing two hours later on Deutschlandsender I that the Führer would speak to the nation later that night. And at one a.m. it was Fritsche's voice that cut through the Wagner to say simply: 'Der Führer spricht'. And then that grating voice, slurred with dementia – 'My comrades, men and women of the German nation . . .'

On 21 July the Gestapo's grip tightened round hundreds of men, their wives and families. In basement cells men screamed in agony as their bodies were tortured beyond endurance, and they lay on concrete floors their torn clothes *soaked in blood. Hands smashed, faces pulped, some died in a matter of days and others survived and appeared as silent ghosts in the travesties of trials in the so-called People's Courts. The verdicts were never in doubt and Hitler had ordered a film record of their deaths. Time and time again he had sat watching the flickering screen, the bodies turning slowly, their necks almost severed by the piano wire that hung them from the meathooks set in the concrete ceiling.*

*The death roll was a long one. 4980 names long. One of the names was Hans John, brother of Dr Otto John.*

*It had been in one of those strange limbo periods that had haunted the afternoon when Otto John had gone to the Bendlerstrasse on 20 July. The story that Hitler was unharmed had come through from Rastenburg, but von Stauffenberg had sworn that it was a lie. Nobody could decide what to believe. Orders were being sent out to initiate Valkyrie, but there was little telephone or radio traffic back. He had left about 8.45 and gone straight to the home he shared with his brother in Dahlem.*

*He had heard Hitler's broadcast at one a.m. and there was no doubt that the voice was genuine.*

*The next day he phoned number after number. At some, strange voices answered and he hung up quickly. And at others there was no reply.*

*On Monday 24 July Otto John booked himself on to that morning's Lufthansa flight to Madrid. There were no difficulties either at Templehof or Madrid.*

# 14

It was 1945, and with the war in Europe drawing to an end most of the embassy staff had moved down from Ankara to enjoy the cool nights of Istanbul and the breezes from the Bosphorus, so the consulate was well staffed.

The short, stocky man walked through the main door to the consulate, over to reception, and asked to see one of the senior diplomats. He gave the name of a particular man. He was an important man. But you don't get to see British diplomats as easily as all that. But he was eventually interviewed briefly by the Acting Consul-General, and something about the visitor inclined the AC-G to arrange the further interview that the man demanded.

Morton Hallam came into the interview room. He had been warned that his visitor spoke with a heavy accent but with a reasonable vocabulary. He shook hands and pulled up a chair to face the sitting man.

'Would it be easier if I sent for an interpreter?'

'I am not Turkish.'

'I see.'

'My name is Volkov. Konstantin Volkov. I am Russian.'

'I have a Russian speaker on my staff if you wish.'

'No. No. Is not possible. What I discuss with you is private. Absolutely private and confidential.'

'I understand, Mr Volkov.'

'I am newly appointed Soviet Consul in Istanbul,'

Hallam nodded. 'I thought I had heard the name recently. What can we do for you?'

'In real fact I am head of NKVD for western Turkey. I have a proposition to make if you are interested.'

'Tell me, Mr Volkov. Tell me your proposition.'

'I wish to leave. To live in Cyprus. I offer information for your help.'

'Why do you want to leave, Mr Volkov?'

Volkov shook his head. 'Is not NKVD plot I assure you.'

'Of course not. But why do you want to leave?'

'I wish for myself and for my wife. She is ill.'

'How ill?'

'She is neurotic. From worry. We wish to leave quickly.'

'What was your proposition?'

'You give me twenty-seven thousand pound sterling, and permission to live in Cyprus. I give you information.'

'What kind of information?'

Volkov reached into his jacket and brought out an envelope and held it in his hand.

'I let you read for a few moments only.'

He leaned forward and handed the envelope to Hallam who opened the unsealed flap and slid out a dozen or so pages of notes.

He read them through quickly, memorizing what he could. Volkov had obviously been in Moscow recently, and equally obviously had deliberately collected information so that he could defect. The notes and sketches were handwritten. They gave addresses and details of a number of NKVD buildings in Moscow. Offices, private houses and safe-houses. Guard and security details, and profiles and sections of keys. There was a list of Soviet agents in Turkey and their means of communication with Moscow. And on the last page there was a single scrawled sentence that said, 'I give names of three Soviet agents operating in government in London.'

Hallam was almost sure then that Volkov was genuine. It would be so easy to check on the three alleged agents. And

118

*Volkov would know full well what would happen to him if the information was false. If the NKVD were playing games it would have to be something fantastic for them to sacrifice three agents as a cover for a penetration exercise. It was possible of course, but highly unlikely. He looked across at the Russian.*

'This isn't really my field, Mr Volkov, but I think we could be interested. It would have to go to London for them to decide.'

'Is not enough time for that. I wish to go quickly.'

'I'll send a signal to London tonight.'

'No.' The Russian looked scared. 'All your cyphers are known to us. Is too dangerous. It must be by word of mouth.'

'You mean all our codes have been broken. The security codes as well as the diplomatic codes?'

'All. The papers please.'

He held out his hand and Hallam gave him back the papers and the envelope.

'Why are you in such a hurry, Mr Volkov?'

'I have waited too long. Is dangerous to wait longer. I am not escaping from some crime if that is what you think.'

'Can I ask you about the Soviet agents in London?'

'I give you three names as part of our arrangement.'

'How is it possible for Russians to be working for the British Government?'

*Volkov looked at the Englishman.* 'I think you not understand. The agents are British.'

'You mean they are naturalized British?'

'For God's sake, mister. They are Englishmen.'

'How long can you give me, Mr Volkov?'

'If I not hear from you in three weeks, twenty-one days from today, is too late. You will not contact me after then.'

'What government department do these agents work for, Mr Volkov?'

119

*Volkov sat looking at Hallam's face. He sat silently for several minutes before he spoke.*

*'Two are diplomats with Foreign Office. One is head of intelligence department.'*

*Hallam was stunned, and he said slowly, 'Would you wait while I consult a colleague?'*

*Volkov shrugged. 'Of course.'*

*Sir Maurice was already dressed for dinner but he agreed to see Hallam in his temporary office.*

*The ambassador sat behind his desk, his face grim as Hallam outlined Volkov's offer. When he had finished Sir Maurice leaned forward, his finger jabbing in Hallam's direction.*

*'Time and time again I have made clear that I will not have either the embassy or this consulate turned into a nest of spies. If you wish to go ahead with this . . . with this charade, you must do it direct with London. I will not have the embassy mixed up in these . . .' At a loss for words the ambassador stood up and waved towards the door.*

*Back in the interview room Hallam said, 'I think we shall be able to help you, Mr Volkov. But as I thought, it would be a decision for London. I would need some time.'*

*Volkov nodded. 'Is under these conditions. First. When you report to London you write yourself by hand. Is not to be typed in embassy.'*

*'That's OK, Mr Volkov.' Hallam said quietly. 'But why do you say that?'*

*'Is Soviet agent on your staff.'*

*'Can you give me the name?'*

*Volkov shook his head. 'No. Maybe later I tell you.'*

*'And the other conditions?'*

*'Is not transmitted by radio or telephone. Only by hand. And is decision in twenty-one days. No longer.'*

*'It will be treated with the utmost urgency, Mr Volkov.'*

*Volkov stood up and when they were both at the door*

120

Hallam said, 'The Englishmen who are agents. Can you give me some identification to support my report?'

Volkov hesitated for a moment and then said with a half-smile. 'All three are young men. One of them sometimes wears a cloak not a street coat. You understand?'

'I understand,' Hallam said softly. He and Volkov made elaborate arrangements for further contact.

Hallam worked through the night preparing the handwritten report for the Foreign Office to pass on to SIS.

Even though it was August there was a gusty wind, and the sky was grey as he walked along the path at the edge of the lake in St James's Park. He walked across Birdcage Walk to Buckingham Gate and eventually turned left into Petty France.

The two files on his desk both dealt with administrative matters. The first was a breakdown of proposed expenditure by his section of SIS in the next year. The second was his own draft suggesting that in the case of his section, which dealt with anti-Soviet and anti-Communist intelligence, the present SIS structure was too restrictive. The division of responsibilities country by country should not apply to his section; a case involving the Soviets in Canada could have implications in France or Poland, but with the present system they might never be linked. He recommended that his section should operate across the board, their remit to be all anti-Soviet and anti-Communist operations, anywhere.

He was checking the draft when the messenger brought in the sealed envelope with the two broad red bands from corner to corner. There was a note from 'C' stapled to the envelope. It instructed him to read the contents and report on them to 'C'. He signed the receipt and handed it back to the messenger.

Sliding the papers from the envelope on to his desk he

*checked that there was nothing left inside, and then tossed the envelope into his 'Pending' tray.*

*As he finished reading the papers he closed his eyes, trying to think coherently. This was it. There would be no way out of it this time. He had always known that there would be such a day. When some carelessness, some idiocy, would bring the whole thing crashing down. And this was that day. One way out would be to suggest that Volkov's defection was a plant. A provocation by the NKVD to test what the British reaction would be. But if he did that and 'C' ignored his advice and put someone else on the operation it would compromise him when Volkov's information was subsequently analysed. From the dates on the embassy papers ten days of Volkov's twenty-one had already gone by.*

*By mid-day he was calm again. He had sorted it out. It was like a game of poker. You had to play the cards you were dealt. How you played them was up to you. Late in the afternoon he sent his written report into 'C'. The documents from Istanbul, he wrote, were of the greatest importance. He would like a little time to dig into the records.*

*It was six o'clock that evening before 'C' phoned him and told him to go ahead and report to him the next morning.*

*At exactly nine o'clock that evening he let himself into the flat in Wedderburn Road. Stein was waiting for him, and two whiskies were already poured and standing on the low table.*

*As Philby sat down and reached for the whisky he said, 'Have you done your transmission to Moscow yet?'*

*'No. I'm not due on network until just after eleven to-night.'*

*'You'd better tell them that they've almost certainly wiped me out.'*

*Stein looked shocked. 'What do you mean?'*

122

'What do you know of an NKVD man named Volkov? Konstantin Volkov.'

'Never heard of him. But there must be hundreds of Volkovs, it's a common enough name.'

'He's recently moved to Istanbul.'

Stein shrugged. 'I've still never heard of him. What's the problem?'

'He's offered to tell the British the names of three Soviet agents working in London. Two work for the Foreign Office, the third is head of a counter-intelligence section.'

'You're joking, Kim.'

'I'm not. He's asking for nearly thirty thousand pounds to defect.'

'How the hell did he get this information anyway? There are fewer than half a dozen people who know.'

'He knows all the same, my friend.'

'My God. Some heads are going to roll in Moscow when I go through tonight.'

'Don't touch Volkov himself.'

'Why not?'

'Sergei, Sergei. How would it look? An NKVD man offers to expose as a Soviet agent a man who's in charge of a counter-intelligence section. The papers come to me and the next day the informer is killed or called back to Moscow.'

'But he could talk.'

'Sure he could. I want him to talk. To me. I'm going to recommend that I fly out and deal with it myself.'

'Will they let you?'

'Maybe not. But I'm going to try.'

'What do you want me to do?'

'Inform Moscow. I shall take as long as I can before I interview Volkov. I'll let you know when I arrive, and you deal with Volkov later. But not before.'

'Shall I warn the other two?'

123

'Warn Guy but not Donald.'

Stein sighed. 'I'm sorry about this, Kim. I'll make plans tonight for you in case it goes wrong.'

'It won't go wrong.'

'But whatever happens they are alerted. They'll be suspicious of everyone. You included.'

'I can handle them. They couldn't prove a thing that would stand up in court. There is more to do when the war is over than ever before.'

'Will you stick it out for us?'

'Of course.'


'Today is the twenty-first day.' Hallam's eyes were angry and accusing.

Philby stood with his bag in his hand.

'How did you arrange to contact him?'

'By phoning their Consulate-General and giving a code-word for a meeting place.'

'So phone him now.'

Hallam moved to his desk and reached for the telephone. He dialled a number and watched Philby as he waited for an answer. Then, suddenly, he leaned forward.

'Konstantin Volkov please . . . thank you.'

There was a pause and then Hallam frowned.

'Is that Mr Volkov . . . I see . . . Mr Volkov, we have two visa applications from Soviet citizens who want to travel to London . . . of course . . . there are no complications provided that . . . OK, if that is what you want . . . goodbye.'

Hallam hung up and looked across at Philby.

'I asked for Volkov, the operator said she was putting me through. A man came on, said he was Volkov. He wasn't Volkov. I know Volkov's voice. It wasn't anything like Volkov.'

'Ring again. Ask for him again.'

'I think you're too late.'

Hallam dialled and waited. He asked for Volkov and listened and then hung up.

'The operator said that Volkov was out.'

'Have you really got two visa applications from them?'

'Yes.'

'Use them as an excuse. Find some query on them and go round yourself.'

It was nearly two hours before Hallam came back. Philby was sitting on the bed in his room.

Hallam noticed the bottle of whisky on the bedside table and the almost full glass.

'Any luck?'

'They sat me in reception. I was there for almost half an hour. I'm damn sure they photographed me. Finally I was told that Volkov was in Moscow.' Hallam stared at him. 'Why did it take so long for you to get here?'

'There were things to be checked. And there were problems about leave rotas.'

Hallam made no effort to disguise the anger and disgust on his face but the man from London was by a long way his senior, looking back at him calmly as he lifted his glass.

'Cheers. I'll hang on for a couple of days in case he turns up.'

Two days after Philby had gone back to London the embassy staff returned to Ankara. And Hallam heard the news just after he had waved the retinue of embassy cars on their way. It was the lead item on the radio news-bulletin and a translation was sent straight in to him.

A Russian military aircraft had made an unscheduled landing that afternoon at Istanbul airport. It was an unauthorized landing as well as unscheduled, ignoring the instructions from the air-controllers. And while the control tower was giving the pilot hell, a car had raced across the *tarmac out to the plane. A heavily-bandaged man on a stretcher had been hurriedly put on board and the aircraft had immediately taken off. The car was now in the custody of the Turkish police, and the three Russians had already claimed diplomatic immunity when they were taken to the airport control office.*

# 15

Philby had said that a car would be waiting for him at Shere-metyevo but he was surprised and disturbed to find Philby himself waiting for him at the airport. And he was apprehensive when Philby stood alongside the immigration officer and said something in Russian that made the man hand back his passport without even opening it. It looked too official, too privileged, bearing in mind the motive for his visit.

Philby himself drove them back to Moscow. His talk was inconsequential; of Wimbledon, and the first Test Match against the Indians. Why had Lever been dropped when his form was so good?

At Philby's flat everything looked much the same as before, except that a girl was there. She was in her late twenties, pretty, in a Slav sort of way. Big, sad, brown eyes, and a full soft mouth. Tall and well-built, wearing a T-shirt and blue jeans. Philby introduced her as Nina and explained that she spoke no English.

Philby stood there in a striped shirt and baggy trousers. 'Why don't you stay here for the night?'

'I'd have to notify the embassy.'

'Of course. We can telephone them after you've eaten.'

The girl had brought in a plate of cold meat and a bowl of salad, and left them to eat alone.

Philby said, 'I gather that you want a long session this time.'

'If you've no objection?'

'I'm at your disposal.'

'Do the KGB know that I'm here?'

'Of course.' Philby smiled. 'I'm a KGB officer.'

'Do they know *why* I'm here?'

'I don't imagine so. It doesn't matter anyway.'

'Surely they would stop you from going back.'

'That's my worry, not yours.'

'It could be mine, eventually.'

'How?'

'Getting you out.'

Philby smiled. 'If I go, I shall go openly. There'll be no problem for you.'

'Tell me about Volkov.'

'Who's Volkov?'

'The NKVD man in Istanbul. He wanted to defect.'

'Ah yes. But that was a long, long time ago. What do you want to know about him?'

'You sold him to the Russians, didn't you?'

'Do you mean I received money for reporting him?'

'No. I mean sold as in "sold down the river".'

Philby leaned forward, his arms on his knees, his hands hanging loosely. There was a glint of anger in his eyes.

'Volkov was offering to betray his country's secrets for twenty-seven thousand pounds. He was a Judas.'

Powell looked back at Philby. 'You betrayed your country's secrets. What's the difference?'

'The information I passed to the Soviets was information to our allies. Information that should have been passed to them anyway. Officially. But it wasn't. Old women in Whitehall passed on what suited the British and Americans. And held back what they chose to hold back. The Russians were fighting their war for them, but what did it matter if another hundred thousand Russians died bloody deaths for want of a few snippets of vital information.'

'Who were you to decide what they should know?'

'I was a man, my friend. I didn't want them to die. The

128

British did. The only reason they co-operated at all with the Soviets was to keep the Germans off their own backs.'

'You were a British citizen nevertheless.'

'I was also a KGB officer. Right from the start.'

'But still a traitor.'

'If I was a traitor why did they still keep me on after Lipton had denounced me in the House of Commons?'

'Nobody knows why.'

'Oh but they do, my friend, they do.'

'Tell me. I'm trying hard to understand.'

Philby sighed, and leaned back in his chair.

'What status are you?'

'Grade one.'

'John Powell, officer grade one of SIS. Why do you think they fixed for me to go to Beirut after I'd been denounced by Lipton and after I had been questioned by Mr Justice Milmo?'

'I just don't know.'

'I said why do you *think* they kept me on the payroll right up until I came to Moscow?'

'I don't know, Kim. It doesn't make sense.'

'It does if you look down the telescope the right way.'

'How do I do that?'

'That's for you to work out.'

'Why did you insist that your request went to Arthur Padmore?'

'Because he must know what went on in those days.'

'You say he *must* know. You mean he *ought* to know or he was part of it?'

'He wasn't anything to do with SIS in those days. I mean he *ought* to know. There are people who can tell him.'

'You mean people like Patrick Walker?'

Philby shook his head. 'No.'

'Who?'

Philby looked at him. A strange disbelieving look.

'Did *anyone* agree that I should be allowed to go back?'

'No. But maybe I didn't speak to the right people.'

'Why do you think I became a Communist?'

'I'd guess for three reasons. I understand those all right.'

'What were the three reasons?'

'You saw what the Nazis were doing and were going to do. You saw what was happening in England. The unemployment. The indifference. The failure of socialism. And lastly because you're a romantic. What the Arabs were for your father the Soviets were for you.'

Philby smiled. A slow amused smile. 'Not bad. Not bad at all. So what's the problem?'

'The problem is that most young men thought as you did. But they changed their minds when they saw what the Soviets actually did.'

'Like what?'

'Sign a peace treaty with the Nazis while we were fighting them. Grabbing Poland, Czechoslovakia and the rest of the satellites. Stalin murdering millions of Russians in the purges. And now the Soviet Union is a vast prison.'

'The Soviets weren't prepared for war, that's why they signed the treaty.'

'That's crap, Kim. We weren't prepared for war either, but we fought them all the same. I know all the old, old, Party excuses. You're too intelligent to believe them. You know too much to be deceived by the Party line. You mix with the people who are doing these things.'

'I care about these people.'

'Which ones do you care about. The ones in the Gulag, or the ones in the Kremlin?'

'Both. I understand them both. I care for both. It won't always be like this.'

'Did you ever meet Gehlen?'

Philby looked surprised. 'Why do you ask?'

'People mention him as part of your background.'

'I never met him or had any dealings with him.'

'Not even after the CIA took him over?'

'No.'

'What about Otto John?'

'What about him?'

'Did you ever meet him?'

'Only once. Do they mention *him* as part of my background?'

'Yes. Those two names go together like Laurel and Hardy.'

'You might understand why I want to go back if you found the connection between them and me.'

'You tell me.'

'I can't. I'm not sure that there is a connection. I think there is. All my professional instincts say there is. But I don't *know*. There are bound to be things that I wasn't told.'

'Why not tell me what you think?'

Philby reached for a whisky bottle.

'D'you want a drink?'

'No thanks.'

'Some wine?'

'No. I don't need anything.'

Philby took a long drink until the tumbler was two-thirds empty, then he put it down with extravagant care on the glass table-top before he looked up at Powell.

'Gehlen died last week. Otto John is still around. Try him.'

'It's wasting time. Your time as well as mine.'

'You don't understand, Johnny. Whatever I say about Gehlen and Otto John you won't believe me. You've seen what it was like even in SIS in London. Way back and now. They all have theories, they all have suspicions. Those who know what happened keep silent.' He leaned forward again. His face earnest and almost pleading. He said softly, 'I don't know myself, Johnny. I really don't.'

'Tell me about Gehlen.'

*The sun beat down on the mountain, glinting on the lenses of the binoculars. He could see right down to the mouth of the valley. Morning after morning he had climbed up from the hotel to the chalet and watched for the first American jeep to signal the arrival of the US Seventh Army. Lieutenant-General Alexander M. Patch would be in command. He had heard on the radio that morning that the Red Army had smashed its way into Berlin. Reinhard Gehlen was beginning to get anxious.*

*It would probably not be an exaggeration to say that General Gehlen was the only man in Germany that morning who was basing his future career, and even his life, on an assumption that could seem to others the wildest fantasy. Gehlen took it for granted that within one, or at most two months of the war ending, the Americans and the Russians would be at each others' throats. And that as the officer commanding the only intelligence unit in the whole of Europe that had successfully penetrated the Soviet Union at all levels the Americans would welcome him with open arms. Even open pockets.*

*When, eventually, he met the top Americans his welcome was more controlled and less rapturous than he expected. But his basic premise was correct. Gehlen was a realist and he put down the coolish welcome in Washington to the fact that the US intelligence services were inexperienced, and to the fact that so many of their German-speaking officers were Jews. It would be easy to say that his views were based on typical Nazi prejudices but it wouldn't have been entirely true. Many of them were Jews, and were not yet ready to wipe out their memories of the Nazis, even for the sake of combatting a new enemy. And they were inexperienced intelligence officers, not yet inured to the special pleading and the glosses of their new profession. They had not yet*

132

absorbed the dictum that the end justifies the means, no matter what the means might be.

But in Allen Dulles he found an admirer, even a soulmate. For it was Dulles's responsibility to counter the new danger – Communism – by any and every means he could lay hands on.

The newly formed CIA set up Gehlen and his old team in their own top-security area just outside Munich, at the small town of Pullach. And Hitler's highly efficient Foreign Armies East was operating again. The same old enemy but new masters. And now they were better paid and better loved than they had ever been. There was still no intelligence organization in the world that was more successful or more efficient at penetrating the Russian scene for intelligence at all levels.

Political, economic, scientific, military, it was all obtainable, and Gehlen and his team brought it in. They gave the CIA better value for money than the CIA gave itself. And Reinhard Gehlen worked his operation as if the money were his own. He was a born intelligence chief, and his interest in money was minimal. There were, of course, a good number of Americans, in politics and the intelligence organizations, who found using dedicated Nazis distasteful, or worse. But the Soviet Union's appetite for expansion and aggression was too obvious for the niceties of civilization to be observed all that closely.

Some politician once said that 'a week in politics is a long time' and a few years can seem a lifetime when the politics are international. The British looked at the Pullach operation with a jaundiced eye, and Adenauer himself had ordered the setting up of other intelligence organizations directly under the West German government's control. By 1950 Bonn had established the BfV, the Office for the Protection of the Constitution, and the ominously titled 'Amt Blank', named after its chief. Both of these operations' responsibilities covered intelligence and counter-intelligence. It was obvious to Gehlen that the BfV was the real rival. A deadly rival. His only supporters left were the CIA. It was of prime importance that he should influence the appointment of the head of BfV. It must be one of his sympathizers. Somebody malleable and controllable.

One after the other he put up names of candidates, and one after the other they were rejected by Adenauer or the British High Commissioner, or both. The British were determined that this crucial post should not go to yet another ex-Sicherheitsdienst or Gestapo man. The kind who populated the Pullach organization. There would be no Nazi taint in this new organization.

When Gehlen heard the name of the man who had been appointed he was at first incredulous and then black with anger.

Otto John had been the first man to be interrogated by British intelligence who knew the inner details of the bomb plot, and after three intensive weeks of interrogation in Madrid he had been passed on to London.

He had co-operated whole-heartedly with the authorities, and was allowed to settle in London, and eventually he practised as an international lawyer. In 1948 he married the well-known German opera singer, Lucie Manen.

And nobody was more surprised than he, when, years later, in 1950, he was nominated and appointed as the first head of the BfV.

It is easy enough to appoint a liberal, intellectual and honest man as the head of an intelligence organization but unfortunately it doesn't make him an experienced intelligence man at the same time. Gehlen had little difficulty in infiltrating his own men into strategic posts in the BfV, and Otto John was furtively thwarted and overridden by the ex-

*Nazis who soon controlled, and successfully ran, the various
sections of his operation.*

*The summer sun slanted through the big windows across the
faces of people gathered in the hall. There were vases full of
red roses and white carnations along the front of the platform. As the Bishop read the passage from St Mark, Otto
John looked from the platform at the faces in the front rows.
They were senior politicians, army officers, journalists and
broadcasters, actors and writers.*

*It was 20 July 1954, and those present had assembled to
honour the memory of all those murdered by the Gestapo
after the abortive bomb plot ten years earlier. Otto John had
been invited both as head of the BfV and as the brother of
one of the victims. Gehlen had been invited as a matter of
protocol but John couldn't see him anywhere. He recognized a few other ex-Nazis who must have attended very
reluctantly. But what was good enough for the West
German Chancellor had to be good enough for them, if not
for Gehlen.*

*It seemed longer than ten years since that morning when
he had packed his bags in haste and headed for Templehof.
He had made no plans for escape. They had constantly
worried that the opportunity to place the bomb might never
occur, but the possibility of the bomb exploding and not
killing Hitler had never been considered. None of the group
had escaped except him, and he was certain that God must
have been on his side. Only his status with Lufthansa had
made it possible. The next day would have been too late.
Even for him.*

*Thinking of those days made him feel faint, and for a
moment he closed his eyes. So much had changed, and yet,
incredibly, so much had stayed the same. The Nazis still
held key posts in every part of the government, from the*

135

Cabinet office to the police, from the politicians to the industrialists. Sometimes their past was known, and sometimes not. Where it was known the excuse was always the same. Men were needed with administrative experience, and unfortunately there were too few experienced men who had not been Nazis. It was true enough, but in his view it would have been better to suffer some inefficiency rather than rely on men who had done Hitler's dirty work for him. He had tried to clear them out of the BfV, and failed. There were too many people of influence ready to protect them.

When his mind came back again to the service in the hall they were singing the last verse of the hymn. It was one he recognized, 'Gott rett' uns'. God save us. And for a brief, sickening moment he thought of the film he had once been shown. The film Hitler had shown at private parties, the bodies still jerking in reflex, after death had come, the corpses turning slowly like carcasses in a slaughter-house from the butchers' hooks in the ceiling.

When the ceremony was over he made his way along to the open doors, and walked in the late afternoon sunshine through to the Kurfürstendamm. Despite all its problems there was still something special about Berlin.

At his hotel he bathed, and ate a meal alone in his room. Sipping his coffee reminded him of his date with Wohlgemuth. He had promised to go round to him for a chat and a drink. Wohlgemuth was an amiable, lively man, and they generally met for an hour or so whenever he was in Berlin. They had originally met during the war, when Wohlgemuth was a Wehrmacht doctor, and he now had his consulting rooms in Kantstrasse. John guessed that Wohlgemuth was doing well as an established surgeon.

As he pressed the door-bell at Wohlgemuth's apartment he turned casually to look at the man reading a newspaper leaning up against the wall at the far end of the corridor.

136

*Then the door was opened by Wohlgemuth himself. Smiling and welcoming as usual, he ushered him inside.*

*Otto John took off his cotton jacket and sat in the comfortable armchair.*

*'How did the commemoration service go, Otto?' Wohlgemuth's face had a look of concern that was ready to change to a smile.*

*John shrugged. 'I hardly felt I was there. I was thinking about those days and now. I guess it went all right.'*

*'When are you going back?'*

*'Tomorrow. Mid-day. How are things with you?'*

*Wohlgemuth waved his hands, smiling. 'Fine. There's always someone with an appendix, or a hernia, or a hysterectomy, to be dealt with.'*

*'Must be the Berlin air.'*

*Wohlgemuth stood up, heaving his big body out of the comfortable chair.*

*'A drink, Otto?'*

*'I'd prefer a coffee if it's handy.'*

*'There's always coffee. I bought this damned machine so that I can help myself when Frau Bencke isn't around.'*

*'Is this her night off?'*

*'Night! Three nights a week and Sundays she has off. And tonight's extra. Gone to see Marlon Brando in* On the Waterfront, *with German sub-titles. Courtesy of the insurance man. Sugar or saccharin tablets?'*

*'Sugar please. One.'*

*'Right. I haven't stirred it.'*

*Otto John took the cup of coffee and stirred it slowly as he looked around the room. He sipped the hot coffee. It had a bitter taste and he pulled a face.*

*'Tastes like war-time acorn coffee.'*

*'Perhaps it's been boiled a bit too long. I probably haven't got the hang of the machine yet.'*

*He drank a little more and then leaned forward to put the*

137

cup on the low table. Suddenly everything seemed to slow down, and he saw the cup sliding in slow motion from the saucer, and that was the last thing he saw before he became unconscious.

There was daylight coming through the windows and net curtains lifted and fell in the summer breeze. His arms lay heavily on the flat arms of the chair and his body was held under the weight of his inertia. He felt swollen, his body too big for his skin, and his eyes stayed half-closed at the edge of sleep. He saw what he thought was a bright red geranium on the window-sill, and the vague outline of a man at the edge of his vision. He wanted to look, but the effort was too much. And slowly he sank back into unconsciousness like a log floating just under the surface of the water.

He heard voices the next time that he came to. They were speaking in Russian, or Polish; some Slav language that he couldn't understand. He couldn't open his eyes but his body felt lighter. He tried to move his arm but it wouldn't respond. He breathed deeply and slid back into the darkness.

There was an ache in his eyes but he could see. He could see the two men sitting watching him. And a woman, a nurse in a white and blue uniform, was standing beside him. She was holding out a glass of water to him, and a green capsule in the other hand.

'Take it,' she said in German. 'It will clear your head.'

His hands trembled as he reached out for the glass and the capsule. When he had put the capsule in his mouth he swallowed the cold water. The nurse took the empty glass and walked to the door.

The man in the blue shirt leaned forward. He, too, spoke in German, with almost no accent but with a harsh voice.

'Are you feeling better, Dr John?'

'What happened. Where is Herr Wohlgemuth?'

138

'He's at his surgery.'

'Where is this. Where am I?'

'We are in East Berlin, Herr Doktor. We want to help you and we want your help too.'

'I don't understand. How did I get here?'

'We brought you here so that we could talk with you privately.'

'You kidnapped me?'

'It was the only way.'

'Do you know who I am?'

'Of course.'

'There will be official protests at the highest level. You realize that?'

The man nodded. 'There have been inquiries.' He half-smiled. 'They have not been, shall we say, strenuous. Not all your colleagues regret your absence.'

'Is there anything in the newspapers?'

'Of course. You are referred to as a defector. A Soviet spy who has been recalled by his paymasters.'

'But that's ridiculous.'

'Certainly. But your enemies will all have their little incidents to recall that show that you were always pro-Soviet.'

'Nonsense. I'm not pro-Soviet. And I never have been.'

'You are an anti-Nazi of long standing. For ex-Nazis that means you are a Communist. You acted as a legal adviser to the British at the Nuremburg trials. You removed faithful ex-Nazis from the BfV so you are a disloyal German. You complained in public about ex-Nazis in high office. You pointed a finger directly at Gehlen and Pullach. So you are a trouble-maker. An embarrassment to your government. Freedom of speech does not include freedom to criticize Nazis or ex-Nazis. You know that, my friend.'

'Do you realize what you are doing? You have kidnapped a senior West German official. You've drugged me. You are holding me against my will.'

139

*The second man who had been silent until then said, 'I assure you that you will not be harmed in any way. We have real and genuine respect for you, and for your fight against the Nazis. We will support you in that fight. We also want to show the people of the German Democratic Republic that there are men in high places in West Germany who are willing to speak out against Nazism.'*

*'I feel very tired. I must think about what you have said.'*

*'By all means. Let us meet and talk again tomorrow.'*

*'How long have I been here?'*

*'This is the third day.'*

*The pressures put on Otto John were subtle and effective. The Russians were not asking him to say anything that was untrue. In fact very little that he had not already said many times in public in Bonn and Cologne. He had given newspaper interviews in Bonn that had said the same things. Kowalski, the second man, had readily agreed that the Soviets and the East Germans would benefit psychologically by him airing his views in public. But Kowalski had countered that by asking if the truth was only the truth when it was said in West Germany. If there were any views or any facts that he disputed in the proposed speech he could omit them. They asked for nothing more than the truth.*

*With much reluctance he gave the press conference and made the broadcast. It was a week after the broadcast that Kowalski visited him at the guard house. He told him that they were both going to a Black Sea resort for a short holiday. They were at a villa just outside Sochi for almost a month and then he was flown to Moscow.*

*He had been accommodated in a flat on Moskvina Ulitsa with Kowalski; and it was on the second evening that they were there when Kowalski had raised a new subject. They were eating together at the time, and despite Kowalski's*

140

*casual approach he sensed at once that it was a matter of importance to the Russian.*

*Kowalski had pushed across the big, glass bowl of fresh fruit.*

'Help yourself, Otto. When you were with Lufthansa you were frequently in Lisbon and Madrid, yes?'

'It was an important route for us in the war. The most important neutral capitals in Europe.'

'And that was how you were able to contact British intelligence in Lisbon about the assassination plot?'

'Yes.'

'Did they believe you?'

'It's hard to say. I made no progress with them.'

'Who was your contact at the British embassy?'

'I don't remember his name.'

'Was it Philby. Kim Philby?'

'Yes. I think it was. A youngish man. I heard his name later when I was in London.'

'Was he based in Lisbon?'

'I don't think so. I think he came in from London.'

'Did he give you any encouragement?'

'Yes. But no practical help.'

'Did he indicate what London's view was about negotiating with your group after the assassination?'

'Nothing specific. General verbal support. Nothing more.'

'Did you ever get the impression that the British had other contacts with your group apart from you?'

'No.'

'You're quite sure about that. None of them spoke of another contact with London?'

'I'm quite sure that I was the only contact.'

'So where do you think your people got the bomb?'

'They made it themselves, or got it made.'

'Do you actually know that?'

'No. I never heard it discussed. I wasn't interested in the bomb itself.'

'Nobody told you that it was made and supplied by British intelligence?'

'No. Was it?'

'Yes.'

'How do you know?'

'We've got the original analysis of the fragments of the bomb by the German explosives experts who examined the room and the bits and pieces. Where do you think they could have got it from?'

'It could only be through Madrid, Lisbon or Stockholm. But I was the only contact.'

'Except for Philby. He could have made some other contact secretly with your group. Did he know any of their names?'

'Only von Witzleben.'

'So it's possible?'

'I suppose so. But I don't see the point.'

'Maybe Philby or his people in London might have been suspicious that you were a plant. An agent-provocateur.'

John shrugged. 'For what purpose?'

'They could think that you were working for the Soviets checking whether the British would sign a separate peace with the Germans.'

'But the British and the Russians must have known even then that Germany was going to lose the war.'

Kowalski seemed to lose interest in the subject and they watched a late football match on TV before they retired for the night. But the next day, and every day for the next three weeks he was questioned. Not only by Kowalski, but six or seven others including a woman. They questioned him for hours every day. Going over the same ground again and again. Trying to make him remember every word that he and

*Philby had exchanged. Every expression on Philby's face. Every detail of the pick-up and the meeting.*

*It was December when he was taken back to East Berlin. They seemed to have lost interest in him suddenly. He saw Kowalski from time to time and he was paid as a consultant to the East German Information Ministry, but was never asked to do any work. He was allowed to visit the Press Club and his movements were virtually unrestricted. He had a small modern flat near the site of the new TV tower.*

*It was at the Press Club that he had met one of the Scandinavian journalists whom he knew from Bonn, and he confided in him that he was hoping to escape back to West Berlin. On 6 December the journalist took him through the checkpoint in his car. And got almost a world scoop on the story.*

*On the West Berlin side the car was stopped for what he assumed would be the usual routine check. There were four police officers. Two of them frontier police, and the other two Kriminalpolizei. One of them opened the car door on his side.*

*'Herr Doktor John?'*

*'Yes.'*

*He was amazed that they recognized him so readily.*

*'You're under arrest.'*

*'You know who I am?'*

*'Yes.'*

*'What is the charge?'*

*'Acts of treason against the Federal German Republic. Would you get out of the car please.'*

*'I must ask to see a lawyer.'*

*'We have orders to take you to the airport. You will be escorted to Bonn. I'm sure that you will be allowed to contact a lawyer there.'*

143

*They had kept him in custody for eight months before they charged him. He was put on trial on 22 November 1956.*

*He was found guilty of treason and sentenced to four years' imprisonment. Dr Wohlgemuth sent a letter to the court apologizing for his non-attendance, and confirming that on several occasions Dr Otto John had told him that he intended to defect to East Germany. And that it was by Dr John's personal wish that he had driven him to East Berlin. He had merely been doing his friend a favour.*

# 16

Powell looked across at Philby.

'Was Volkov already dead when they put him on the plane?'

Philby smiled. 'The old routine.'

'What old routine?'

'Keep changing the subject. Get the suspect on the run. Get him confused. Then go back to square one and see if the answers are the same. Blow hot and cold from "let me be your friend" to "why are you lying to me?" '

'So what's the answer to my question?'

'I've no idea. I shouldn't think he was dead.'

'Why not?'

'They would want to interrogate him in Moscow, to find out what he knew, and who had told him about me.'

'The people at our consulate were the only people who spoke to Volkov in Istanbul?'

'Yes.'

'And he told them that all their cyphers had been broken by the Soviets?'

'Yes.'

'I've checked their signals records for the next eight months and they didn't change the codes. So why did they go on using them when they knew they were no longer secure?'

Philby smiled. 'I wasn't the only friend that the Soviets had in the Foreign Office area you know.'

'I can't believe that.'

'Oh for God's sake, Johnny. Who do you think covered

up for all the other Soviet spies? George Blake, Britten, Cloude, Dorschel, Fuchs, Bossard. How do you think George Blake could be got out of Wormwood Scrubs without inside help and co-operation? Blake was SIS, they thought they were using him against the Soviets. The information he passed to Moscow ripped NATO security to shreds. He was sentenced to forty-two years and stuck in the Scrubs. You don't really think that the KGB could have "sprung" him out of that place without top-level inside help do you?'

'The story at the time was that Moscow paid the IRA to do it.'

Philby laughed. 'What rubbish. Anyone who would believe that would believe anything.'

'Where did the help come from?'

'Ask Patrick Walker. He could tell you. Are you going to stay here for the night?'

'I'd have to inform Coles at the embassy.'

'Phone him. The phone's over there. The number's 231-95-55.'


Philby waved towards the bed. 'It's rather spartan I'm afraid.'

'Looks fine to me.'

'Do you want something to read in bed?'

'No thanks. I sleep pretty well.'

Philby moved across and sat on the bed watching Powell unpack his bag.

'Tell me about you, Johnny.'

'What do you want to know?'

'Your background. Your home. Your parents.'

Powell was arranging his brush and comb and shaving gear on the shelf over the small handbasin.

'I was an orphan.'

'What happened?'

'Nothing.

'Were your parents killed, or what?'

'I was left as a baby at a police station.'

'My God. How terrible. How sad. Who brought you up?'

'An orphanage.'

'Are you married?'

'No.'

'Why not?'

Powell turned round to look at the man sitting on the bed.

'I guess I'm afraid of having responsibilities for other people. I wouldn't want to let them down.'

' "He travels the fastest who travels alone." Was it R.L. Stevenson?'

Powell smiled. 'No. It was Rudyard Kipling. And the previous line is just as important.'

'What is it?'

'The quote is, "Down to Gehenna or up to the Throne, he travels the fastest who travels alone".'

'Ah yes. Gehenna. The hell-fire. In a way I envy you.'

'Why?'

'No responsibilities. No father and mother to set their stamp on you. Nobody to mourn. Nobody to make unhappy. No child to protect.'

'And no one to rejoice with.'

Philby shook his head. 'It's a long time since I rejoiced.'

'When was it?'

Philby looked towards the small, barred window and sat silently. Eventually he said, very softly without turning his head. 'I don't think I ever have really rejoiced. It's a big word.'

'Didn't you rejoice when you passed something vital to the Russians?'

'Who would I have rejoiced with?'

'Burgess and Maclean? Your Russian controller?'

'I never worked with Burgess and Maclean. And my

Russian contact had a wife and two children besieged in Leningrad. He wasn't a man for rejoicing. He was a pessimist. He expected them to be killed by the Germans. He was right. They were. They weren't times for rejoicing. It was a long, grim, grey period.'

'Did it worry you giving Moscow our secrets?'

Philby smiled and shook his head. 'What I told Moscow helped them, but it did us no harm. It was no more than telling a friend that you had heard on the grapevine that his house was going to be burgled, when you had heard it in confidence from one of the burglar's friends. Anything that I told them during the war we ought to have told them anyway.'

'You never felt any guilt?'

'Good God no. Never. Not for a moment. There was a war on, and the real fighting was in Russia.'

'And after the war?'

Philby stood up, slowly.

'Do you want a night-cap?'

'No thanks. I'll sit with you while you have one if you want.'

'Have you got many friends?'

'No. A girl-friend, that's all.'

'Are you happy?'

Powell smiled. 'Like you said about rejoicing. Happiness is too big a word. I prefer contentment. Contentment can last.'

'Are you content?'

'More or less. Are you?'

'I would be content if I were back. Passively content.'

'Would you risk being put on trial?'

'They would never do that, I assure you.'

'I wouldn't rely on that, Kim.'

'I'd be interested to know who would throw the first stone.'

'An old colleague of yours named McNay.'

'James McNay?'

'Yes.'

Philby smiled and stood up. 'See you in the morning. Sleep well.'

Powell had only vaguely heard the telephone ringing but a few moments later Philby had knocked on the door and walked in.

'It's Coles from the embassy for you, Johnny.'

He slung his dressing-gown over his shoulders and walked to the phone in the sitting room.

'Powell.'

'I've just had a signal from London. They want you back right away.'

'What is it?'

'I've no idea but I've booked you on to an Aeroflot flight to Heathrow. You need to be at Sheremetyevo in two hours' time, 11.15.'

'Can you drive me out?'

'Sure. I'll be there in an hour. I'll wait outside in the car.'

'Just come up.'

'The guards wouldn't let me through the entrance. You'd better ask our friend to tell them that I'm authorized even to park outside.'

'OK. See you.'

He had washed, shaved and dressed and then he had sat with Philby at the low table. Philby was wearing an old Paisley dressing-gown and seemed disturbed that Powell had been recalled.

There was a plate of warm toast, a dish of butter and a jar of Cooper's Oxford marmalade. Coarse cut.

'When will you be back?'

'I don't know, Kim.'

'Is your recall to do with me?'

'I genuinely don't know.'

'I've written out my new phone number. You can phone me if you want.'

'Thank you.'

Down in the street something made him look up before he got into the car and he saw Philby's white face at the window high up above him. It looked wan, and lonely, and sad.

There had been an hour's delay at Amsterdam and a long wait at the luggage carousel at Heathrow. When he finally shoved through the crowds to the main hall he saw Mills, one of his own men, waiting for him. Mills took his case and they walked across to the multiple car park.

When they were on the M4 he asked Mills why he had been called back.

'There's a flap on. A real flap.'

'What?'

'Somebody's been murdered.'

'Who?'

'Lord Harpenden.'

'My God. When did it happen?'

'As far as we can tell it must have happened two days ago. But he was only discovered yesterday evening. The quack hasn't seen him yet.'

'How was he killed?'

'Two shots. One behind each ear.'

'Where was he found?'

'At his farm in Kent.'

'Anything taken?'

'Not that we can see.'

'Who's in charge?'

'Kenrick, but he's been told to hold everything until you've gone over it.'

'Who do I report to?'

'Nobody. There's an envelope from Sir Ian for you in the glove compartment.'

150

Powell tore open the envelope and read the brief note on the stiff, white paper. Kenrick was in charge of the scene of the crime investigation. The local police would not be informed until Special Branch and Five had been put in the picture. He was to investigate the security aspects and keep them to himself. The notification of the death could not be delayed beyond seventy-two hours and it would be his responsibility to use all means to prevent public knowledge of the murder before the police were notified.

'Milord' had had several homes but the farm at Wittersham had always been his main base. There was another farm in East Anglia, a farmhouse and shoot in Scotland, and dozens of small cottages with a few acres of land scattered over the Kentish countryside. His commercial interests were administered from a Georgian house just off Portland Place within sight of Broadcasting House. And the Polish Embassy.

Powell slept fitfully as he was driven down towards the coast, and only woke when they left the Hastings road for Tenterden. Parson's Farm lay off the main road, except for the double oast that flanked the road leading to Rye.

The big double gates were closed but one of them was opened as they halted in the drive. The plain-clothes man walked over, checked their identity cards, spoke briefly into his mobile radio, and then waved them on towards the big house.

There were lights on already in the downstairs rooms, and the golden light of the setting sun made glancing, diamond patterns on the leaded panes of the windows. It was a beautiful house. William and Mary, and only inverted snobbery could have described it as a farmhouse. It would have been a manor house in its time, and none of its owners had been philistine enough to add or subtract from its elegant lines.

Kenrick was waiting for him at the big oak doors. Kenrick had been in SIS at the start of the war, but despite his long service he was junior to Powell. They had worked together from time to time, and he was allocated to the 'Milord' surveillance. There had never appeared to be any resentment on the part of the older man. He was a professional and got on with his assignments. Powell guessed that to be passed over for promotion so often, with Kenrick's long and varied experience, meant that somewhere along the line somebody had put some 'stopper' in Kenrick's 'P' file.

Kenrick's hair was still mainly black and only the wings above his ears showed signs of grey. His face was leathery, his body was lean and trim. He was in good shape for a man who must be only a few years away from retirement.

'Good-evening, Mr Powell. Would you like a meal and a bath before you get started? It's all laid on if you'd like it.'

'Where's the body?'

'In the study.'

'Let me have a look in there first, just to get the feel of it.'

Kenrick nodded and turned to Mills. 'Get Mr Powell's bag and bring it inside will you please.'

Kenrick walked with him across the vast hall, through a dining hall, a large sitting room, and into a room that was panelled in walnut. Its curtains were drawn. The body was in a low-backed leather chair, the torso slumped forward, the head lying, as if asleep, on the surface of the leather-topped desk. The shape of the broad shoulders was distorted by the left arm that was trapped between the chest and the desk top. The right arm hung down between the legs.

Powell leaned forward and sideways to look at the face. A large piece of bone at the front of the skull hung forward, held only by a narrow flap of skin. It looked like a broken Easter egg except for the grey-blue Medusa-like loops of brain tissue that had been forced out. There was blood down the cheek, and a pool of dark brown, dried blood on the desk itself.

Powell moved round the chair and knelt to look at the

wound behind the left ear. It was quite small and he guessed it had been from a .38. The wound behind the right ear was larger, as if the shot had been fired a little further away from the skull. When he stood up Powell rubbed his knees absent-mindedly.

'What's been touched?'

'Nothing at all, sir. But I've had extensive photographs taken.'

'Who discovered him?'

'Jessop. The plain-clothes man on the gate. I've got a statement but it looks useless.'

'Where are the servants?'

'There were none here apparently. That's what made Jessop suspicious. We think they must have left a few hours before the murder.'

'How many were there?'

'Five including our chap, the gardener.'

'What about the farm staff. The farm-manager?'

'They weren't ever allowed over here unless they were sent for.'

'Any views, Tom?'

'It's professional. There's no doubt about that.'

'You mean the two head-shots?'

'Yes.'

Powell looked at Kenrick's face. 'Who do you think?'

'Us or them. Nothing's been taken.'

Powell turned his eyes to the wall beyond the desk and Kenrick said, 'Whoever did it removed the slugs before they left. They went into the wall at both sides of the window frame. It looks as if they knifed them out. I've had the holes photographed but it won't help. They were in a hurry and they prised them out pretty crudely. You can see blade marks on the paint.'

'Let's eat, Tom. I'm starving.'

The three of them ate together and Powell told Kenrick

153

what to do if the servants came back. Mills said that one of Jessop's men had heard down in the pub that the servants had gone off in a coach.

Powell lay on the covers of a bed in one of the guest rooms. His last thoughts before he slept were on the obvious fact that either the SIS or the KGB had killed 'Milord'. Why should *either* of them want him dead? Whichever one of them it was, it had been well planned. There were all the usual signs of a professional killing. It had been tidy, precise, and successful.

He woke at four, and bathed and shaved before he went down the broad oak stairway. The lights were still on everywhere and Kenrick was writing notes at the big dining-table. He looked up as Powell pulled out a chair and sat down.

'What would you like to do first, Mr Powell?'

'Any news of the servants?'

'Yes. Our gardener man phoned London. They were given a holiday at 'Milord's' instructions and expense. A signed note was given to the general manager. It seems he did the same a couple of years ago.'

'Where are they?'

'At Pagham just outside Chichester.'

'Was any reason given?'

'Reward for loyal service.'

'Did they believe it?'

'No. It was done in a hurry. Only an hour's notice. The rumour was that the previous time that had happened there had been some sort of orgy. And they assumed that this was the same again.'

'Why an orgy?'

'Nylons and panties in unusual places last time.'

'Those were probably planted by his lordship.'

'So why did he want the servants away?'

'People coming here that he didn't want anyone to see.'

'Could be.'

154

'That filing cabinet in the corner of the study. Have you got the keys?'

'No. I haven't touched anything. Those were my orders. Just to hold the fort until you got here.'

'Get Owens down here will you. Tell him it's urgent.'

'There's Dr Shires at Eastbourne. He'd be much quicker.'

'I thought he'd retired.'

'He has, but he still consults for us in emergencies.'

'OK. He'll do.'

While he waited for the doctor to get over to them Powell went through the whole house. Opening cupboards, checking drawers, tapping walls. In the end he was satisfied that 'Milord's' papers could only be in the filing cabinet, the desk or the safe in the study wall.

Dr Shires had come and gone by the time he had finished his general search. Death, he confirmed, had been instantaneous, and caused by the two shots in the head. Death had occurred approximately sixty to seventy hours before, and there were no visible signs on the body of a struggle or any other wounds.

Powell nodded as Kenrick gave him the report.

'Ask Mr Mills to search his clothing and put everything on the side table. Do you know if Sammy Watts is available?'

'I'll check for you. Do you want him for the safe if he's on tap?'

'Please.'

Ten minutes later Powell picked up the bunch of keys that Mills had taken from the corpse and opened both drawers of the filing cabinet. The bottom drawer was empty and the top drawer held nothing except seven or eight files. He lifted them out carefully and carried them over to the side table.

Powell listed the titles that had been scrawled on the buff-coloured covers. There were three files titled NATO 1, 2, and 3. A file marked HARP. Two marked WASHINGTON A and B. And a file without a title but marked 97413.

He opened each file in turn. The basic material in each of them was the same. Photo enlargements of micro photographs direct from the negatives. The text, a white typewritten face reversed on a black background, the paper thin and flimsy, brittle with age. Each page consisted of four columns of letters and figures in five-digit groups. They were blow-ups of standard microfilm coded messages. And they were old. Very old.

Slowly and carefully he went through them page by page. But there was nothing unusual. The cryptographers could go through them, but he suspected that they were too old to be of much interest. He shoved them on one side and went through the stuff that Mills had removed from the body. There was nothing of any particular interest.

There were three drawers on the right-hand side of the desk, and a single door to the left. He opened the door first. Inside were three bottles of whisky, a half-empty bottle of gin, and half a dozen glasses. And right at the back a box of cigars that was still sealed. Powell broke the seal and cracked open two of the cigars, then pulled them apart. They were quite normal.

In the bottom drawer on the right-hand side of the desk were envelopes, stationery and unused file covers. In the centre drawer there was a plastic tray holding pencils, paper clips, two erasers and a couple of elastic bands. Alongside the tray was a bottle of ink, a pencil sharpener, and a small pile of visiting cards in 'Milord's' name. In the top drawer was a cheap note-pad and a Parker ballpoint. And what looked like two books of raffle tickets. Powell turned one of them over casually and lifted the outer cover. It was a one-time code pad. The five-figure groups were printed in red. The other pad was similar but printed in black. He gathered up both pads and the note-pad.

Sitting at the table he counted the number of leaves in each pad. There were twenty in the black and nineteen in the red. He walked across the room to stand under the main light and held the note-pad sloping away from him. He could see the impressions on the smooth shiny surface of the cheap paper. The KGB generally used red pads for encoding and if he was lucky the impressions on the pad were the original message. And if he were luckier still it would be in English.

Back at the table with one of the pencils and the sharpener, he ground up a small pyramid of powdered carbon from the lead of the pencil. He knew that Forensic would go berserk when he told them, but his instinct told him that this could be all that he needed. He gently puffed the black powder across the paper, tapping the edges to spread it evenly. He tapped the surplus on to a loose page from the note-pad. He could make out several figures and random letters. It was written in block capitals and the letter repetition made him almost certain that it wasn't in English.

He piled the file covers together, the one-time pads, and the leaf from the note-pad and shoved them to one side as he called out for Kenrick. When he came Powell indicated that he should sit down at the table.

'I don't think we need any more, Tom, do you?'

'Have you got what you want?'

'I don't know whether it's any use or not, but I think I've got all there is. Unless Sammy finds anything in the safe.'

'He's due any minute.'

'Fine.' He looked at Kenrick's face. 'Who do you think did it, Tom?'

'I'd say KGB.'

'So would I. Why do you think so?'

'Because if it was our people they wouldn't have left anything around that could interest you.'

'It was old stuff. Encoded microfilm and a couple of one-time pads.'

'Our people wouldn't have left stuff like that around for

the police to find, but the KGB wouldn't give a damn what was found.'

'Any idea why either of them would have done it?' Powell's eyes were on Kenrick's face.

'I guess somebody thought he might talk. And again it could only be the KGB who would want to prevent him from talking. Our people would have been delighted if he had talked.'

'All of them?'

Kenrick looked across the table at him. 'If you knew, why did you go along with it up to now?'

'Go along with what?'

'The committee.'

'I don't understand.'

'Well you ought to.'

'For heaven's sake what are you on about?'

'I'd better leave it. They could claim it was a breach of security.'

'Are you willing to talk to me off the record?'

'Provided it really is off the record.'

'It is. As of now.'

'What do you want to ask me?'

'Why you wondered why I should go along with the committee. Why shouldn't I?'

'Because it was phoney.'

'In what way?'

'In my book it was a cover-up.'

'For what?'

'Why did "Milord" matter so much?'

'Because he was the man who recruited Philby.'

'That's rubbish. Harpenden was only one of a score of men in high places working for the Soviets.'

'So why was the committee formed?'

'Maybe to keep the heat off some of the others. If the investigations about Philby's background are concentrated on one man, then the others can relax and carry on working for Moscow.'

'Were you around when Philby was operating, before he was exposed?'

'All the time. Except when he was in Washington.'

'Did you suspect Philby before he bolted?'

'Long before then.'

'When?'

'After the Volkov incident. There were too many indications to be ignored.'

'Did you know who the others were?'

'I was pretty sure. I didn't *know*. I couldn't have proved anything.'

'What happened to them?'

Kenrick shrugged. 'Some are dead. Some are retired. Some are still there. Helping the Soviets.'

'Who are you thinking of?'

'I'm not naming names, Johnny. I'd like to retire peacefully, not end up like "Milord".'

'Tell me what areas you're thinking of?'

'You know already don't you?'

'I guess so. But tell me all the same.'

'One Tory Minister. Three ex-ministers. Two historians. A bundle of scientists. One still at his old university. One member of the Queen's entourage. Four trades union leaders. D'you want me to go on?'

'No.'

'All Tories and establishment except the trades union people.'

'That was his background.' Powell looked at Kenrick as if expecting a denial.

'And Maclean's and Burgess's.'

'What made you think of them?'

'I think Moscow sacrificed Philby all along the line to save Maclean. He was the man who mattered.'

159

'You'll be re-assigned now that Harpenden is dead. I'll tell them I want you for research for a few weeks if that suits you.'

'What are you working on?'

'Philby. I can't tell you any more until they clear you.'

'They won't agree without a struggle.'

'Why not?'

'Because I was around in those days.'

'You were assigned to me for "Milord".'

'That wouldn't worry them. They knew it was a dead end. It was a game. A diversion. It kept people's thoughts away from other things and other people.'

'Who will resist?'

Kenrick smiled. 'Padmore and Walker. But it may not be direct.'

'We'll see. Meantime, phone Special Branch liaison and tell them that it's OK to let the police find Harpenden's body. When you've phoned, tell the others to get back to London. I'd like you to drive me to Hastings Station and I'll make my own way back.'

'OK. You've got my home phone number?'

'Yes. But it'll be a couple of days before I contact you. Maybe longer.'

# 17

The first-class carriage in the train from Hastings was empty, and Powell leaned back in the corner seat watching the oasts and farmhouses slip by. His mind had lost its usual evenness. There was a kind of dreamlike feeling about what he was doing. Most of the people who had worked a long time in the intelligence service had been aware that the three defectors had had their social misdeeds covered up by friends and colleagues, both in government and diplomatic circles. And for some reason Burgess and Maclean had been remembered more for their sordid failings of drink and crude homosexuality than for their treason. They had achieved legends as not much more than outrageous play-boys. P.G. Wodehouse characters taken to extremes. Upper-class aberrations. Foolish rather than treacherous. Their supporters were seen as upper class elite Establishment men from the ruling classes who covered up for the offenders because they came from good families. And with some of them that was undoubtedly true. But there were others, men from the same background, who covered up for them for different motives. Men whose loyalty was suspect but well protected by the laws of libel and slander; and other men whose loyalty was mistakenly taken for granted. It wasn't just a handful of men, there were scores of them, maybe hundreds. Men whose allegiance was to Moscow. Men who were patient and tenacious, who accepted that destroying their own country would take time, and was best done covertly rather than openly.

As the soft countryside passed by, even the facts that he

knew seemed only dreamlike rather than nightmarish. The snug farmhouses, the apple orchards, the sunshine, were still there. It was England. And these men held high office. They were members of the Reform, the Athenaeum, the Garrick, and the Travellers. Men of that background couldn't really sell their weak but amiable country to the grim grey Soviets. Their minds were too logical, too civilized to actually do it. To have talked about it long ago on Sunday mornings in their rooms in college perhaps. But not now when their hair was grey and their knighthoods already history, and their seats in the Lords not solely due to Labour Prime Ministers' whims. Nevertheless they had done it. And were still doing it.

In odd, fleeting moments it came into focus, sharp and horrifying, clear and deadly. But it wouldn't stay long enough in place for him to hold on to. He was tired and confused, but he felt that after a couple of days he could start working things out more clearly. But he was slowly coming to the conclusion that the antagonists like James McNay were right. Philby should not be allowed back. If he came back, unchallenged, it would be proof that you could get away with treason. Not just Philby, but all of them. He guessed the identity of half a dozen of them but that wasn't enough. He would have to walk carefully, and he would tell nobody what was in his mind. He would play along, reluctantly appearing to be concluding and recommending that Philby should be allowed back.

'There's a pile of mail for you. I was tempted to open it.'

He laughed. 'Why?'

'Your letters always look so much more interesting than mine.'

He sat opening the letters one by one, reading them casually and then putting them in a pile. There were ten letters and not one of them was personal. Invoices, receipts, statements and reminders; and book club offers.

'Anything interesting?'

'No, sweetie. The usual rubbish.'

She reached down beside her chair and picked up a flat, rectangular parcel.

'That's from me and Lydia.'

'Did he let you see her again?'

'Yes. He was in town on business and he phoned. Said I could have her for the afternoon. Nanny would pick her up at five.'

'Did it go well?'

'Not bad.'

But he knew from the corners of her mouth that she was covering up. She raised her eyebrows in a kind of challenge for him to doubt her, and when he smiled she relaxed.

'You haven't looked at your present.'

Slowly and carefully he tore off the decorated paper. It was a framed picture. An old mezzotint of an officer in the full dress uniform of the 42nd of Foot. The Black Watch. He suddenly felt very tired and very vulnerable. He hadn't had half a dozen presents in his life, and he was at a loss for words.

'You've got a very good memory, Van.'

She shrugged. 'Well, do you like it for Christ's sake? I can change it if you don't.'

'It's perfect, sweetie. Thank you both very much.'

'You like it?'

'It's marvellous.'

'Is it how you always imagined it?'

'Yes.'

'You're a funny man. It's a shame.'

'What's a shame?'

'You, you great idiot. You should have had a family and Christmas trees and all that jazz.'

He smiled. 'You're my Christmas tree, Van.'

She put her face in her hands and sobbed. He sat there

looking at her, full of compassion but with nothing in his heart or his mind that made him reach out a hand. He sat there silently, holding the picture on his lap. When she looked up her face was blotched with tears.

'We're such a queer couple, Johnny.'

'In what way?'

'We're so different from one another but in one way we're the same. We just don't fit in with the rest of the world. You in one way, me in another.'

'It only matters if we dwell on it, sweetie.'

She shook her head slowly. 'Everybody else seems to have their lives worked out. They know where they are, and they know where they're going.'

He smiled. 'They don't really, Van. They just don't look down when they're walking along the high wire. They're full of doubts. Just like you and me. Different doubts maybe, but doubts all the same.'

'Do you really think so?'

'I know so, honey. Now let's go to bed.'


There had been only money in the safe, and he handed it over in the cardboard boxes to Facilities. 30,000 dollars in ten-dollar notes, 40,000 Deutsche Marks in large denominations, and a canvas bag that was heavy with Krugerrands and sovereigns.

He passed the files to Cyphers and asked for a report, and then walked down to Forensic. They set up the quartz lamp for him, and he wrote down the groups of letters slowly and carefully.

Back in his office he looked at what he had written.

TWÓJ SYGNAŁ 79191420 NIEMA POWTARZAM NIEMA WATPLIWOŚCI MY PRZYSZLIŚMY DRUDZI DO HARFY KROPKA PRZYNAJMNIEJ DWA LATA ZA PÓZNO KROPKA PABLO KONIEC SYGNAŁU

Powell reached for the telephone and asked for Anders' extension, then dialled it himself. Anders was in a meeting but would be available in an hour's time. He spent the hour phoning Special Branch liaison. 'Milord's' body had been found, and the local police had called in Scotland Yard. Powell asked the duty liaison officer to keep him informed if any suspects or information on suspects came to light. The KGB hit man would be in Amsterdam or Prague by now but he would like him identified if possible. Just for the record.

Anders came in an hour and a half later.

'You wanted me, Johnny?'

'Sit down, Tad, I want you to read me some Polish.'

'Is it technical?'

'I don't know. I shouldn't think so.'

Powell passed across the sheet of paper and Anders sat reading it. Frowning slightly as he read it again.

'Doesn't make sense, Johnny, but here goes. "Your message 79191420, no repeat no possible doubt we came second to harp stop at least two years late stop Pablo message ends." ' Anders looked at Powell. 'Make any sense to you?'

'Not at the moment. Maybe it will later. Are you still on Port Security?'

'Yes. I've got another four months to go.'

'Any Soviet hit men been through in the last few days?'

'Which way?'

'Both. In and out.'

'I'll need to check. Any particular dates?'

'Yes. Just before and just after last Thursday.'

'Did they do anything?'

'Maybe.'

Anders smiled. 'OK. I'll check. How urgent is it?'

'Today if possible.'

It was late that afternoon when Anders phoned him.

'There's a possible, John. Two of them. Came in through

Folkestone on the hovercraft with an accredited group. Delegation of Soviet miners on invitation from NUM. Landed on Tuesday, left on Friday from Heathrow for Helsinki. Both of them on our register as KGB. Not seen at NUM meeting. Said to be indisposed. Last seen by us four months ago in Sydney, Australia. Went in as part of a trade mission but seen on violent picket line and warned by State police.'

'Have you got descriptions and names?'

'Yes. And photographs. D'you want copies?'

'Please.'

'I'll send them up to you in half an hour if the copier's free.'

'OK. Thanks.'

'Any time.'


When he phoned Padmore he was invited down to Oxford for lunch the next day. Padmore sounded almost ingratiating.

That evening he took Vanessa to a new restaurant in Kings Road. They had a taxi there and walked back. They called in on the way back at Victoria Station for an evening paper. He bought an *Evening News* and a *Standard*, and a copy of *Vogue* for Van.

The story of Lord Harpenden's murder was on the front page of both papers. A fuzzy photograph and about six column inches in bold type that showed they had nothing to say. Harpenden had never been in the public eye, and he had none of those characteristics that endear the wealthy and titled to the general public. He had a wife who lived somewhere in the South of France and if there were other relatives they probably still lived in the small Polish village where he had originally come from in 1930. There were brief details about his commercial success, and his friendship with the late Prime Minister. The inquest was to be held in three days' time. The police had set up an incident room in the village hall. No official statement had so far been made.

They had made love, but he was still not asleep at two o'clock. He could hear the far-off clanging of trains at Victoria Station, and he knew it must have rained because he could hear the swishing of tyres as solitary cars went by in the road.

Slowly and quietly he slid out of their bed and walked through to the sitting room and switched on the reading-lamp. He could hear the gusts of rain blown on to the windows and it made him think of the orphanage on Sunday nights. Sunday nights had always been the bad times, and as he remembered it it had always seemed to be raining. In those days he would know that another week stretched out ahead of him, the clock ticking loudly, remorselessly and solemnly, as if someone had died. And all those years ago he had been sure that one week would follow another for the rest of his life, and he had wanted to scream, to shout out in protest. But it wasn't possible. They relied on him. He was the boy they pointed out to visitors. The boy who proved that it all worked. Food and shelter and a pat on the head *were* enough. You *could* get by all right without a father and a mother. How could they possibly know that they were wrong. The others, who pined and fretted, were the real ones. They weren't the exceptions. He was. He was always frightened. What, they would have asked, are you frightened of? Everything. Frightened of ticking clocks and Sunday nights, of other people, of being alive, of not knowing. Of everything.

As he sat slumped in the chair he closed his eyes and shook his head. It was one of his turns. It would go. Something good would happen and the black clouds would lift. Two or three times a year he would feel himself being drawn near the edge of this chasm for a second or two but eventually he would escape. Maybe no more than once a year it would steal up on him. Suddenly, secretly. Waiting in an airport cafeteria. Why was he there? What was he doing? Driving the car along a familiar route he would have to stop because he didn't know where he was, or where he was going, or why he was there. Sometimes it would be a couple of hours, sometimes a night and a day, before his batteries were charged again. It was like on TV when the movement was stopped and the figure was frozen for long seconds until the credits had run and the figure moved on, the arms and legs unfrozen.

Van was right in a way. Other people at least thought that they knew what they were doing and where they were going. But he didn't. Philby knew where he was going. Knew what was going to happen. He knew with an assurance that brushed aside facts and attitudes, the McNays and the Padmores, the Walkers and the Powells. Philby wasn't guessing. Philby knew. Knew he was coming back. Angered only by the delay.

He got up slowly from the chair and walked into their small kitchen and made himself a cup of tea. He carried it into the sitting room and found himself a pad and a pen. He moved to the dining table and started writing. He wrote himself a report and it took him an hour. At the end of that time he read it again, then burned it and flushed it down the toilet.

Some people were happy to see Philby come back. Why? Some people were strongly against his coming back. Their reasons were obvious. Philby was a traitor. Philby himself wanted to come back. He had no doubt of that now. But he wasn't sure *why* Philby wanted to come back. Did the KGB know of Philby's intention, and if they did why did they let him make contact with London? If the KGB were playing games did Philby know? Was he party to some KGB ploy? And if he came back, with or without London's agreement, would he be put on trial?

Those were the only questions he really needed to have answered. The killing of 'Milord' was undoubtedly KGB. A piece of standard insurance to stop somebody from talking. If the KGB had found out, or had been informed, that the man who was in charge of the surveillance of 'Milord' was the man in contact with Philby, they were probably just making sure that that door was closed and bolted. If 'Milord' had been arrested and interrogated, and had talked, then a lot of pieces of the ragged SIS jigsaw might have fallen into place.

He listened to the farming programme as he shaved and dressed, left a note on the table for Vanessa, and let himself quietly out of the flat.

In the fresh air he felt his black mood fading, like when brandy blots up pain; and by the time he was at Paddington station he was back in the world again.

The train was on time, but he took a taxi out to the Woodstock Road to just past the Radcliffe infirmary, and then walked the rest of the way to St Anthony's.

Padmore welcomed him effusively, and insisted on showing him first the new painting that he had bought. It was a minor pre-Raphaelite. A gentle, delightful painting of a small girl in a field of daisies. It was unlike what he would have expected Padmore to admire or desire. Padmore was overjoyed that he had only paid £300 for his prize, but his pleasure in the painting itself was real enough.

When they were both seated and the coffee had been brought Powell raised the subject of 'Milord's' murder and Padmore had come down to earth.

'I don't see it as significant, do you?'

'What's your theory, sir?'

'A routine KGB killing. No longer useful to them. They would know he was under constant surveillance. Tales to tell. Better to silence him.'

Padmore looked at him quizzically, as if he expected some rebuttal of his answer, his head half-turned like a wary cockerel on a midden.

Powell said, 'You don't think it had anything to do with the current Philby affair?'

'No. I shouldn't think so. A coincidence I should think. Now tell me about Moscow. What have you decided?'

'I think he genuinely does want to come back.'

'I ask myself why, Powell, why?'

'I think he's homesick. He's had enough.'

Padmore nodded slowly. 'Understandable enough. He was very English you know. Strange. Like his old father. But I couldn't see him settling in Moscow. Never could. Like the Soviet defectors over here. Never settle. A few months honeymoon and they're criticizing the West, and swearing everlasting love for Mother Russia.'

'But they don't go back.'

'Pride, my boy, stiff-necked pride. And from what I have heard, Moscow would have 'em back like a shot. Wonderful propaganda. Example to others of the same mind.'

'What would happen to Philby if he came back?'

Padmore put his hands together like the Dürer drawing, and pursed his lips to show that he was reflecting. Powell's instinct told him that Padmore was putting on a bit of an act.

'Let us look at it both ways. There would be a few hot-heads for putting him on trial. Old scores to be settled. That sort of thing. They would have to be dealt with. We couldn't tear open all those old wounds again. And the public don't like it, you know. Like all this chasing after elderly Nazis by the Jews. They're tired of it. No. If Kim came back he would have to come back incognito. Settle down in Sussex. A cottage or something like that. And we close the book.'

'D'you think the Soviets would let him?'

'They're going along with it so far. They understand this sort of thing. The homeland ... they're very sentimental people underneath.'

'Is that what you would recommend, sir?'

The old man's shrewd eyes turned on him. 'Be a damn sight more sensible than having him step off an Aeroflot flight at Heathrow and calling a press conference.'

'What conditions would you want to lay down?'

Padmore shifted around in his chair making himself more comfortable.

'Make rules and conditions and everyone wants to break 'em. Common sense would be enough.'

'There would always be the threat of deportation hanging over him.'

'What? Oh yes. I suppose that could be borne in mind. A bit tricky though.'

'Do you think we should call the committee for a final meeting, sir?'

'I don't think so. Talk to them individually yourself. Sound them out and make your recommendations.'

'You would back me, sir?'

'Of course. One hundred per cent. So would the others.'

'Even if my recommendation was negative?'

Padmore's head turned sharply. 'Ah. Well. In that case we should have to consider the implications.'

'Such as?'

'Such as that he storms into Heathrow full of wild allegations. Or a press conference in Moscow to stir up trouble between us and the Americans.'

'Can you give me the name of any of our people who were in Washington at the same time as Philby?'

'Patrick Walker.'

'What was his job in those days?'

'I don't remember. Something quite junior.'

He waited for Kenrick by the Reptile House so that he could watch the main Zoo entrance. Kenrick came in at the tail-end of a party of schoolchildren, bought a Zoo guide, and then walked over towards him. He nodded to Kenrick as he approached and watched him turn left up the main walk.

Powell glanced around then walked down the side of the Aquarium building, along the bottom pathway and on towards the Children's Zoo. Kenrick was already there, sitting on one of the wooden benches looking towards the rabbit village. He sat down beside him.

'Sorry to interrupt your leave, Kenrick.'

'That's OK, skipper. What's the trouble?'

'Has anyone given you new instructions?'

'Yes. I was told to report to Century House tomorrow for a new assignment. I asked them to clear it with you first.'

'They haven't contacted me.'

'I didn't think they would.'

'Why not?'

'Because something's going on.'

'Like what?'

'God knows. But I can smell it. I've been at this game a long time. I've smelt this smell before.'

'What do you think it is?'

'I'd say that we're digging up Philby again.'

'Why do you think that?'

'It's a long time since we've done it. It's a routine every few years. A new government, a new "C", or the KGB send him somewhere he can be seen by us or the CIA. They like playing games with us. Just teasing. And it uses up resources trying to find out what he's doing in the Yemen or Turkey. He's a kind of Martin Bormann. Nobody can draw a line and forget him. He's Banquo's ghost in a cloth cap.'

Powell smiled. 'Who can tell me about his time in Washington?'

'The CIA and the FBI.'

'Who can tell me who isn't CIA or FBI?'

Kenrick sighed. 'Are you asking me officially or unofficially?'

'Both.'

172

Kenrick smiled. 'OK. Officially I've no idea. Unofficially I should try Grant Mayer. He's retired from the CIA now.'

'Where does he live?'

'I've no idea. Washington, I should think.'

'What about people on this side of the water?'

'If they know they won't tell you.'

'Why not?'

'Kim had more protection in Washington than he had in London. And he did more damage there. The Americans wouldn't be negotiating Salt II if it wasn't for Philby's time in Washington. The Russians were crazy to sacrifice him.'

'How do you mean – sacrifice him?'

'They threw him away for the sake of Maclean.'

'And Burgess.'

'For God's sake. The Russians would have wiped out Burgess if Maclean hadn't panicked, and passed on his panic to Moscow.'

'Why would they have sacrificed Philby for Maclean?'

'Maclean was more important to them.'

Powell remembered that somebody else had said that. He couldn't remember who, but he would check his notes.

'Who protected Philby in London?'

'Everybody outside Five. Diplomats, members of parliament, the usual top society gang. Five suspected him, but they couldn't touch him because he was SIS.'

'Who protected him in Washington?'

'The same kind of people plus three or four in Washington who really mattered.'

'Because he was a nice guy?'

'No. He was a charmer all right, but that wasn't why they protected him. They knew what he was up to. Not the details. But they knew he was a Soviet agent. They were working for Moscow too. Some of them still are. Putting a word in here, pulling a string there. Just keeping the pot

173

boiling. There were a few innocents who were on his side without knowing what it was all about. They thought he was a true-blue patriot and a hard worker.'

'Everybody says he *was* a hard worker.'

'He was during the war. It was easier then. Afterwards he wasn't so active. He passed on information but didn't get involved with actual operations for Moscow.'

'He wants to come back.'

For a moment there was sudden, shocked surprise on Kenrick's face, and then he smiled. 'It figures I suppose.'

'Why?'

'Well, Philby was recruited very young. He mixed with communists at Cambridge. Cambridge was full of them. And the timing was right. The Labour Party wanted disarmament, and the upper classes saw Hitler and Mussolini as doing a good job. Building roads, finding jobs and all that. It was like a red rag to young men like Philby.

'They recruited him. He did their dirty work but he had the excuse that there was a war on and they were doing the fighting. But when it was over Philby wasn't an evangelist anymore. He would know too much about what Moscow was up to. He was too bright not to see it. But he was, after all, an NKVD man. And you don't resign from that. He was stuck. I'd say that from then on he just served his time. He hears that the finger's on Maclean, and Moscow tells him to get him out. And that was the beginning of the end for Kim. The finger only pointed at him after those two had turned up in Moscow.'

'So why didn't he go too?'

'Didn't want to, skipper. He liked the flesh-pots. Luckily for him the Soviet stooges protected him and the innocent fools did too. He didn't go over the wall until he had to.'

'Have you told anyone else your theory?'

Kenrick laughed. 'No way. I wouldn't know who to tell. But if I can see this others can see it too. If *they* don't say it out loud I ain't going to be the one who does. Like I told you, I'm looking forward to growing roses in Bexhill in a few years' time.'

'Tell me what it was like in SIS in those days.'

'You mean in 1939 and forty?'

'Yes.'

Kenrick looked down at the ground between his well-polished black shoes and it was several minutes before he lifted his head and turned to look at Powell.

'It'll seem crazy to you. Everything about it made me wonder if it had really been like that.

'When the war started SIS was just a handful of people. Ex-colonial policemen. Ex-Indian police. That sort of chap. They had been good policemen but they were kind of innocent. They didn't really know what was going on in the world. They didn't even recognize what was going on in this country. The intelligence they collected was not much more than travellers' gossip. Seldom of any significance and seldom supported by any evidence. They passed it on to the Foreign Office and the General Staff and I'd guess that it was never read.'

'Why not?'

'It was rubbish, out-of-date chit-chat from unreliable sources. The FO could have got more from reading *The Times, le Monde* and *Völkischer Beobachter*. To say that SIS was not respected is flattering them. They were figures of fun. And, by a good many, despised, they just didn't count.'

'How did they survive?'

'The war saved them in two ways. First of all they had to recruit a lot of new people in a hurry. Some of them were very bright. Philby was one of them. But the most important life-belt was the cryptography set-up at Bletchley. The Ultra people. Purely for administrative convenience they were made a part of SIS. The material they produced was vital.

175

SIS distributed the material and the kudos brushed off on to them. They played almost no part in Ultra but they got a lot of the praise.'

'But surely the new people made a difference.'

'Not all that much actually. They looked at their superiors, couldn't believe what they saw and the clever ones just soldiered on. They settled down in whatever foreign country they were sent to and survived.'

'Including Philby?'

'Oh no. Philby looked at his bosses, drew the same conclusions but kept them to himself. He never openly criticized the old China hands. He got on with his work and they liked him. And remember one important point when you assess friend Kim. He was the only SIS officer to be decorated at the end of the war. That was obviously the old boys' way of saying "thank you".'

'How did you get on?'

'I wasn't as bright as the new boys. I wasn't university trained or sophisticated. I didn't criticize the establishment because I didn't see any cause. It's only hindsight on my part what I'm telling you now. I did as I was told. I saw it as a privilege to be in the SIS. And despite some of them, I still do.'

'I'd like to talk to you a bit more about those days some time.'

'Any time you want.'

'What did you think of Philby?'

Kenrick smiled. 'I never really weighed up any of those new boys. They were a world apart from me. He was always friendly and whether he was doing it for us or the Soviets there was no doubt that he worked hard. I think he and the others saw me in the same way they saw a senior club servant. I was given orders and I got on with it.'

'I'll make application for you during the next few days.'

'I hope they agree.'

'They will.'

Powell made no application for Kenrick until he had seen where he was to be assigned. When he heard that they were posting him to Canberra. Powell claimed him. If they wanted him that far away he was the man he wanted as back-up.

At mid-day the files had been returned from Cryptography with a brief note. The codes were a mixture of pre-war and war-time codes used by Soviet Naval Intelligence. The material was already on file and was of no intelligence value. The note suggested that the files could have been kept as some sort of souvenir. They suggested that he pass them to Archives or Central Registry. As he pressed the bell for the messenger he heaped the files together and pushed them to one side on his desk. Then, hesitating, he picked them up and counted them. There was one missing. He looked through the titles, and then leafed back through his notes. The one that was missing was the one with the title ;Harp', scribbled on the front. And he remembered the word 'harp' in the message that Tad Anders had translated for him. Anders was Polish and 'Milord' had originally come from Poland.

His hand reached out for the telephone and then some instinct made him hesitate. When the messenger came for the files he asked him to sign an official document receipt listing each title. He didn't call Cyphers for the missing file.

He waited for Kenrick to report to him, and then asked him to check with Central Intelligence and the Ministry of Defence if 'harp' had been allocated as the code-name for any military or intelligence operation since 1939.

Facilities booked him a Concorde flight direct to Washington and he briefed Kenrick on what he wanted checked while he was away.

# 18

There had been no problem in tracing Grant Mayer. His name was in the telephone book with an address in Georgetown.

He took a taxi to the corner of O Street and Frederick, and then walked. Mayer's address was a pretty house between an antiques shop and a small art gallery. The woodwork was newly painted in pale blue, and the brickwork in white. It was obviously well cared for. Walking up the three stone steps he pressed the brass door-bell and waited. He looked at his watch. It was noon exactly.

The man who answered the door was well over six feet, broad shouldered and white haired.

'Mr Mayer?'

'Yes.'

'Could I have a word with you, sir?'

'What about?'

'I'd rather talk in private if it's convenient. Or I could come back later.'

The pale blue eyes looked at his face.

'Are you a journalist?'

'No.'

'What are you?'

'A security officer. I'm from London.'

For a moment Mayer hesitated and then he said slowly, 'Come on in.'

'Thank you.'

Mayer led him through a narrow hall to a back room.

Two tall French windows stood open to a small stone paved garden and Mayer pointed to a wicker chair.

'You like a drink.'

'I'd be glad of a soft drink.'

Mayer busied himself at a glass side-table and brought back two drinks. A fresh orange juice, and a whisky for himself. The chair creaked as he lowered his big frame into it.

'You got an ID card, son?'

Powell reached into his inside pocket and passed his leather folder to Mayer who looked at it carefully. Reading the text and then turning it on to its side to look at the photograph. He handed it back after he had looked again at Powell's face.

Mayer had a battered face. An old-fashioned, manly face. A big jaw, a flattened, broken nose, and his white hair was crew cut.

'OK. What can I do for you?'

'I want some background information on Philby when he was in Washington.'

Mayer smiled. 'Why come to me. Langley could give you that.'

'One of my people recommended that I should see you. And I didn't want to go through official channels at this stage.'

'What's your guy's name?'

'Kenrick.'

'Don't remember him.'

'He's about your age. Tall, thin and . . .'

'Yes. I know the guy. Got an accent. Well dressed. A bit of a Dapper Dan.'

Powell wondered what Kenrick's reaction would have been to the description. It was different. But accurate.

'That's the one.'

'Didn't he marry an American girl?'

179

'I don't know.'

'Never mind. What do you want to know about Philby?'

'What was your impression of him? What do you think he did for the Soviets while he was in Washington?'

Mayer moved around in his chair and then reached for his glass.

'Cheers. Tell me, Mr Powell, when the British are looking at those times, why is it always Philby?'

'He was the central figure.'

'Crap. Philby was just a dogsbody, a high-class ass-end Charlie, a desk man. Maclean was the man who did the damage. *He* was the spy.'

'OK then. Tell me about Maclean.'

'A raving queer, a drunk, high-society, arrogant, America-hating, and a son-of-a-bitch.'

Powell remembered reading somewhere that Sir Archibald Clerk-Kerr, the British Ambassador, had said that he thought that 'Donald was a sweetie'.

'When did Maclean come to Washington?'

'Before the end of the war. Must have been 1944. Early 1944.'

'What was his job?'

'Second secretary at your embassy. Something like that.'

'How did he last so long in Washington? I think he didn't go to Cairo until 1948.'

'He wasn't obvious for the first year. I guess when the first atom bomb was exploded in New Mexico was the start. Stalin would have been really putting the pressure on their stooges when he learned about the bomb at Potsdam.'

'What did the Soviets get from Maclean?'

'In a nutshell they got all the atom secrets. And they killed any chance of co-operation between the British and the US of A.'

'But the Soviets had their own physicists.'

'Sure they did. But Maclean saved them five years' work and billions of dollars on research.'

'How did he do it?'

'God knows. Of course, when you look back at it it doesn't seem possible. If it wasn't so serious it could be a Marx brothers' film. In 1943 there was a secret agreement between Britain and the United States called the Quebec Agreement. It made the exchange of atomic information between the two countries mandatory. But it was so secret that when Congress passed the MacMahon Act in July 1946 forbidding the passing of any nuclear information to Britain, they didn't even know, and they weren't told, that there was such a thing as the Quebec Agreement. So you got the crazy situation of the MacMahon Act making illegal what the Quebec Agreement made obligatory.

'The Quebec thing had set up a committee called the CPC. The Combined Policy Committee to facilitate the exchange of information. And believe it or not the British nominated Maclean as their representative on that committee.

'He was in the Atomic Energy Commission building. And that bastard had a pass, a non-escort pass, that let him into any part of that building any time of the day or night. And let me tell you that General Groves, commander of the American atomic programme didn't have such a pass, and could not get such a pass. The records show that Maclean was there night after night, after hours, free to look at anything he liked. How crazy can you get? He'd got all the British secrets and all the US secrets. What was Philby compared with that?'

'Were you suspicious of him at that time?'

'We all were. We raised hell with the British. They wouldn't listen to us. Then Strauss had Maclean's pass removed and only then did they realize that we really meant business. But we never trusted the British again. They were

181

supposed to be the masters of intelligence and counter-intelligence. The models for the CIA. Behaving like innocents. We couldn't understand it. But one thing we did understand, and that was that we wanted them out. We haven't trusted them since. The KGB must have dined out on it for years.'

'What was Philby doing all this time?'

'He was the chief British intelligence representative in Washington.'

'Was he trusted?'

'We didn't trust any Britisher. Information was leaking out of America to Moscow in buckets. Scientific, political, you name it, they were getting it. The Russians were fully informed on everything we were doing, planning and thinking. It was a nightmare.'

'What damage did Philby do?'

Mayer sighed. 'The CIA mounted an operation in conjunction with London against Albania. It was a total disaster. Men's lives were lost. The Soviet knew they were coming, knew where they were landing, and who they were. Philby was in charge of the operation, the Washington end of it anyway. Is that enough?'

'What else did he do?'

'The Soviets exploded their first A-bomb in September 1949. You can imagine the shock here and in London. We set up a special unit to evaluate the new situation. Philby saw almost everything that passed between the two governments. So the Soviets were given a blow-by-blow description of our thinking and planning. Every day was Christmas for those bastards.'

'But you still feel that Maclean was more important to the Soviets?'

'He sure was. He was their nuts and bolts man. He got them the bomb. The drawings, the technology. Philby only kept them informed on policy. They were both valuable.

Apart from that the Soviets recruited Maclean well before Philby. They never had doubts about Maclean.'

'You think they had doubts about Philby?'

'They sure did.'

'Why?'

Mayer smiled. 'You tell *me*, son. Your MP Lucas, Lipton, whatever his name was, denounced him in Parliament as the "third man". The Foreign Secretary, no less, denied it. Some lawyer has a kind of unofficial private trial of Philby but nothing happens. But he gets the big heave-ho and a pay-off. He goes to Beirut as a correspondent for the *Observer* and the *Economist*. You can't tell me that they took him on after all that scandal without pressure from SIS. He's in Beirut for over five years before he skips to Moscow. You don't suppose that was only stupidity do you?'

'What else was it?'

'You tell me. If the Soviets were sure about Philby why did they kidnap Otto John and spend all their time asking about Philby. Otto John couldn't have known all that much, but it shows how much they wanted his few crumbs. Those broadcasts and the press conference about ex-Nazis in West Germany were a lot of crap. Just a cover for what they really wanted to know. *Was* Philby theirs, or not?'

'What do you think?'

'I don't know. Philby wasn't our interest. It was Maclean we wanted. We damn near got him too.'

Powell looked at the battered face and the angry eyes.

'Tell me.'

'You tell me something first.'

'If I can.'

'Why do you want to know all this?'

'I can't tell you. I'm sorry. It's highly classified.'

'So talk to Langley.'

'I'm not here officially.'

183

'Aw, come off it. You didn't come over just for a gossip with me.'

'I did. I'm investigating Philby's background. What he did in Washington is important.'

'If you level with me then I'll tell you about Maclean.'

'Maclean's dead so far as our interest is concerned. Philby's still alive.'

'In our book Philby was just a British shit. Maclean was a top spy.'

Powell smiled. 'You sound like one of my colleagues.'

'Who's that?'

'You wouldn't know him.'

'Try me.'

'His name's McNay.'

'James McNay?'

'Yes. *Do* you know him?'

'Sure I know him. Why is he like me, or me like him?'

'He describes Philby as an out and out bastard.'

Mayer turned his big body to look at Powell, frowning.

'You mean Jimmy McNay said Philby was a bastard?'

'Yes.'

Mayer stood up and walked to the French windows, staring out at the small garden. A Siamese cat walked past his legs, looked at Powell and then leapt elegantly on to Mayer's chair. Mayer turned to look at him.

'How long are you staying in Washington?'

'I only came to see you.'

'Are you hungry?'

'No.'

'I'm going to take you out to Langley. I want to show you something. I'll have to get clearance first. Is that OK?'

'Whatever you say, sir.'

Mayer was out of the room for almost ten minutes and when he came back he nodded. 'It's OK. Let's go.'

Mayer had quizzed Powell discreetly on the journey but

he seemed to accept the non-committal answers with good grace.

At Langley Powell had been given a temporary pass and a plastic card was pinned to his jacket. A young man who obviously knew Mayer conducted them to an office at the far side of the building. There was a girl secretary in the outer office and a strip on the inner door said Deputy-Director L. Swenson.

They were shown into a large office almost immediately, and the man behind the desk smiled, and nodded to the two chairs in front of his desk. Mayer introduced Powell and briefly related what they had talked about. The man's face was impassive as he listened, his eyes on Powell's face. When Mayer had finished the man leaned forward.

'Can you tell me what particular aspect of Philby's time in Washington interests you most?'

'I just wanted a general impression of him and his activities when he was here.'

'Most of the papers concerning Philby are now in the public domain. You would be entitled to apply to see those under the Freedom of Information Act.'

'I think Mr Mayer has told me most of what I need to know, sir.'

Swenson sat silently for several moments.

'Does London have a particular interest in Philby at the moment?'

'I can't answer that, sir.'

Swenson smiled. 'I guess that's answer enough.' He turned to look at Mayer and nodded. 'OK, Grant. I've told them what can be shown.'

The office they were escorted to was quite small. Sparsely furnished, it looked to Powell like an interrogation room. There was a plain teak table with a couple of thick files and some larger papers alongside them. Stencilled on the top file cover were the words 'Operation Angel'.

Mayer pulled out a chair. 'Look through this stuff. There's no hurry. I'll be back in half an hour.'

At first he read with disbelief, but after ten minutes he realized that it was no escapade, it was a fully worked out operation. 'Operation Angel' was the kidnapping of Maclean from his house in Moscow and his abduction to the United States. There were detailed plans of the exterior and interior of his house. Drawn to scale, and including the garden and its surrounding wall. Sheet after sheet giving hourly reports on his movements for days on end. There were documents that appeared to be genuine. Travel passes. KGB identity cards. The addresses of safe-houses in Moscow, Leningrad, and Kiev. Photographs of Maclean walking in the streets, getting into cars, entering buildings and standing with others talking. The same details were available of the KGB officers supervising him. Even a photograph of Maclean at his desk in the Soviet Ministry of Foreign Affairs. The backgrounds of the men who would carry out the operation were given in full, and the maps showed the escape method and the exit route. And three alternatives.

In the second file was a minute-by-minute programme for the actual operation, with details of the radio network to be used and the hardware required for the operation ranging from sets of keys to the helicopter specification.

He hadn't read it all by the time that Mayer came back but he'd read enough.

Mayer sat down alongside him. 'I just wanted you to get the message. For us, Maclean was the man we wanted.'

'Why did you want him this much?'

'We just wanted the bastard. We wanted to show that slipping off to Moscow would never again be the end of the story. We wanted to put him through the wringer and get every last detail of what he did. Who recruited him and who

186

controlled him? And I guess we wanted to show the British what we thought of them.'

'Why didn't you do it?'

'Look at the proposed date of the operation.'

Powell looked, but it had no significance for him.

'I don't get it.'

'That day was ten days after Nixon resigned.'

'Tell me about McNay.'

'What about him?'

'Why were you surprised that he shared your views about Philby?'

'Who did he say it to?'

'Me.'

'Was anybody else there at the time?'

'No. We were alone in a room at his club.'

Mayer looked at Powell's face for a few moments. Then shook his head, slowly, 'I'll just say you've got problems, mister. Let's leave it at that. D'you want a lift to Dulles?'

'If it's convenient.'

'Sure it is. Let's go.'

Mayer had waited with him until his London flight had been called, and Powell suspected that it was part friendliness and partly a check that he was actually leaving.

# 19

The house on Nebraska Avenue had an elegant frontage; ramshackle but spacious, at least it had character.

There was a line of cars outside the front of the house and lights from all the windows. Somebody was playing 'Ain't misbehavin' on a piano that was slightly out of tune.

Inside there were a dozen or so people. The room they were in was sparsely furnished, and the furniture itself had the same worn look as the house. But there was no shortage of drink, there were bottles and glasses on every shelf and ledge.

In the small kitchen a thin, pale woman leaned against a large refrigerator. Its enamel chipped, and rust around its hinges. She held a tumbler in her left hand and there was very little water in the gin.

The woman standing with her had a rasping Bostonian accent but her voice was cautious and lowered.

'Tell him to get the hell out, Aileen. It's your goddam house.'

'Kim would be furious. He wouldn't have it.'

'You'll crack up, honey. Jesus, you've got five kids to cope with. That's enough without a drunken bum like Burgess on your neck.'

'Kim always makes excuses for him. I think he's sorry for him.'

'Aren't we all. But I wouldn't give him house room all the same.'

'We'd better go back in.'

Aileen Philby stood in the doorway of the smoke-filled

188

room and above the noise she could hear what he was playing. 'Some enchanted evening'. A few drunken voices bawled out the words, and she saw Kim turn and smile, then reach up with his left hand to the top of the piano. He took a quick gulp of his drink and went back to his playing. She noticed that the bald patch that so annoyed him looked a little bigger these days.

She walked into the room so that she could see his face. He looked podgy and strained, but it was a nice face. An amiable face. A cosy, lived-in face. And, as always, he was intent on what he was doing. She admired his concentration but she was afraid for him. His responsibilities seemed to be getting him down. And despite their boisterous camaraderie she knew that Guy Burgess's unannounced arrival three weeks ago had added to the strain. And at that moment he half-turned his head and looked at her. For a moment he didn't seem to recognize her, and then he winked, and smiled. That special smile he kept for her. A small boy's smile. A mischievous, small boy. And he looked so cuddly. Like one of the children's well-worn teddy-bears.

He had stopped for a whisky at a bar on his way in to Washington. But he was at his office just before eleven.

It was one of his bad Washington days. Klaus Fuchs had been arrested in England and London and Washington were busy co-operating, putting together their separate pieces of the jigsaw. It was too late to save Fuchs. Moscow hadn't even told him about the man. But as the clues fell into place the fingers were inevitably going to point to Maclean. Moscow's instructions were that Maclean should be protected at all costs. They expected him to do it, despite the fact that Maclean had long ago been moved by the Foreign Office from Washington to Cairo and from Cairo to London.

His own relationship with Aileen was desperately bad and

189

*it added to his depression that it was so patently clear that Moscow were prepared to sacrifice him to ensure Maclean's safety. Moscow had indicated that Maclean was not aware of his danger and that he was not to be warned. They obviously wanted Maclean still operating until the last moment.*

*But the net was closing in. The file marked 'Homer' on his desk was being added to daily. The British had intercepted radio signals between New York and Moscow five years earlier. They had only broken enough of the messages to learn that a Russian agent in the USA had a sister at an American university.*

*It was an apparently useless scrap of information until the Soviets had exploded their bomb; then it became obvious that the leak could only have come from the scientists at Los Alamos.*

*The obvious suspects were the British scientists, and as the various reports had crossed his desk Kim Philby saw them gradually closing in on Fuchs after they had noted that his sister, Kristel, was studying in the United States.*

*When they traced and identified Harry Gold, Fuchs' courier to the Soviet Consulate-General in New York, it was a matter of routine to pinpoint Yakovlev as the final contact. All the time that Maclean had been in Washington his wife, Melinda, had stayed in an apartment in New York. That had provided him with a reason for frequent visits and a cover for his meetings with Yakovlev. Those visits would be remembered now.*

*And from their investigations came the clear indications that a senior diplomat at the British Embassy in Washington was a Soviet agent. And although Maclean had long ago left Washington for Cairo, there weren't all that many senior diplomats at the embassy during the time they were investigating. They were working back through the list. And the code-name they had given to the unknown traitor was 'Homer'.*

*But the routine of his work allowed him to carry on with his job despite the pressures that bore in on him from every direction.*

*The report of Volkov's allegations about Soviet spies in the Foreign Office was in the 'Homer' file and that morning a new document had been passed to him. An early Soviet defector from Red Army intelligence, the GRU, named Krivitsky, had claimed that the Soviets had long ago recruited an agent, a well-educated British diplomat who served in Washington.*

*It was obvious that London were not passing on all the information they had but they had asked for his comments. He had no choice but to go along with it if he was to maintain his cover. No matter what happened, this time he needed the record to show that his recommendations had been constructive.*

*He took all afternoon to draft his report and gave a list of diplomats who he suggested should be considered suspect and investigated immediately. Maclean's name was the third on the list.*

*He had left his office at 5 p.m. and it was an hour and a half later when he entered Rock Creek Park. Lynski's car was already there when he pulled up at Pierce Mill. There were no other cars, and as he looked around he checked that there were no other people in sight. He turned and walked slowly towards the trees and when he was just inside the woods he waited.*

*Lynski was small and dapper, and looked like a department store sales clerk. And that was no disadvantage for a man who was a KGB colonel.*

*Philby gave him the roll of undeveloped film and Lynski slid it into his pocket without taking his eyes from Philby's face.*

*'How are you, Kim?'*

*'Tired.'*

'Is too much gin, comrade.'

'You didn't come here to lecture me on my drinking habits, Alexei.'

'Moscow say it may be very near time for our friend to leave. They ask that you warn him if you have indications of real trouble for him.'

'Warn him or make the arrangements?'

'Just be ready to give the warning.'

'Why don't you get your people in London to warn him?'

'He take real notice if it is you, Kim. Anyway those are the orders from Moscow. They expect you will be the first to hear if he is in danger.'

'How soon must he go?'

'As soon as you have positive information that he is a target.'

'Who will help him?'

'When the day comes you go direct to Guy. He will make the arrangements.'

'Anything else?'

'Yes. They say you make plans for yourself. Be ready for when the time comes.'

'Any more. Who's Krivitsky by the way?'

'He's not KGB, he's GRU.'

'So how in hell does a GRU man know about Maclean and me?'

'We're investigating right now.'

'A bit late, Alexei. They're getting careless.'

'Do you want to pull out now?'

Philby leaned back against the tree, his eyes closed as he thought. It wouldn't do to give a quick answer. Especially a negative. They wouldn't expect him to want to hang on to the flesh-pots, but they wanted him in place to give the warning. He opened his eyes.

'Not just yet, Alexei. There's a lot more I can do. I expect *after this lot the Americans will clamp down and I'll be posted back to London.'*

*'It's up to you, comrade. We should understand.'*

*'Thanks.'*

Philby had let Lynski leave first because he was right on the edge of the area that Soviet diplomats were allowed to move in without special permits. He waited twenty minutes before he drove off himself.

The first report claimed that three storage tanks in the Kucova oilfields had been destroyed, and the second claimed that the refining plant at the copper mines at Rubik had been seriously damaged.

Philby initialled it as noted and put it in his tray. He guessed that he was probably the only man in Washington outside the Albanian Embassy who even knew where Kucova and Rubik were. Apart, of course, from his opposite number in the CIA, jointly responsible for playing games in Albania. He wondered if they would call it a day now.

But a week later they had called a meeting at CIA headquarters at Langley. There was to be a new operation, almost a miniature invasion involving hundreds of men and substantial back-up. SIS had already agreed to it and he and an officer of CIA were to be in joint charge.

The scenario was deceptively simple. The Greek Communists were being remorselessly defeated in the civil war. Yugoslavia had broken with Moscow, and the Balkans had suddenly become the weakest area of the satellite states. Churchill had always called it 'the soft underbelly' of Europe and it was beginning to look as if he had been right. Albania was in turmoil. Badly administered, its reconstruction programme a shambles, and its people in a ferment of discontent. What SOE had done in France could be done in Albania. And the disruption of a Soviet frontier would be

193

reward enough. The people would rise in revolt, and from that one operation the Soviet satellites would see that Soviet might could be overthrown.

The earlier guerilla groups parachuted in had been low-grade and ill-trained and their small numbers had not impressed the locals. They saw the hit-and-run raids on minor targets as merely bringing reprisals on the towns and villages where the guerillas sheltered.

Three natural leaders from the exiled King Zog's Royal Guard were given the task of building up a fighting force of seven hundred patriots in exile. The three had fought against the Nazis and there were enough Albanians in the refugee camps of Greece and Italy for them to choose their fighters carefully.

SIS had a sophisticated radio listening post in Cyprus and that was the base used for training the resistance army.

Ex-SOE officers and infantry officers trained them in using modern weapons, and in standard tactics and night warfare. Radio operators were instructed in sending, receiving, maintenance, coding and decoding. Their parachute course was careful and thorough. Those who were to infiltrate across the Greek-Albanian border needed no parachute training. They could have found their way blindfolded. The beach landing parties practised day after day.

At the end of each three-month training period men were grouped into units of fifty and sent to camps spread over the island. It was officially claimed that they were segregated for security reasons but there was more than that behind the planning.

The first fighting teams had been dropped in the mountains north of Tirana, and the Albanian militia had been waiting for them. Thirty had been killed on landing, and stragglers had died of wounds as they made their way to the Greek frontier. The same thing had happened to the two first beach parties. They had landed safely from their landing craft and were past the tide line before the waiting machine-guns mowed them down. In the camps in Greece there were murmurs of betrayal and traitors.

Captured radio operators forced to operate under duress had used their security checks to show that they were operating under enemy control and found that the militia already knew their warning check-words. Some refused to send and were shot immediately, others co-operated and signalled that the area was clear for reinforcements.

In one night at Elbasan the planes came over and circled the marker flares as the parachutes floated down into the darkness. The militia had held their fire until the planes had gone and then killed every man of the landing party. Ninety-two men had died that night. After the debâcle the word had got back to the units in Cyprus. The police and militia were always there. Ready and waiting. Hundreds of troops in isolated areas that wouldn't normally warrant a single policeman. And they didn't come weeks ahead, they came on the afternoon of the landing, killed the landing party and left the next day. Neat and tidy. Economical and efficient.

McNay sat on the bleached wooden table, under the canvas awning. Two men stood holding a blackboard upright on the table beside him. It was a large-scale map of two square kilometres north-east of Elbasan. He had a pointer in his right hand and he mopped his face with a towel in the other.

Sitting on the sand in front of him were about seventy or eighty men in a semi-circle. A tall, thin man with a face from a Roman coin stood alongside McNay watching the men, as McNay looked around at them, speaking slowly and distinctly.

'If any of you don't understand what I'm saying, either ask somebody who does, or put up your hand and ask me. Understood?'

There was a low mutter and a hand went up. And a man

195

spoke words that McNay couldn't understand. He was from southern Albania and he spoke only Tosk. McNay turned to the man beside him.

'What did he say, Hamit?'

'He ask you show him again the formation of the landing flares.'

McNay pointed at the map.

'The one to the north is here at the edge of the woods. At the base of the cone we have one here on the left at the edge of the farm buildings. On the right there is a lake, and at the tip of the lake is the third flare.'

He paused and then continued. 'When you land you will not carry out your training procedure regarding your parachute. That can be ignored. Abandon your parachute on landing. You will see on the map the collecting points for your three sections. They are marked A, B, and C and you will assemble at those points with utmost speed. You will report to your section-leader. Does anyone not know who his section-leader is?'

Nobody put up a hand and McNay continued.

'I want to impress on you that silence is vital. You will not speak, you will move carefully, you will not load weapons. They must be loaded on the aircraft. Your section-leaders will give you your orders. And now Hamit Matjani is going to talk to you.'

The tall man, still an officer in the Royal Guard, talked to them about a free Albania and the fighting and sacrifices that that would entail. Then the men were dispersed in sections to their tents. It was the last few hours of their time on Cyprus. And although they didn't know it, for most of them it was the last few hours of their lives.

At the landing area the militia men were climbing down from the personnel trucks and lining up for their last meal before they got into place for the night's action. They were cheerful and in good spirits. It was like shooting quail in a *pen and when it was over there would be two weeks' leave in Tirana. And a couple of parachutes each. The girls in Tirana would give a man a lot of loving for a panel of parachute silk. That night's operation was slightly unusual because they had been ordered to take five prisoners. And one of them was a particular man. The information they had had from Moscow said that he would be the first to drop.*

*Hamit Matjani looked at the men on the floor of the aircraft and on the long, wooden benches fitted to the fuselage. He had been dropped seven times into Albania and had made his way back each time over the Greek frontier and then on to Cyprus. But most of these men had never even been in a plane until they did their parachute training. Some slept with their heads on their bent knees. Others took deep breaths to overcome nausea and fear, and others just stared unseeingly as their bodies jerked and shook from the turbulence of the thermals as they came in over the coast.*

*The warning light came on and Matjani crawled over to the hatch and unscrewed the big wingnut and turned the hatch on its swivel. He nodded to Zenel Shehu who would be dispatcher for the rest of them, going last himself. What the British army trainers called 'Arse-end Charlie'.*

*He sat to attention and looked at the light panel. The green light came on and he straightened his body and the slipstream turned him on one side until the weight of his pack and his boots swung his legs down as the canopy opened. He could see the flares, exactly like on the blackboard map. But although there was almost no wind he was veering to the right towards the lake. He pulled on the cords but the 'chute continued on its course. He could see the ground rushing up and seconds later he was in the water, his parachute canopy dragging him on to his back as it was caught by the surface wind on the lake. He punched the release and the harness jerked away from his body and he was in water up to his chest. And almost half a kilometre from the outer edge of the dropping zone.*

*He waded through the mud to the reeds, struggled up the bank, and saw the darkness of the wood that had looked like a field of mushrooms on the map. And then he froze. There was the clatter of machine-guns and they sounded more like Schmeissers than Brens. There was the thud of grenades and the quick-firing burst of sub-machine-guns.*

*He stood quite still at the edge of the wood, his eyes closed as he tried to think what to do. His hands clenched and opened slowly as he stood in the moonlight. All his instincts were to go to his men but he knew that that was a hopeless gesture. It was obvious that once more they had been expected. There was no doubt in his mind that they had been betrayed. And it had happened too many times. He had spoken with the survivors in the camps in Yannina and Athens, but he had only half-believed their stories. He knew now that they were true. He must get back and warn the British officers, and stop the slaughter of the brave and loyal men. He would go down the valley to the river. The beautiful Schkumbin where he had learned to swim as a boy.*

*He walked just inside the wood and sat listening to the firing. Except for sporadic bursts it was over in fifteen minutes. There were a few small-arms shots that echoed in the night air, and he shuddered at the thought of what they represented. The* coup de grâce *for the injured and dying.*

*The next morning he walked through the woods before sunrise and looked through his binoculars to the area where they had dropped. There was nothing there. No bodies, no parachutes, no militia. It had all come and gone in five hours. He walked slowly forward to where the early morning mist curled up from the ground in the first rays of the sun. He stopped at the finger of the lake and saw where the militia must have mounted two machine-guns, a heap of brass shell-cases glinted in the sun. Hundreds of them. For the militia it must have been more like an exercise than a battle. He remembered a phrase from the Koran, 'Would that you knew what the Disaster is! On that day men shall become like scattered moths and the mountains like tufts of carded wool.'*

*It took him four weeks to make his way to the frontier and he sent a message from Athens to McNay while he waited for a boat. Five of his men had been taken alive and were on trial in Tirana. A typical Soviet show-trial. Two were sentenced to death and shot, and the others jailed for life; and the Soviet Union denounced the US and British governments and their intelligence services.*

*The guerillas rotting in the camps in Greece were an embarrassment for all concerned and SIS finally pressured the Home Office into allowing them to come to Britain. A welcoming party was mounted at the Caxton Hall for the 'refugees' from Communism, and the Ministry of Labour found them jobs with the Forestry Commission and in government factories.*

*Despite the inquest on the series of disasters, and the suspicions of treachery, similar operations were mounted in actual Soviet territory. Ukrainian nationalists were backed with training and finance. It was not long since the Ukrainians had been fighting the Nazis, and their discontent with Moscow was permanent and continuous. The men sent into the Ukraine by the CIA to ferment revolt suffered the same fate as the Albanians. They were expected. Their names, their routes, and their times of arrival, were known in advance to the KGB. None of them survived.*

*Wheeler's Restaurant in Old Compton Street was bathed in its usual flattering pink glow from the red plush décor, and the three people at the banquette table were celebrating with scampi and champagne. A married couple and an odd man out, they were celebrating the odd man out's birthday. It was 24 May and the man's thirty-eighth birthday. His name was Donald Maclean and the next morning Herbert Morrison, the Foreign Secretary, would sign the paper that would allow MI5 to arrest and confront him with passing vital secrets to a foreign power. Being Britain, and the 25th being a Friday, the pick-up would not take place until the Monday morning. After he had paid the bill Maclean was left with only a few shillings in his pocket.*

*The three of them strolled to Charlotte Street and Schmidt's for something to eat.*

*The couple were relieved that Donald was in one of his good phases. Calm and relaxed.*

*'How are things with Melinda, Donald?' The woman asked. And she stopped eating to hear the answer.*

*'Much better. Definitely improving. The baby's due in two weeks time and that will be a relief all round.'*

*'What are you going to do while she's in the nursing home?'*

*'Heaven knows.'*

*'Come and stay with us.'*

*'Now that would be marvellous. But are you quite sure that it's convenient?'*

*'Of course it is, don't be silly.'*

*Maclean smiled at her. 'I've got over that stupid affair with the fellow at the Moonglow.'*

*'Thank God for that.'*

*Maclean shrugged. 'He was rather nice, sweetie. I really cared you know. No. For Christ's sake. I loved him. I suppose I was jealous.'*

*'In what way, Donald?' It was the man who spoke and Maclean looked at him, shrugging as he smiled.*

*'He was always making eyes at other men. He drove me frantic whenever we were together. They were always big*

200

*butch types who wanted to protect him from little old me.'*

*He called in at the Travellers' to cash a small cheque, and then walked through to Trafalgar Square. As he walked into the main concourse at Charing Cross Station he looked at his watch. It was 5.10 and he bought a* Standard *at the W.H. Smith bookstall before he headed for platform 6 and the 5.19 to Sevenoaks.*

*At Sevenoaks the two Special Branch men got out and watched him through the ticket barrier. That was as far as their orders required them to go.*

*Maclean looked around to check that Melinda had not come with the car and then walked towards the queue for taxis. Burgess had stopped him before he got there.*

*'Get in the car by the railings. The white A70. Don't look around.'*

*He opened his mouth to speak but Burgess had turned away to look at the time-table on the notice-board.*

*They were out of the town on the Hastings road before Maclean spoke. He could sense Burgess's agitation.*

*'What's up, Guy?'*

*'We've got to get out tonight. Morrison signed the orders this morning.'*

*'Who in hell is Morrison?'*

*'Your boss, sweetheart. Herbie. The little man with the quiff. The Foreign Secretary.'*

*'Jesus. Where are you heading for?'*

*'Tatsfield. Your place.'*

*'But the bastards will be there waiting for me.'*

*'No they won't. It's not effective until Monday morning.'*

*'Where after Tatsfield?'*

*'This is it, Donald. We're on the way to Moscow.'*

*'But they'll have put a stopper on all ports.'*

*'No they won't. Have they asked for your passport?'*

*'No, of course not.'*

*'You'd better put Melinda in the picture.'*

201

*Maclean looked at him. He wondered how much Guy Burgess knew of Melinda.*

*The three of them ate together at the house in Tatsfield. Special Branch had found the Austin A70 at Southampton docks the following Tuesday.*

# 20

The restaurant was almost empty, Vanessa was away doing up her face and the small girl was eating an éclair. There was chocolate round her mouth as she looked at him. She looked so like her mother that it was hard to imagine that her father's genes had influenced her features in any way.

'*Is* she wild?' The little girl's eyebrows were raised in query.

'Is who wild?'

'Momma. Daddy says she's wild.' She sniffed. 'Have you got a tissue?'

'Your mother's got them in her bag.'

'That's why they were divorced you know. I heard Aunt Jean telling somebody. D'*you* think she's wild?'

'I think she's a very nice lady. That's what I think.'

'Are you an actor?'

'No. Why did you think that?'

'Aunt Jean said the other man was an actor.'

'Yes. I hear you've just had a pony.'

'Yes. My daddy's going to teach me to ride. He's got lots of ponies. Well, horses. He's going to be the Master of the hunt next season. Costs thousands you know.'

'What would you like to do this afternoon?'

'Can I drive your car?'

Powell laughed. 'When you grow up you can.'

'I drive the Land Rover at home. On daddy's lap. I drive it down to the farm.'

'That must be good fun.'

'Oh it's not fun. Daddy says people who want fun all the time are stupid.'

'How about we go to the river and fish?'

'Have you got rods?'

'A couple.'

'That would be nice.'

They caught a roach with weed by the weir, and a perch on a spinner, and put them both back in the river. Then they drove back to the small hotel. And after the goodbyes Powell drove the small girl back up to the Hall. It was one of the conditions imposed by her former husband that Vanessa should never come to the Hall. Ralph Gower came out as they drew up.

He was a burly man, big built, with an amiable, podgy face that went oddly with his small shrewd eyes. Gower looked at his watch.

'Back on the stroke I see. Well done.'

He helped his daughter out of the car and as she turned to run to the house he called after her.

'Lydia. What do you say?'

The small girl stopped and turned, blushing. 'Thank you for having me, I had a lovely time.'

'That's better. Off you go.'

He turned to look at Powell. 'She behave properly?'

'Perfectly.'

'What did you all do?'

'Had a meal. Fished. Pottered around.'

'You need a day ticket to fish you know.'

'Yes. I've got one.'

'Jolly good show.' He laughed uncomfortably. 'Got to look after the village interests you know. Sitting on the bench and all that.'

Powell nodded. 'Well I'll be off.'

'How's . . . er . . . how's Vanessa these days?'

'Pretty well. She gets by.'

204

Gower laughed. A forced jolly laugh that went with rugby dinners and hunt balls.

'I expect you keep her on a short rein.'

Powell looked at Gower. When the marriage broke up his relatives and Van's would have all told him that he had nothing to blame himself for. But he would have a suspicion lurking at the edge of his mind that there would be some who thought otherwise. He was a dolt, but behind that fleshy face he would have doubts.

'No. She's a grown woman. She must live her own life.'

'Quite. Quite. I suppose we all learn a thing or two as the years go by.'

'When can she see Lydia again?'

'Just say the word. Any time.'

'I'm not always around.'

'She can phone herself, surely.'

'She can't, Ralph, she's scared of you.'

Gower looked amazed. 'Scared of me. She was *never* scared of me. Always gave back more than she got.'

'It's not that kind of scared, Ralph. She's scared you'll rebuff her. Scared you'll punish her by saying no.'

'That's ridiculous.'

'It isn't. I've been there when she phoned you in the early days. She used to be ill for days afterwards when you rebuffed her. Really ill.'

'You don't mean that.'

'I do.'

'My God. I'd no idea. Didn't think she cared that much about the child.'

'She cares, but maybe not the same way that you do.'

'And how do I care that's so different?'

Powell closed his eyes for a moment then opened them to look at Gower.

'I know you care very much for your daughter. Honest, consistent caring. She obviously loves you too. Like children

205

do love their parents. Without analysis and without criticism. You and Van had much the same background but you're a man and she's a girl. Men do well from your upbringing, girls don't. They're taught how to land a husband but not how to live happily ever after. I'm sure you never realized that.'

The big unshapely man stood there in silence looking at Powell. And Powell thought he looked a bit like Pooh Bear caught with his paw in the honey-pot.

'What made you say that, Powell?'

'Say what?'

'You said kind things about me. About caring for my daughter.'

'I said it because I think it's true. And I'm not scared of you, Ralph. Only scared people are unkind.'

'Did Van say this?'

'No. It's all my own work.'

'Does she ever talk about me?'

'Sometimes.'

'Does she miss me at all?'

'She never said so in so many words but yes, I think she misses you.'

'What does she miss?'

'The whole bag of tricks, I think. She lost her home ground. You. Her home. Her parents. Her daughter. A girl can't lose much more than that.'

'It was her doing. She played the fool.'

'I'm sure she did. But what did you expect with that superficial bitch of a mother of hers. Plus the fact that you didn't love her.'

'For God's sake. I chased all over the countryside after her. Getting her out of one scrape after another.'

'That isn't loving her. That's owning her. If you loved her she'd still be your wife.'

'That's not true, old man. It was she who wanted out.'

'Rubbish. She just wanted to matter more than your farm, your horses and your business.'

'She never said that.'

'Jesus, Ralph. How old are you? Forty-four, forty-five? Your bloody horses don't tell you when they've got the croup or whatever horses have. You have to notice the symptoms and then apply the Band-aid.'

'What about you and her?'

'What about it?'

'Does she come first with you?'

'I haven't got your wide sweep of competing interests, sweetheart. There's just my work and Van. And I work to earn a living, not to pass the time. And we're not married either.'

Gower looked up at him and sighed.

'I wish I'd known all this before.'

Powell hesitated and then said softly, 'You could always try again, Ralph. You've got a bridge.'

'How do you mean, a bridge?'

'Your daughter.'

'I don't understand.'

'Why don't *you* take her out with Van, instead of me. And she might see that Lydia doesn't grow up to make the same mistakes that she made.'

'Would you mind if I invited her here?'

'Of course not. Like I said, she's a grown woman.'

'Maybe there's some way I could help you sometime, Powell. I appreciate what you've said.'

'Just remember, Ralph. She ain't a man, she's a woman, and despite appearances her parents weren't much good to her. Neither were you in the end.'

Gower nodded and stood back as Powell started the engine, his arm half-raised in a wave, or a salute, it was hard to tell which.

When he rang Tom Farrow's home number he was told that he could be contacted at his office and Powell checked the number of the *Financial Times*, dialled and waited. When he got through to Farrow he was willing to meet him that evening and they arranged to meet at the Royal Court in Sloane Square.

Farrow was waiting for him, whisky already in hand.

'Not back in Moscow yet, Tom?'

'I did ten days there to cover the Senator's visit to Brezhnev. I'm waiting for my replacement to have his credentials cleared and then I'm off to Washington, thank God.'

'Did you attend the press conference that Philby gave after Macmillan cleared him in the House?'

'Yes.'

'Where did he hold it?'

'At his mother's flat in Drayton Gardens. He'd gone to ground there after the piece in the *People*.'

'Who was there?'

'I don't remember, but there was a heavy turn-out. He was very hot news. They were all top guys. I was easily the most junior correspondent there.'

'Was he questioned?'

'He gave a prepared statement first. Everybody was given a copy and he read it out.'

'Can you remember what he said?'

'It was absolute crap. He said he hadn't been able to speak out before because he was bound by the Official Secrets Act, and went on about the damage that could be done to the security organizations by publicity of any kind. Embarrassing for foreign relations and all that sort of jazz. It was smooth as cream and just as bland.'

'How did he look?'

'Oh, very pleased with himself. Good humoured, no stammer. A bit like a newly elected politician. Relieved that the election was over and savouring the first fruits of victory.'

'What were the questions like?'

'Quite tough. Somebody asked him about his relationship with Guy Burgess and he said that it had been imprudent but he didn't intend indulging in mud-slinging. Hearts and flowers stuff about fair-weather friends.'

'What about Maclean?'

'He said he thought he must have met him a couple of times over the years but he couldn't put a face to the name.'

'Did anyone ask him if he had ever been a Communist?'

'Yes. I think it was either James Cameron or Alan Whicker. He said he never had been and that the last time he had knowingly spoken to one was in 1934. He said he had always been a bit left of centre but nothing more.'

'What was the general feeling about him?'

'Well I think most of us were taken in. After all he had been completely cleared by Macmillan, publicly and officially. He was a bit like a journalist himself. He had been a journalist in Spain and France; amiable and boozy. He played the martyr pretty well.'

'No dissenting voices?'

'Oh yes. There were some very cynical old hands there. Three or four of us went for a drink afterwards and I can remember somebody suggesting that MI5 had set a trap for Philby and he was walking right into it. It was accepted that SIS were defensive about Philby. They were on his side. Most of them, anyway.'

'What was the trap supposed to be?'

'Build up Philby's confidence. Make him feel he'd got away with it while they kept their beady eyes on him. He'd be over-confident and then they'd pounce on him.'

'What were the others' reactions to this?'

'They didn't think that MI5 would dare to mount a surveillance on an SIS officer. Apart from that, they didn't think Philby was the kind of man to be over-confident. Too cool for that.' Farrow smiled at Powell. 'There must have been at least a dozen people in SIS who knew that he was lying when he said he hadn't spoken to a Communist since 1934. He was married to one until at least 1941.'

'There were plenty outside SIS who knew too.'

Farrow laughed. 'It's incredible really. Those outside SIS *knew* he was a traitor, and those inside SIS weren't sure which of the scenarios was the real one. And even now I suspect he's got plenty of old friends who swear he was misunderstood.'

'He's a self-confessed traitor.'

'That won't stop them. They'll say that that's just part of his cover story.'

Powell smiled. 'You've grown more cynical since those days.'

'You bet I have.' He looked at Powell's face. 'Are your people letting him come back?'

'You know I can't answer that. What would *you* do if you had the choice?'

Farrow laughed. 'Sign up an exclusive with book rights, film rights, the lot.' He stood up. 'I must get going.' He paused. 'Do I get any privileges on this story when it breaks?'

'I can't promise anything, Tom. I'll put in the word of course but by that time it will probably be the PM's decision. You've got to remember that even if he comes back it may not be announced. And there are bound to be a thousand and one conditions surrounding him. We shan't forget your help anyway.'

# 21

Day after day they had grilled him. *Helenus Milmo KC, Skardon and White. And they made little attempt to hide the fact that they considered him guilty. But as he knew, and they knew, it was one thing to think that he was guilty, and quite another to prove it.*

*As he had expected they started with Burgess and Maclean. It was 1952 and only a year since they had defected. How did Maclean learn that he was being watched? How did Burgess find out? Had Philby told Burgess? He denied telling either of them and pointed out that as instructions had been passed in the Foreign Office that Maclean should not be on the distribution list for top-secret papers in the weeks before he defected it would not be surprising if he had realized that he was under suspicion. Had he provided any protection for Maclean? Philby referred them to his own list of suspects sent to London. Maclean's name was on it. That answer in no way convinced his interrogators but they knew full well that it might convince a judge and would almost certainly convince a jury.*

*They moved on to the Volkov incident. Somebody had provided them with a time-table and they went over it in detail. The abduction of Volkov at Istanbul airport just after his departure could have been a coincidence, and that was what he maintained, but he had been surprised that they had dug back into the Bletchley radio monitoring records. The records showed that exactly two days after Volkov's offer to defect had reached London, the Soviet embassy radio traffic from London to Moscow had doubled, and that a similar increase had occurred between Moscow and Istanbul.*

Philby had professed ignorance as to why that should be. He maintained that he was as mystified as they were. When they followed up by pointing out that the same increase in signals traffic between Washington and Moscow had happened the day after he had been warned about a suspect in the Washington embassy he knew that his time was running out.

Despite what had happened there were people in SIS who saw him as an efficient, hard-working officer who had become an innocent victim of a witch-hunt by MI5. They had worked alongside him for years. They had seen with their own eyes the long hours he put in, and they had used successfully, against the Nazis, many of his evaluations and suggestions. There were a dozen explanations for any of the incidents that MI5 were trying to pin on one man. And most damning of all there was nothing, absolutely nothing, on Philby's record that spoke against him. And the sheer improbability of all these incidents being attributed to one man didn't make sense.

The interrogation eventually ended, and the file was closed, with a verdict agreed by the interrogators as 'guilt unproven but suspicion remaining'. Philby was given a payment of £2000 and a promise of the same amount in six-monthly instalments over the next two years. There would be no charges and no trial. He had been quite sure that there wouldn't be a trial but he hadn't projected his thinking far beyond that fact.

There had been a price to pay for keeping up the steady voice, the co-operative attitude while still maintaining his defences. When they had come back from Washington he had rented a tatty little bungalow at Rickmansworth, and night after night he would return there aggressively drunk. The failed relationship with Aileen was now open, and

212

*charged with tension. Wild-eyed and hysterical they shouted their pain at each other. With little money, abandoned by their friends, the antagonism bordered on violence. And Kim Philby bore one more burden that nobody knew. After Washington he had been ordered by Moscow to break off all contacts with them until he was contacted again. He had heard nothing from them for a year.*

*His search for work was hampered by his condition. He was down and out, and it showed. A fruit importer offered him a job, and war-time service friends who felt he had been ill-treated put words in for him for more suitable jobs. But it was obvious that M15 had not forgiven or forgotten. Their intervention was never pressing. It didn't need to be. A vague hint from that source was always enough.*

*Shocked by the condition of her daughter, Aileen's mother bought her a large house in Crowborough. Kim Philby seldom visited the place and when he did he lived in a tent in the garden. But most nights he spent in London with his new girl-friend, Connie.*

*Aileen, wild-eyed, unwashed and unkempt, lived a life of demented fantasy. A wraith of a woman almost completely out of touch with the world, she sometimes raved of spies and secrets, but nobody took her seriously. Nobody outside the tight inner circle had heard of Philby, and Burgess and Maclean were, to the public, just a couple of drunken queers who had gone missing. Aileen Philby was a lost soul, abandoned and ignored. On the morning of 15 December 1957 she was found dead in her bed by her daughter.*

*Too many members had read the piece in the* People *that Sunday in September 1955 not to know what was coming when, on the 25 October at Prime Minister's question time, Lieut. Colonel Marcus Lipton, Labour MP for Brixton, caught the Speaker's eye and stood up. All they wondered was how far he would go. He went all the way.*

*Has the Prime Minister made up his mind to cover up at all costs the dubious third-man activities of Mr Harold Philby who was the First Secretary at the Washington Embassy a little time ago, and is he determined to stifle all discussion on the very great matters which were evaded in the wretched White Paper, which is an insult to the intelligence of the country?*

The Prime Minister brushed the question aside and said that the Foreign Secretary would make a statement at an early opportunity.

Every newspaper in Fleet Street had known that Philby was suspected as being the 'third man', and most of them knew that reports to that effect had been circulated inside M15. But the English laws of libel prevented them from informing the public.

After Marcus Lipton's blunt question in the House it fell to the Foreign Secretary, Harold Macmillan, to make the eventual statement to the House in reply. A White Paper was prepared and the Foreign Secretary received a brief to go with it.

As Foreign Secretary, Macmillan had responsibility for the reply because Philby was an officer in SIS, and SIS 'belonged' to the Foreign Office. So the brief was prepared by SIS. It contained only what its compilers knew could be proved against Philby, and there was no mention of merely suspicious or dubious incidents, like Otto John, Volkov or his interrogation by Milmo. If M15 had been asked to supply a brief it would have been a very different story. Philby, to them, was a prime suspect. But M15 'belonged' to the Home Secretary and protocol militated against any cross-referencing without ministerial requests. The fact that there were suspicions by others was only mentioned to make the point that 'mere suspicion' was not enough on which to condemn an officer who for years had proved himself to be

214

*efficient and hard-working, and whose promotions had been only a just reward for his services – an officer who had been awarded the Order of the British Empire. And Macmillan, a sophisticated and patrician man was too used to the back-biting and internecine warfare of politicians not to take the point.*

*When Harold Macmillan, the Foreign Secretary, stood up in the House of Commons on 7 November 1955 the House was crowded and silent. The Press gallery and the Strangers' gallery were full.*

*For the most part he read from typed notes.*

*He said that he thought that many criticisms in the Press and elsewhere of the handling of the case were based on a misapprehension of the rights of a citizen in a free society in time of peace. Whilst action against employees, whether of the State or of anybody else, arising from suspicion and not from proof, might be taken with good motives and might avert serious consequences, it seemed, judging from what happened in other countries, that the practice soon degenerated into the satisfaction of personal vendettas or a general system of tyranny, all in the name of public safety. It had also been said that the statements on the case made by Foreign Office spokesmen or by Ministers had been disingenuous or obscure. But inquiries by the security service had continued for several years, and while they were in progress a full statement would have indicated to the world the real degree to which they were meeting with success, thereby possibly compromising the investigation itself.*

*With regard to the conduct of Maclean and Burgess while they were in the Foreign Service, Mr Macmillan said that it was important to realize that the quality of Maclean's work, prior to his appointment in Cairo in 1948, had been 'not only good but outstanding among his*

215

*contemporaries'. During his first fourteen years in the Service his conduct had given rise to no adverse comment, and his behaviour in Cairo had been interpreted at the time as a result of a prolonged period of overwork and strain. As regards Burgess, Mr Macmillan refuted suggestions that he had been promoted after having been found guilty of serious indiscretions. In actual fact, from the time of his establishment (i.e. ceasing to be a temporary employee) he had remained a member of the fourth grade of the junior branch of the Foreign Service. He had been recommended for promotion to the Senior Branch by the late Mr Hector McNeil, but as there was a good deal of doubt about his suitability, in view of his slight experience of the ordinary duties of the Foreign Service, it had been decided that he should be given a thorough trial on routine work in the Far Eastern department. While he was working in that department allegations were made that he had been guilty of a serious indiscretion about intelligence matters; after these had been fully investigated, he was severely reprimanded and informed that he would be transferred and that his prospects for promotion would be diminished. He had thereafter been transferred to Washington, but the Ambassador had reported unfavourably both on his office work and on his behaviour outside, and he had been recalled and the conclusion reached that he would have to leave the service. Nevertheless, until the day of his disappearance there had been no grounds to suspect that Burgess was working against the State; he had been indiscreet, but indiscretion was not generally the characteristic of a secret agent.*

*Dealing with the security investigations, the Foreign Secretary said that diligent inquiries had been started in January 1949 immediately after a report had been received that certain British information had become available to the Soviet authorities a few years earlier. In the*

*course of the next two years the security services had nar-*
*rowed the field of suspects to one, namely Maclean, but*
*even then the evidence was inconclusive and cir-*
*cumstantial. The best, and perhaps the only, chance of*
*obtaining evidence which could have been used to sup-*
*port a prosecution lay in obtaining admissions from him.*
*There was, however, no firm starting-point for an inter-*
*view, and it was highly desirable to obtain further infor-*
*mation about his contacts and activities which could be*
*used as a basis for questioning him. A watch had there-*
*fore been kept on him, though this had not been extended*
*to his home at Tatsfield because of the technical*
*difficulties of keeping him under observation there, and*
*the consequent risk of putting him on his guard. Turning*
*to the question of whether the two men had received a*
*warning of the investigations into their activities, Mr*
*Macmillan said that whilst the circumstances of their dis-*
*appearance were certainly explainable in terms of a warn-*
*ing, it was quite possible that they had fled because one or*
*the other had noticed circumstances or a combination of*
*circumstances which aroused their suspicions. Never-*
*theless, the possibility that they had received a warning*
*had to be seriously considered, and searching and pro-*
*tracted investigations into this possibility had been under-*
*taken and were now proceeding.*

*In this connection the Foreign Secretary referred to Mr*
*H.A.R. Philby, temporary First Secretary in the British*
*Embassy in Washington from October 1949 to June 1951,*
*whose alleged 'dubious third-man activities' had been*
*mentioned in a parliamentary question by Lt.-Col. Lipton*
*(Lab.) on 25 October. Mr Macmillan said that although*
*Mr Philby had been friends with Burgess from their time*
*as fellow undergraduates at Cambridge, and although*
*Burgess had been accommodated in Mr Philby's home in*
*Washington from August 1950 to April 1951, it should be*

217

*realized that at no time before he fled was Burgess under suspicion. It had been found, nevertheless, that Mr Philby had had Communist associations before and after his university days, and in 1951 he had been asked to resign from the Foreign Service. He had subsequently been the subject of the closest investigation, but no evidence had been found that he was responsible for warning Burgess and Maclean. While in Government service he had carried out his duties ably and conscientiously, and there was no reason to conclude that he had at any time betrayed the interests of Britain, or to identify him with the so-called 'third man', if there was one.*

*As regards others whose names had been associated with the affair, Mr Macmillan had caused them to be carefully studied and investigated. No one was being shielded. Had any evidence of guilt been forthcoming, he or his predecessors would not have hesitated to take appropriate action, but no such evidence had been found.*

*When Macmillan came to the end of his speech, Herbert Morrison, the previous Foreign Secretary who had signed the order for Maclean's interrogation, caught the Speaker's eye and stood up.*

*He said that although he agreed with most of what the Foreign Secretary had said, he was not as fully satisfied as Mr Macmillan appeared to be. He was inclined to think that Maclean had been warned by someone, because it was a remarkable coincidence that he should have given the order for the questioning of Maclean on 25 May and that the two were missing on the same night. In this connection Mr Morrison said that he had received a letter from a friend whose judgement of men and affairs he respected. The person concerned had asked that his name should not be mentioned – though it was available to the Foreign Office if they wanted it – because he did not want to be pursued with publicity in this matter. This letter said:*

*'I was very interested to read your remarks about Maclean and Burgess . . . because I know them both and actually lunched with Maclean the day before he disappeared. The point I wanted to mention to you was that on the day I am sure he had no intention of leaving in the way he did. He spoke to me so normally as to his private affairs, his wife's confinement, and his plans for the immediate future, that I am convinced he was not then intending to leave the country. This makes me feel that, subsequent to meeting me on 24 May, he received some warning that he was under suspicion, and immediately left the country with Burgess. It may be, therefore, that someone in the Foreign Office told him on 25 May that you had authorized him to be questioned. Of course, it was not until the Foreign Office knew, that the security service knew as well.'*

*At the end of Herbert Morrison's short speech there were several Labour MPs clamouring to catch the Speaker's eye and he let three of them make short comments. There was an obvious feeling on the Opposition benches that Morrison had gone easy on Macmillan as a fellow Foreign Secretary who knew the problems his successor was facing. The Opposition would have none of it, all their comments were sharp and acid.*

*Mr Richard Crossman (Lab.) contended that the White Paper, instead of defending the Foreign Service, had 'put it far deeper into the mire'. If, after four years, 'this tissue of palpable half-truths and contradictions' was the best they could produce, then the impression of a 'cover-up' was more strongly substantial than ever.*

*Mr Tomney (Lab.) alleged that the White Paper was 'an attempt to cover up something within a circle of associates in the Foreign Office, to protect somebody from their follies and mismanagement, misjudgement and neglect'. He maintained that there would be no reassurance unless there was an independent inquiry.*

*Mr Robens (Lab.) similarly said that the public and many MPs were sure that there was a close circle of people in the Foreign Office who 'covered up' for their friends. 'How else could it be,' he asked, 'that a couple of drunks, a couple of homosexuals, well known in London, could for so long have occupied important posts in the Foreign Office?'*

*On 10 November Lt.-Col. Lipton MP in a personal statement to the House said that as a result of further examination of the question he was satisfied that there was no justification for his allegations against Mr Philby, that he deeply regretted having made them, and that he unreservedly withdrew them.*

*Almost two weeks later, on 21 November the last ripple in the parliamentary scenario edged its way to oblivion when Mr Turton, Joint Under Secretary at the Foreign Office, stated in a parliamentary reply that 'no officials had been dismissed or transferred as a result of the inquiries into the Maclean-Burgess case. One official, however, had been asked to resign and had received a financial settlement in accordance with the terms of his engagement, whilst another had been permitted to resign in view of his relationship to one of the persons involved, and had been given a gratuity.'*

# 22

He had walked the same route every day. Away from the village, along the empty road, through the woods, higher and higher up the hill until he could look across the lake. The fresh air, the good food, gradually did its work on his body and the peace did its work on his mind.

There were small mounds of springy pine needles at the crest of the hill and he sat there focusing his glasses on the water's edge. The reeds were already turning red and brown, and a small flight of swallows swooped over the water as if rehearsing their autumn flight to the south.

He sat for over an hour, gazing across the lake to the soft hills beyond. And beyond the hills themselves was the sea, where the green fields of County Waterford swept down to the Irish Sea. Eventually he took out the stamped postcards and wrote something different for each child. Just as he had done every day for nearly two months.

Later he walked back slowly to the road. There was a man at the stile in the last field. He nodded to him as he clambered over and the man said, 'Top of the morning, Kim.'

His mouth opened, then closed as he recognized the man, and he managed a smile.

'What brings you here, Jimmy?'

'Oh, let's say, Auld Lang Syne.'

'Let's not, Jimmy. Let's say what it's all about.'

'What are you doing these days?'

'I've got a temporary thing. Writing a book for a friend of mine. A history of his company.'

'*Do you want work?*'

'*Of course I do. I'm broke. Flat broke.*'

'*We can put the word in for you.*'

'*Too bloody true. It's already been done. I get on a short-list of two, you people put the word in, and the other fellow gets the job.*'

'*We can get you a retainer as a Middle-East correspondent.*'

'*Who for?* Old Moore's Almanac?'

'*For the* Economist, *doubling up for the* Observer.'

'*Why the sudden solicitude?*'

*McNay shrugged. 'We want to help.*'

'*Where should I be posted?*'

'*Beirut.*'

*Philby smiled. 'And what else do I have to do?*'

'*We'd pay you for regular reports.*'

*Philby turned his face away, the gentle breeze ruffling his thinning hair as he looked across the fields without seeing. He would just be a freelance stooge. The kind he had used so casually himself to get in a few more crumbs of information. But he had no choice. He desperately needed the money, and it was at least a way of life that he knew. It was incredible that they were still prepared to use him, even in this minor role. Or was it just a way to keep him under surveillance until they had gathered enough evidence to charge him. Or make it easier to put a knife in his back in the dark in some Beirut backstreet.*

'*When do you want me to start?*'

'*As soon as you can. Put in your applications and we'll talk to the two journals and you'll get offers in ten days. They'll pay retainers.*'

*He wanted to ask what was happening in SIS, but he knew he wouldn't get an answer. He was no longer an insider. But he would have liked to know how he stood. He had taken it for granted that he would remain permanently under*

222

suspicion, and McNay's approach surprised and puzzled him. He wondered who his contact would be.

McNay walked on ahead of him, and didn't stop at Philby's temporary home.

Philby could see a car at the bottom of the road opposite the post office.

It was only five days later when he got the postcard with the Stockholm postmark. The picture was of the crowds on a summer's day on Kungsgatan, and the message was innocuous to an innocent eye. He had taken the train to Dublin six days later and they met in the back office of the shop in Dawson Street.

The man had made no mention of their two years' silence, and took up the threads as if they had never been broken. He was a stranger to Philby but he was obviously cool and efficient, taking for granted his co-operation. He was to accept the Beirut offer and would receive his instructions from a KGB officer already in the area. The addresses of two safe-houses and half a dozen dead-letter drops were given to him. All except one were in Beirut. There were no commendations for the risks he had run, or the sacrifices he had made. The fact that he was back in the business had to be taken as their only sign of approval.

He had put in his application to the two journals, had been interviewed and taken on. He felt no elation, and for almost the first time in his life the future looked grim and forbidding. A dull treadmill of routine until he died. A rusting hulk of a ship that wasn't worth breaking for scrap, left for time and nature alone to do the work.

Not even its regulars would rate the bar of Beirut's Hotel Normandy as anything more than convenient. Philby had his mail addressed there, although his room was at the Hotel Bassoul. He was popular with the small English and American community. The men found him an amiable drinking *companion and the women were rather taken by the helpless man with the wry smile and the untidy, uncared-for clothes.*

*If the stories he filed back to London read more like Foreign Office reports they were at least accurate, on time, and informative; and that in itself was uncommon enough with Middle-East correspondents to commend him to his masters.*

*Even for that community his drinking had gradually become an embarrassment, and his behaviour in private become cruder. But those who were generous-minded put it down to loneliness and the traditional occupational hazard of journalists.*

*Probably Sam Brewer was the only journalist in Beirut who didn't realize that Kim Philby was paying court to his wife. He was an American and so was his wife Eleanor.*

*Although Eleanor Brewer had lived abroad continuously since the war she had no interest at all in world affairs or politics. With a small daughter, and a vague interest in sculpture, she went on her placid way until the day she met Kim Philby.*

*It wasn't long before the secret notes became secret meetings in the flats of mutual friends. And it was obvious to onlookers as well as to Eleanor Brewer that although Philby's passion might be considered as over-romantic it nevertheless was real. As if he desperately needed the romance and tenderness that he had not had for a decade he poured out his soul into those daily letters.*

*He wore no false appearance of regret when he got the news of Aileen's death and he proposed to Eleanor Brewer before he left to go back to England to wind up the last details of his former life.*

*Shortly after his return Eleanor's mother died, and she combined a journey to the United States to put her father in an old people's home, with the ritual of a Mexican divorce. She and Kim Philby were married in 1958.*

224

*There was a daily routine. They had a small place that gave a fine view of the harbour, and rising mid-morning they would stroll down to the Normandy for their mail. Then drinks as their friends drifted into the bar.*

*He always appeared to his fellow journalists and his friends to be the least energetic of them all. He chatted to scores of people but he seldom asked direct questions. And probably because of his easy-going attitude he numbered dozens of diplomats and Arab leaders among his contacts.*

*SIS made no complaint about his routine reports and seemed satisfied with his answers to the specific questions that they sometimes raised with him.*

*His role with the KGB was far more useful. Their intelligence-gathering network in the Middle East was highly efficient but the apparatus was weak in its evaluation processes. Philby had the experience of the senior diplomat that was necessary to 'read' documents. He could decide whether some document was the vague thoughts of some minor official, or a first draft that would never see the light of day, or the final version of some policy suggestion that would have to be seriously considered by the writer's superiors in London, Washington, Amman or Ankara.*

*Philby's notes on the copy of some document from the State Department in Washington or the Foreign Office in London made the eventual evaluation in Moscow ten times more valuable. And for the local KGB network to be able to arrange for a trusted informant to spend a couple of hours talking to Philby was invaluable.*

*On 30 September 1960 Kim Philby's father died. The first of two blows that were to disrupt the even tenor of his life with Eleanor.*

*On his way home to Riyadh from London the seventy-five-year-old man stopped off in Beirut to see his son. There had been a party for his friends and admirers and the old*

225

*man obviously enjoyed himself. He had died the following day from a heart attack, in his room at the St George's Hotel. He had been buried with a Muslim ceremony at the Beirut cemetery and Kim Philby's own obituary on his father appeared in the* Observer *on 2 October.*

*Eleanor Philby had been frightened by the drinking bout that followed his father's death. It was almost a relief when, in December, he had had to travel to Riyadh to clear up his father's affairs.*

*For two months after his return the drinking bouts were less frequent until an afternoon in early April 1961. A man who sometimes came to their house had brought her husband home in a taxi. His clothes filthy with vomit, his eyes closed, his legs helpless. The man had spoken in poor English, she asked him where he had found her husband, and he had shrugged and said, 'In the coffee-shop.' He had helped her get her husband to bed.*

*For two days Philby had kept to his bed. He had drunk only coffee, and he had eaten only dry biscuits. He lay there without speaking, his eyes looking up at the ceiling, his head turning sometimes to watch the curtains moving gently in the breeze at the small open window. He had warned Moscow that if George Blake responded to London's request to return as soon as possible from Beirut, he would be walking into a trap. They had listened, but rejected his advice on the grounds that if SIS suspected Blake they would never have sent him to the Arab studies centre in Beirut. And apart from that, if they were really suspicious they could have picked him up in Beirut or at the centre in Shemlan. George Blake had gone back, and they had arrested him at the airport the moment he landed. And now they would interrogate him for months, and the fingers would start pointing at him once again. There would be no chance now of working his passage back into SIS. They'd debriefed Dolnytsin and that was how they had uncovered*

226

*Blake. Dolnytsin would have pointed at him too, and with
Blake interrogated they would have enough.*

*The Armenian restaurant named 'Vrej' was in one of
Beirut's backstreets. It was never patronized by Europeans.
Its food and clientele were strongly ethnic but they had
become used to Kim Philby. He had influential friends
among the Armenian community in the Lebanon, and he
knew from the past the mountain paths into Armenia better
than some Armenians knew them. They were well aware too
that the man he met there on Wednesday nights was KGB.
But he was dark-skinned, and spoke Arabic with an Armenian accent. Wednesday wasn't the only day that Philby
patronized the restaurant but the KGB man was his only
regular contact.*

*Philby had his usual table in the corner furthest from the
door, and his companion that day was a Saudi trader who
covered most of the Middle East, buying and selling skins,
civet, and small lots of coffee. He had news of discontent in
the Iraqi army, and of secret meetings with Syrian politicians by junior officers.*

*Philby half-filled his own glass from the bottle of anis and
then filled the Saudi's glass. It was when he was putting the
cork back in the bottle that Philby saw him. He was pushing
aside the bead curtains at the door and looking slowly
around the dimly-lit interior. Then their eyes met. They
were the same blue eyes that had once looked at him with
mild benevolence at Westminster School. The eyes were
benevolent now, but the face was fuller and the hair well-
laced with grey.*

*Philby knew that it would not have been an accidental
meeting. They would have watched him when they could
spare the time, but he was surprised that they knew about
the 'Vrej'. He had tried to keep that secret. A place of last
resort. But there was no point in dodging the issue. He*

227

*excused himself to the Arab and bade him goodbye and pushed the bamboo table clumsily to one side as he walked across the room.*

*As he held out his hand to the man at the door he said, 'You must be looking for me. How are you?'*

*Patrick Walker smiled back. 'It's good to see you, Kim. I'm fine. How about you? Can we talk here?'*

*Philby turned. The Saudi had left and the table was empty.*

*'Let's go back to the corner table.'*

*They had sat talking together for over two hours. Philby would have liked to have heard the gossip in SIS. Not as information to pass on to the Russians but just to know what had happened. Like an old-boys' reunion or a chance meeting with someone from an office where you had once worked. But despite Patrick Walker's smiling amiability he had avoided all mention of SIS and its personalities. Even who was sleeping with whom could be useful to the KGB. But they could talk of politicians and their naughty ways, and the ex-SIS who were no longer in the business, and they could talk cricket and cricketers. Neither of them were cricket fanatics but cricket was summer, a reliable backdrop, a way of being indolently active. You could like cricket without knowing its finer points or caring who won or lost. Philby had once said that 'cricket was like the British at war'.*

*They had spent half an hour on Philby's reports and arranged to meet the next day at Philby's house. When he gave the invitation he deliberately didn't give his address. Walker hadn't asked for it and Philby knew then that they were not just chatting. Walker was a shrewd operator. He hadn't asked where Philby lived because he knew. And he didn't mind that Philby knew that he knew.*

*Walker had stayed in Beirut for three days and had spent his evenings with the Philbys. The relationship was relaxed* and friendly, but Kim Philby knew that among the scores of seemingly unimportant questions that he had been asked there would have been two or three that were more than they seemed. They would have been based on bits and pieces of information they had got from interrogating George Blake. And he had no idea what George Blake had done or what he had confessed to. All he knew was that George Blake was both SIS and a KGB agent. But that was all.

After Walker's visit in October Philby had reverted to his heavy drinking. And all their friends had tales to tell of Philby's crudities. Offensive remarks to friends' wives, he was now a less refined drunk, a bottom pincher and sexual fumbler. Even long friendships can wear thin at the sight of a dishevelled drunk relieving himself in public on a prized Persian carpet. The invitations were few but it said a lot for Philby's personality, and charm when sober, that there were some who took his behaviour in their stride. And there were wives who felt a genuine sympathy for Eleanor who sometimes joined her husband in some drunken aberration as if it might prove her loyalty and love for the distraught and desperate man she had married.

Patrick Walker had returned to Beirut the third week in January and had contacted Kim Philby soon after he arrived. He was staying at the embassy and had suggested drinks that first evening at an apartment that SIS used as a last-resort safe-house. It was owned by a Turk who spent most of his time in Cairo and Famagusta.

Walker had been shocked by the obvious and visible deterioration in Philby. Philby never cared much about his clothes but he looked now as if he slept in them. The bags under his eyes only emphasized the bloodshot eyes themselves, and the puffy, haggard face.

He poured them both a drink and sat facing Philby in the comfortable armchair, and as he raised his glass and said, 'Cheers,' he wondered if maybe Philby was on drugs.

229

'How are things, Kim?'

Philby looked at his glass and avoided looking at Walker.

'The Observer's given me a rise.'

'I've been asked to check a few things with you, Kim.'

'Go ahead, friend, help yourself. Pick the bones.'

Walker looked at the tired face, temporarily diverted from his task.

'Have you seen a doctor recently, Kim?'

'I don't need a doctor, Patrick.'

'You need something, my God.'

Philby nodded. 'That's true. I need some peace.'

'What would give you peace, Kim?'

'To be able to get away from them, and you, and everybody. To start again with nothing on the slate.'

'To do what?'

'To do nothing. I'm done in, Patrick. Burnt out. God knows how I get through each day. I need a grateful government who will just send me the money, and ask for nothing in return. I heard something the other day that sums it all up. The title of a show in London.'

'What show was that?'

'It's called Stop the world I want to get off. That's me, Patrick.'

'Will it wear you out to talk with me?'

'No. Talk away. I'm listening.'

'Do you remember 25 May 1951?'

Philby half-smiled. 'Yes. Of course.'

'They've been drawing diagrams and time schedules and listing names. You'll remember that it was a Friday. On the Friday morning Herbert Morrison gave MI5 the nod to bring in Maclean for questioning. Agreed?'

'If you say so. That's what he said in Parliament in 1955.'

'It's a fact, Kim. So Morrison knew, and the two MI5 men knew. Nobody else. Except you, that is. A coded signal was

230

sent to you for information, at the Washington embassy. D'you remember?'

'I'm sure it's recorded, Patrick, it doesn't really matter if I remember or not.'

'Burgess was living at a flat in New Bond Street. He had just come back from Washington in disgrace for his wild behaviour. He was planning a holiday in Italy with a fellow he met on the Queen Mary. In fact he was due to meet him on the 25th at 10.30 at the Green Park Hotel. Round about ten o'clock that morning he made several telephone calls. Talking with friends about possible routes and places to stay. That was up to ten o'clock. Morrison had given his OK at 9.32 a.m. You received your signal at three o'clock in the morning Washington time. Ten a.m. in London. Burgess kept his appointment at the hotel at 10.30. We have talked to the man concerned. When they met, Burgess was very agitated, and said he might have to put off the holiday. He said that there was a problem. He would let him know by 8.30 that evening whether it was on or off. He never did of course. But what is more our concern is that this chap says that Burgess told him that a friend of his in the Foreign Office was in serious trouble and he, Burgess, was the only one who could help him.'

Philby sat looking down at his glass.

Walker said softly, 'It can only have been you, Kim, nobody else could have warned him.'

Philby looked up. 'Are you telling me, or asking me?'

'Asking you.'

'If I say it wasn't, you won't believe me, so why ask. You'll have to work it out for yourselves.'

'We have.'

'So?'

'We've got Dolnytsin and Blake. It's only a matter of time.'

'And then what?'

231

'Why don't you just talk with me, Kim. And I'll see what I can do. There's bound to be room for some compromise.'

The bloodshot eyes looked back at him unblinking and Philby's body shuddered as he sighed deeply.

'I'll think about what you've said, Patrick. How long are you here?'

'Two or three days.'

'Are you staying at the embassy?'

'Yes.'

'We'll be at the Pauls' party tomorrow night. I'll talk to you then.'

'OK. How's Eleanor?'

'Who?'

'Eleanor. Your wife.'

'Oh . . . yes. She's fine. She's a simple soul, Patrick. She's not involved in anything. You know that don't you?'

'I'll look forward to seeing you both. How are you off for money?'

Philby appeared not to hear him. He sat there silently for several minutes and then he stood up slowly.

'Do you want me to call you a taxi, Kim?'

Philby turned at the door and stared at Walker's face as if he might learn something from it.

'What?'

'Shall I call you a taxi?'

Philby took a deep breath and tried to button his buttonless jacket.

'No thanks,' he said. 'I'll walk.'

# 23

As Kim Philby held open the door of the taxi for Eleanor he turned to the driver.

'The British embassy, driver.'

He smiled as he settled himself beside his wife and took her hand in his. They were going to the First Secretary's party at the embassy.

As they turned from the hill road to the main road Philby said, 'Good God, sweetie. I've forgotten to do something.'

He leaned forward and said to the driver. 'Drop me here will you.'

As the taxi stopped he turned to Eleanor. 'I've got to send a cable from the Post Office. I'll catch you up. Make my apologies to the Pauls, I won't be long.' He kissed her fleetingly on the cheek.

As the taxi moved on she turned to wave to him, but he didn't wave back. He didn't seem to have noticed as he walked past the carpet shop and the taxi passed him.

Eleanor made the apologies to their host when she arrived, but there would have been no problems anyway, embassy people were well used to the vagaries of journalists' lives.

By the time the guests at the party had finished the main course Kim Philby was going through Rayak, heading for Ba'albek; and at much the same time that a distraught Eleanor was being taken home in an embassy car Philby was standing at the frontier post between Lebanon and Syria.

He stood watching as the Syrian frontier guard examined his papers. The guard shone his torch on Philby's face and looked back at the photograph. The papers confirmed that he was Ferit Haluk, diplomatic courier for the Turkish government. The guard nodded and handed back the papers. He walked carefully round the old Chevrolet truck with the Turkish number plates, shining his torch under the mudguards, rapping his hand on the door panels to check that they were hollow, and sniffing inside the cabin for the sweet smell of opium. Finally he waved them over the border.

Kim Philby slept after they turned off the main road at Homs on to the pipeline track to Palmyra. They had bedded down for a few hours that evening on the northern bank of the Euphrates at Dier ez Zor, and had broken camp just after midnight to save the tyres from the heat of the day. They had reached the Turkish border at El Qamishliye at noon. The papers he showed at the guard post confirmed that he was Fehmi Izmen, trader, a member of the Turkish minority in Famagusta, Cyprus. A change of vehicle and another day and night on the mountain roads and he was in sight of Mount Ararat.

He knew the pathways over the mountain as well as he knew the way from Whitehall to St James's but it took him many hours, for he went on foot. But by the morning of the fourth day after leaving Beirut he was asleep in the villa just outside Yerevan, safe in the Armenian Republic of the Soviet Union.

It was late afternoon before he awoke, and he bathed and shaved, and changed into the clothes they had brought for him.

He sat on the balcony at the small white table, looking across the valley towards the mountains. There were lemons growing below the balcony and the air smelt fresh and sweet; and faintly, in the distance, he could hear music; flutes and drums, and some sad stringed instrument. They had been playing that music in Yerevan three thousand years before the crucifixion. The stringed instrument was probably a lyre or a harp. And he smiled to himself at the word and the thought. He remembered the quotation from the Bible, '. . . David took a harp, and played with his hand: so Saul was refreshed, and was well, and the evil spirit departed from him.' They had used that verse so many times as a code. But David's harp was being broadcast now from Radio Yerevan.

He wondered what the children were doing at that moment. He would be able to get a letter to Eleanor but not to the children. He sighed and stood up, and walked into the bathroom, running a few inches of cold water into the bath to cool his hot, swollen feet.

In the weeks after Kim Philby's disappearance the press speculated from time to time on the circumstances, but SIS and the Foreign Office played it cool. They agreed that a journalist who had known Burgess and Maclean many years ago had not been seen for some time, but that was a matter between him and the newspapers who employed him.

It had taken Eleanor some time to grasp the fact that her husband was a Russian agent, but in the third week a loving letter arrived in his neat handwriting. A loving letter without explanations, but saying how much he missed her. It was postmarked Cairo. There were other similar letters with various postmarks over the next few weeks.

Patrick Walker had stayed in Beirut, visiting her most days and was privy to the contents of the letters.

It was almost six months after Philby's flight that a letter was pushed into her hand by an urchin in the street when she was out shopping. It was from Kim. Complicated instructions to get herself and the two children unnoticed to the airport and take a Czech Airlines flight to Prague. She was to write the date of her departure in chalk on the wall in the small alley near their home. If she had problems she was to scrawl a cross on the wall and she would receive help. She chalked up a cross in the darkness that night. And she had said nothing to Walker about the note.

The next morning a man had visited her. He gave her United States and Soviet passports for herself and the children, open-dated tickets to Prague on Czechoslovakian Airlines, two hundred US dollars and 5000 piastres. And he gave her elaborate details about how she should leave the house and get to the airport. She was to mark her date of leaving on the wall as soon as possible so that Kim could fly from Moscow to meet her at Prague airport.

The elaborate instructions, the secretiveness, her doubts and distress about what she was about to do had been too much. She wasn't sure who Patrick Walker was, but he was helping when he could, and he was obviously one of Kim's old friends. She told him the whole story that evening. He had talked to her for hours asking if she was sure that she wanted to make her life and her daughter's life in Moscow. A language they didn't speak, a way of life that was totally alien, ostracized by the British and American communities as the wife of a traitor. He persuaded her to let him get them to London where she could consider her situation more calmly and in a friendly atmosphere. He would take responsibility for her. There was little resistance, and they had flown out of Beirut to London the following night.

Later that night a taxi had dropped an Englishman near the Philby house and waited for him for ten minutes. In that time he had chalked a date on the wall in the alley before he walked back, smiling, to the taxi.

Kim Philby had waited for three days at Prague airport before he realized that they were not coming. The small piece of petty spite depressed him deeply. They had been his friends, or at least his colleagues, and they knew what it would mean to him. To some it would be just a prank, but

236

*there were others who knew how it would affect him. But if
that was how they were going to play it, so be it.*

*In London she had answered all Patrick Walker's ques-
tions about her life with Kim Philby, his movements such as
she knew of them, and his friends. But she didn't tell him of
the letters she was getting that came via a chain of people
from the Soviet Embassy. And two months later she got off
a plane at Sheremetyevo and Kim Philby was on the tarmac
to meet her. A healthier looking Philby. Still the bags under
the eyes, but the eyes themselves were no longer bloodshot.
And the smiles, and the kisses, and the hugs, were genuine
enough on both sides. Her daughter had gone to boarding
school in the United States and Kim's son had joined his
other children.*

# 24

He wasn't sure what he'd expected when he accepted Kenrick's invitation to spend the Sunday with him at his home in Bexhill. He hadn't really had time to think about it, before he drove down with Vanessa. Down the A21, turning off for Battle, and then through to Bexhill.

Even on high-days and holidays the beaches at Bexhill are never crowded, and on Sunday mornings the old gentlemen in their panama hats go out for their Sunday papers, exchanging friendly nods and the wave of a trembling hand holding a walking stick.

Only a fanatic would suggest that Bexhill has any claim to great visual beauty. It bears all the signs of Victorian and Edwardian speculative building. It has none of the postcard beauty of a Martha's Vineyard or even a Bosham or Itchenor, but it has the beauty of peacefulness, homeliness, and belonging. Its people smile at strangers, there's a good bookshop, and no five star hotels. And its public toilets are spotlessly clean. Bexhill is civilized, provided you don't equate that word with cathedrals, museums, and *haute cuisine*.

Kenrick's house was in one of the longish roads that run parallel with the promenade, east of the sailing club and the pier. A terraced house with bay windows up and down, a small front garden, and half a dozen stone steps up to a glass-panelled door with shiny, brass fittings.

Kenrick himself answered the door in a navy-blue blazer and grey flannel trousers. His wife was just behind him in the hall. She was much younger than Powell had expected.

He guessed that she was at most forty. She had blonde hair with a white head-band to keep it in place. A white tennis dress with a close-pleated skirt and white shoes. And two long, beaded necklaces. They could both have been cast at no costuming expense as extras for anything by Scott Fitzgerald, or the chorus in *Salad Days*.

As they were introduced and led down the long hallway Kenrick chatted and his wife twittered. Powell and Van were made at home and given drinks in the sitting room. It was when they had finished the second round that Dolly Kenrick stood up and said, 'They must meet Sammy.'

Kenrick nodded, and looking at his two visitors he said, 'Sammy's my son.'

The Kenricks led them down the steps into the back garden, down a paved path, under a rose arch to a small ornamental pond set in a shady grotto. There was a child in a wheelchair. About ten or eleven years old. A mongol child, a boy, dressed in a white shirt, a grey sleeveless pullover, denim trousers and sandals.

Despite the fact that the child couldn't speak they had been introduced and a few minutes later Dolly Kenrick had left to bring out the picnic meal, then Kenrick himself went off to help her.

Powell wheeled the chair alongside a wooden bench and sat by the boy. Talking to him gently, giving the answers as well as asking the questions. Looking at the boy's face, smiling at his own jokes. After a few minutes the boy jerkily moved his arm and put his hand in Powell's hand. The small hand was warm and soft and trusting. Vanessa sat alongside Powell, pale-faced, silent and still.

Powell was telling the boy about his flights in Concorde when the Kenricks came back, and the boy's head was on his shoulder. He was careful not to move as he ate his sandwiches and when it was time for the coffee Powell suggested that he should take Sammy for a walk on the sea-front while Vanessa talked to the Kenricks.

Kenrick helped him get the wheelchair down the front steps, a ramp had been built at the back of the house, and Powell wheeled the boy down to the sailing club so that he could watch the dinghies being prepared and launched. They both had an ice-cream in a cone and watched the boats, and then went slowly back to the house an hour and a half later.

Vanessa had relaxed and was talking animatedly with Dolly Kenrick in the sitting room. By the time that he and Kenrick had got the wheelchair back into the garden it was nearly six o'clock.

'I'll have to be going, Tom. It's been a pleasant break for me. You've got a nice home down here.'

Kenrick looked at him. 'You really mean that don't you?'

'Of course. Why not?'

There were tears at the edges of Kenrick's eyes and he swallowed and said, 'You're right. I love them both. I love this place, but nobody believes that I do. They think I just put a brave face on it.'

'Then they're fools, Tom. You're very lucky to have Dolly and Sammy, and they're lucky to have you.'

Kenrick took a deep breath. 'I heard you were brought up in an orphanage. Is that why you understand Sammy?'

'I shouldn't think so, Tom. I just like your Sammy. I like gentle people. Are you religious at all?'

Kenrick shook his head. 'No. We went to church at first. Said the prayers and meant them, but of course nothing happened. Nothing could. But he's got us as long as we're alive.'

'Is that what worries you. What will happen when you're not around?'

Kenrick nodded and said softly. 'It's a nightmare. I can't bear to think about it.'

240

'That's why I asked you if you're religious. I'm not either so it could have been a problem. How about I take over if anything happens? Not interfere, but just act as back-up for Dolly and Sammy.'

Kenrick looked down at his shoes and nodded, and said quietly, 'Thanks. We could talk about it.'

Even though it was summer he had put the heater on in the car for the journey back, and Van had slept in the seat alongside him, one slim hand resting on his thigh.

Late the next evening Kenrick had phoned him at the flat.

'Can I see you for a few minutes, sir, tomorrow morning?'

'Sure. Come and have breakfast with us.'

'It's kind of official, Mr Powell.'

'OK. At the office. What time?'

'I'd prefer to see you somewhere else.'

'Where've you got in mind?'

'The buffet at Victoria Station.'

'What time?'

'Would ten o'clock be OK, sir?'

'Fine. Goodnight, Tom.'

Powell walked to the station next morning and Kenrick was waiting for him at one of the tables near the window. Powell waved to him, bought two coffees and walked over with them.

'Morning, Tom.'

'Morning, sir. I've bought coffees already.'

'I guess we can manage both.'

Kenrick shifted uneasily in his seat and moved aside the salt and pepper pots. He looked at Powell's face, his brow furrowed.

'I've got a problem, sir. I don't quite know how to ... er ... how to ...'

'Just come right out with it, Tom.'

'It's not that easy, sir. I've got to ask you to keep it

241

between us. I need to know that you will, before I tell you.'

'Who mustn't I tell?'

'Anybody. It's not just a question of telling anyone, it's a question of going on behaving as if you don't know what I've told you.'

'Sounds interesting anyway.'

'They'll fire me if they find out that I've told you.'

'Maybe you'd better not tell me then.'

Kenrick sighed and looked at him.

'I don't think it was the KGB who knocked off "Milord".'

'Go on.'

'I'd like to know what you think of what I said.'

'You're a very experienced operator. You've been in the business a long time. If you think that, then I'd want to know why.'

'You understand the implications?'

'Sure. If they didn't do it, *we* must have done it.'

'That doesn't fit your evaluation does it?'

'No. But I could be wrong.'

'You *are* wrong, sir.'

'There was a lot of evidence the other way.'

'The two KGB hit men. Leaving the documents and all that?'

'Yes.'

'Maybe that was done just to make you think it was the KGB.'

'Why should our own people be interested in deceiving me. I'm not likely to object or shout it from the housetops.'

'Have you spoken to Mr Anders recently?'

'I spoke to him about ten days ago.'

'He's been posted unexpectedly to Hong Kong.'

'So?'

'It was done in a hurry. He only had two hours to pack.'

'Go on.'

242

'Mr McNay interviewed him the day before he was posted. Asked him to translate a signal in Polish. Anders did so and told him he'd already done the same message for you. McNay seemed agitated and it was after that that Mr Anders was posted. He asked how long he would be out there. He was told that it was an indefinite posting. Anders raised hell because of his family, and then they said not longer than two months. And Hong Kong's Mr McNay's area. Anders is working for him.'

Powell slowly, and quite unnecessarily, stirred the remainder of his coffee again. That meant that McNay had somehow got hold of the original coded message. The one that Harpenden had actually written. He looked back at Kenrick's face.

'Anything else?'

'No, sir.'

'Are you quite sure?'

'No more facts anyway.'

'What about suppositions?'

'I think our people did it. I can't see why they put you over the hurdles without telling you. Or why they didn't tell you when the dust died down.'

'There's a snag to your reasoning, Tom.'

'What's that?'

'If our people did it they wouldn't have left the blank page on the pad with the impression of the message on it.'

'Maybe they were in a hurry or careless.'

'You don't believe that do you?'

'Maybe not, but I still think I'm right.'

'There's something else isn't there?'

'Did you know that copies of our surveillance reports always went to the other members of the committee before you got them?'

'No I didn't. Who gave you those instructions?'

'I got them direct from "C". The old one, not the new one.'

'Why didn't you tell me before?'

'My orders said not to.'

'What did that make you think?'

'I reckoned they were still playing games about Philby, and that they weren't letting on to you.'

'Let's get back to "Milord". I had assumed that the KGB had him killed because they were suspicious about Philby's meetings with me. I even wondered if they had sacrificed "Milord" to indicate to us that Philby was serious about coming back. Wiping him out so that he couldn't get in the way. To show, without saying the words, that they were willing to let Philby come back.'

'I think you were fitting the facts to the case. What Mr Padmore always quotes as "*Post hoc ergo propter hoc*". And maybe you were meant to do that.'

'Could be. I wonder why?'

'In my experience anything in any way to do with Philby is always more than it seems. Never straightforward. Interference. String-pulling. It's as if we were still at Ryder Street or Broadway, with Philby still there, smiling that funny smile of his, watching us all going through the hoops he'd set up for us.'

'Well, thanks for telling me, Tom. I'll keep it all to myself.'

Kenrick stood up. 'Thanks for being kind to the boy, sir. Most people are embarrassed. They don't mean it unkindly. It upsets them.'

Powell looked up at Kenrick. 'It upsets you, Tom, and it upsets me. But for different reasons from the others. He's a sweetie, and we want him protected, but we want him to be in the world as well. What's the medical prognosis?'

'That I'll live longer than he will. And Dolly will live longer than both of us.'

'How does she take it?'

'She's fantastic. Better than I am. She just gets on with it. I wish I could make it up to her.'

'I'm sure that you do, Tom. Some men would have walked out.'

Kenrick stood silently for a few moments, and then he said, 'Maybe you'd better have another look at my "P" file, sir.'

He turned abruptly and walked off.

Powell stirred the second coffee and sipped it. It was cold but he didn't notice.

He knew that Kenrick was almost certainly right. But why should SIS want 'Milord' out of the way. If that was what they wanted they could have done it years ago. Why now? And why leave the documents around? It gave an impression that it was KGB, but who did they want to deceive? The police would have passed the secret stuff straight to Special Branch who would have passed it to MI5. It was old and worthless anyway. But why should they want to deceive *him*? And why had the surveillance reports gone to the others before him? And if that was what they wanted why the hell didn't they just say so? Lay it down as part of the routine. The whole 'Milord' operation was only a low grade piece of routine for all of them anyway.

They had probably waited until the two KGB hit-men happened to be in the country as part of the deception. And the fact that they had left the page on the pad with the impression from the previous page was because they hadn't used SIS operators. They sometimes used outsiders, and whoever it was was bright enough to rip off the page with the coded message but not experienced enough to think of the page below. But it had been a complex operation, not a one-man job. They had had to get rid of the servants.

McNay would know now that he had the message decoded and that he had got Anders to translate it. And for

245

some reason Anders had been hurried away so that he had no contact with him. What more could Anders have told him? And had McNay been acting on his own or for Padmore and Walker as well?

Would it be best to confront McNay or better to keep them guessing? He knew what he was going to do first.

*She put the old-fashioned wicker basket on the draining board and turned to look at him.*

*'I couldn't get any vinegar.'*

*'Why not? They've always got vinegar at GUM.'*

*'I couldn't think of the word for it, Kim.'*

*'Uksus.'*

*'That was what the wretched woman kept saying. I didn't understand her.'*

*Philby stared grimly back at her. Why did she have to call the shop assistant 'the wretched woman'. It was that woman's country for God's sake. It was Eleanor who was 'the wretched woman'. Making no effort to learn the language or fit in with the life of Moscow. Bored at the Bolshoi, indifferent to ballet, music, works of art, she complained constantly that Moscow was not New York.*

*She looked back at him defiantly. 'Have you heard from them yet?'*

*'Who's them?'*

*'You know who I mean. Your friends. The KGB.'*

*'Why do you always have to sneer at them. Everything we get is provided by them.'*

*She shrugged her indifference. 'Have you heard from them?'*

*'Yes.'*

*'When can I go?'*

*'There are conditions.'*

*'What conditions?'*

*'That you don't talk about our life here in Moscow. You*

246

*don't give our address and you don't reveal the name I use. The Russian name or the other name.'*

*'What can I talk about?'*

*'Anything else you like.'*

*'I shan't be wasting my breath talking about this dump.'*

She saw the anger in his eyes behind the smile, and she was glad. She hated their life. Ostracized by all the embassy people. Watched by the oafs from the KGB. The fact that they lived in what were considered in Moscow as privileged conditions was no recompense to her. The apartment, the car, the dacha in the country were inferior in every way to the life-style of any manual worker in America. And she despised her husband for pretending that this was enough for them for the rest of their lives.

*'You won't be just harming me if you talk.'*

*'How do you make that out?'*

*'There's the Macleans. Melinda and Donald.'*

*'I'm not worried about them.'*

*'Maybe not. But that's why they're worried about you.'*

Some instinct made her soften her approach.

*'I want to see my daughter, Kim. She doesn't deserve to be neglected like this.'*

*'What about my children?'*

*'They're your responsibility, not mine. We're here because of you, not me.'*

She saw the white ridge of anger round his mouth as he stood up, and the tears at the edge of his eyes. For a moment she felt a flash of sympathy as he put on his coat and the ghastly workman's cap. He didn't speak to her as he let himself out of the flat.

He didn't come back until mid-day the next day. He was calm and detached as he gave her the envelope.

*'Your US passport. Your Soviet passport. Seven hundred dollars, and your return ticket is at the airport. Just ask at the desk. Your flight's the first one out tomorrow. You need*

247

*to check in by 7.15. If you have any problems ring any Soviet Consulate or the Embassy in Washington. And do what they tell you.'*

*He took a small cardboard box from his pocket and put it on the table.*

*'That's for your daughter.'*

*'What is it, Kim?'*

*'A camera.'*

*She put her arms round him, her head on his shoulder. She sighed and looked up at his face.*

*'You're a sweetie to think of her. I'm sorry if I've been bitchy.'*

*'You need a change. Let me know when you're coming back. Phone the embassy and they'll pass the message on.'*

*'Do you want to eat now?'*

*'No, I'm going out of town for a week or so.'*

*'Where to?'*

*'East Berlin.'*

*'Are you going to see Litzi while you're there?'*

*'I shouldn't think so. I'll be too busy.'*

*'When are you leaving?'*

*'Now. I've come back to pack my kit. The office will be sending a car for you tomorrow morning about six o'clock.'*

*She steeled herself not to care as he silently packed his bag. When he had finished he carried it into the hall-way and came back. But only as far as the door. He nodded to her.*

*'Enjoy the trip.'*

*Then he turned, and a few seconds later she heard the outside door close behind him. She walked over to the window and looked down to the street. She saw the black Zil drawn up outside the entrance, and Melinda Maclean standing beside it. She turned away slowly and stood looking round the room. Without him there it was like a tomb. She looked at the leather armchair as if he might still be there. Intent on some book, reaching for the Russian dictionary from time to time to check a word, sometimes staring across at the bookshelves, his mind far away. She often wondered where his mind wandered. To his children? To some place she didn't know? To his life with Aileen or one of his other women? He never complained, never grieved, never spoke of the past. If she ever asked what he was thinking of he would smile and shake his head, but he never replied.*

*The major who stood saluting was young and fresh-faced. Dressed in full regimentals he stood stiffly as the military band played the 'Internationale'. It was the last week in August 1963.*

*There was only a handful of people there. Melinda Maclean was the only woman. Her husband was standing by the coffin on the bier and she wondered what Guy Burgess's reaction would have been if he could hear her husband's oration at his funeral. '... gifted and courageous man who devoted his life to the cause of making a better world ...' Not to mention screwing young boys and getting smashed out of your mind, she thought. Guy Burgess's* louche *charm had never worked for her. His behaviour in Washington, and his loud public diatribes against America and Americans, had been a constant source of embarrassment. As an American married to his so-called best friend her compatriots sometimes chose to lay some of the blame at her door. She loathed being linked in any way with the arrogant, mischief-making Burgess. Donald called his behaviour flamboyant, she classed it as oafish. Thank God Donald had had little to do with him since they had been in Moscow. She didn't give a damn about speaking ill of the dead. So far as she was concerned he was better dead. She wished that she had had Kim's strength of conviction. He had never for a moment had any intention of attending the funeral.*

*Eleanor sat on the bed at the motel near Baltimore, reading*

249

*through the letters again and again. As always they were typed, although several had postscripts in his neat orderly student's handwriting.*

*The letters were the old Kim, loving and tender, and admitting his loneliness without her. He obviously spent a lot of time with the Macleans and for a moment she felt a brief pang of jealousy as she remembered Melinda standing by the car in the street waiting for him to come down. Why hadn't she just come up and said 'hello'? Why the indifference? Or was it furtiveness?*

*She sorted the letters into date order from the postmarks on the envelopes. They had been posted from Paris, Amsterdam, Moscow, Washington, Los Angeles, and one from New Mexico. They would have been fed into the KGB machinery and sent on by some circuitous route.*

*She had thought it typically furtive when the first two or three arrived, but that was before the US immigration authorities had confiscated both her passports. The Soviet embassy in Washington was fighting the US State Department about them now, but the Americans were dragging it out as long as they could. The Soviet Ambassador himself had sent a letter of protest quoting the fourth and fifth Amendments. The embassy had sent her a copy. She had never realized that her own country could do such a thing. Kim would be amused when he heard. But she didn't feel amused; she felt lost. A small girl who didn't know where the toilets were at the new school. The girl who didn't know the ground rules.*

*At first the confiscation of her documents and the sudden visits from CIA men asking her questions had been no more than disturbing; but as the weeks extended into months they constantly pressed her about whether she really wanted to return to Moscow. Was she under any sort of Soviet pressure to return? Wouldn't she prefer to stay with her daughter?*

250

She had shown one of them, an oldish man with a grey-haired crew-cut, two or three of Kim's letters to show why she wanted to go back.

He had sat there reading each letter carefully and slowly, two or three times each, as if he were trying to memorize them. When he handed them back he had asked her if she hadn't thought that her husband was just keeping tabs on her. She told him the truth; that such a thought had never entered her mind.

The longer they delayed the more determined she became to return. She hadn't been certain at first. There seemed no point. He had ceased to love her, he so often looked at her as if he despised her; but his letters and the attitude of her own countrymen had swung her the other way. She was determined now to go back. It was November 1964 when she eventually arrived back in Moscow.

From the moment she arrived she knew that she had made a terrible mistake. It was as if she had never been away. The flat had become a place for one. A base rather than a home, and from the first hour she felt like an intruder. He had a pattern to his life. She could join it if she chose, but he made clear a dozen times a day that she couldn't alter it in any way. When they were in public he was polite, but he always managed to create the impression that she was a hanger-on, an immature intruder, who had to be tolerated and humoured.

When it became obvious that not only had he been having an affair with Melinda Maclean while she had been away, but was still continuing that relationship, she knew that their marriage was over. There was no kind of pressure for her to leave but she was not offered the slightest inducement to stay.

To add to her misery he was drinking heavily again, and she watched his physical and mental deterioration with growing fear. If anything should happen to him she would be on her own in Moscow. Without influence and without help.

251

*When she told him that she wanted to go back he had looked at her with bloodshot eyes, his head to one side, his hand trembling as he raised the glass to his lips. He hadn't spoken a word and she had wondered for a moment if he had actually heard or understood what she had said.*

*She heard him in the early hours of the morning. The crashing of furniture as he stumbled about, and the sound of the outer door opening to the corridor.*

*Gorsky had rung the bell early the next morning. He told her that Kim had been taken to hospital and was being treated for pneumonia. He also told her that he had been instructed to make whatever arrangements she wished for her to return to the United States.*

*She went to see her husband the evening before she left, determined to be composed and calm. But the sight of him lying there in the hospital bed, his head propped up on the pillows, his face white and bloodless, a drip-line to one arm that lay on the outside of the sheet, his lips dry and cracked, his breathing laboured, had been too much. She sat sobbing on the bed, her face in her hands. Crying for him, as well as for herself. A nurse had gently led her away and the KGB driver had taken her back to the flat.*

*She hadn't slept all that night. At first she had paced the rooms, slowly and aimlessly. Then for what seemed like hours she gazed from the window. The roofs and streets were covered with snow and the snow was still falling. Big, silent, Russian snowflakes drifting down remorselessly as if they would never stop. A solitary car moved slowly in the grey-brown slush in the road, its lights illuminating the heaps of snow at the edge of the pavement where the snow-plough had thrown it aside.*

*For the first time in her life she experienced a tremendous feeling of sadness for her husband. Before, the sadness had always been for herself. She realized that he too must have suffered from the restrictions of their life in Moscow. There was nobody he could talk to intimately. Nobody to share his doubts. Nobody to encourage him to carry on. Like some injured animal he hid his pain and lived from day to day, hoping that some day the wounds would heal. But knowing that they never would.*

*She sat in his leather armchair staring towards the book-shelves as he used to stare. And she knew then why he never could answer when she asked him what he was thinking. She herself didn't know what she was thinking. There was no more room in her head as images crowded in relentlessly. A chalk cross on a wall in dim moonlight, his father sitting in a canvas chair beside the crumbling house in the hills, a pipe and a tobacco pouch on top of a book, a girl's bedroomy voice singing 'You were there – I saw you and my heart stopped beating'. The half-closed, blue eyes of the immigration officer at New York who looked up from her passport to her face as he reached for the telephone.*

*She was still sitting there when the car came for her the next morning. Her cases were stacked alongside the chair but she didn't remember putting them there.*

*A British SIS man had spoken to her in the transit lounge at Heathrow. He had said that his name was McNay and he had asked her questions about Kim. She had refused to answer him, just shaking her head. And when he had persisted she had walked over to an airport policeman and the SIS man had walked away. She realized as she sat down that she was still holding the bunch of red tulips that the KGB man had thrust into her hands at Moscow airport. She walked over to the rubbish bin and threw them in among the cigarette ends and ice-cream wrappers.*

The iron garden-gate squeaked as Powell pushed it open and there was music coming from inside the house. Maria Anders gave piano lessons. She was a Pole with a cockney accent and right from the first lesson you played Chopin.

She had been born in a Polish Army camp in Wales, had been to Warsaw once with a party from the convent where she was educated, and knew full well that when she fell in love with a Pole in SIS she wouldn't ever see Poland again. Chiswick was the next best thing.

She answered the door herself, smiling and beautiful. He had phoned her during the afternoon and asked to see her. She had asked no questions, just told him to come round when he was free. She liked Johnny Powell.

She showed him into the back room. It was an old-fashioned room, good solid furniture and a photograph of Pope John Paul II its only decoration.

'Tad's been sent away, Johnny. I expect you know that?'

'Yes. Have you got a phone number for him in Hong Kong?'

'Yes. He phoned through as soon as he arrived, the day before yesterday.'

'I want you to call him and then put me on the phone.'

She looked at him quizzically. 'Is this all OK, Johnny?'

'Yes, of course.'

'Official?'

Powell shrugged. 'Semi-official.'

'How's Vanessa?'

'She's fine.'

'She still grieving about the little girl?'

'She's up and down, you know. It's not easy for her.'

'Are you two going to get married?'

'I don't think she's ready for another go yet.'

'She likes you a lot you know. She told me. Says you're her rock.'

'That's nice.'

She stood up. 'Let me see if I can get him.'

She walked over to the telephone and he heard her battling her way through the various exchanges. It sounded as if Anders was in a hotel. Finally she got him and there were several explosions of Polish with gaps as she listened. Then she waved him over and handed him the receiver.

'Is that you, Tad?'

'Yes.'

The voice was very faint and there was a lot of static on the line.

'You remember that message you translated for me. The one in Polish?'

'I remember.'

'I understand you did it for McNay too.'

'Did he tell you that?'

'Not directly.'

'Who told you?'

'A friend.'

There was a long pause before Anders replied.

'OK. What's the problem?'

'Did McNay comment on the message at all?'

There was a long gap filled only with static. Powell said, 'Did you hear me, Tad?'

'Yes. I'm thinking.'

'Think hard. It's important.'

'I'm thinking about whether we should be discussing this.'

'I need to know, Tad. I really do.'

'He didn't make any comment.'

'Why did you hesitate answering me then?'

'He didn't comment, but he made an alteration to the text. He had asked me to write it down for him. I only translated it verbally for you.'

'What was the alteration?'

'Are you going to tell him you have spoken to me?'

'Not at this stage. Maybe later.'

'What's going on, Johnny?'

'This is a public line, Tad. I can't say anything. Tell me what he altered.'

'There was the word "harp". He put in a capital aitch.'

255

'Is that all?'

'Yes. Is Maria OK?'

'She's fine.'

'The bastards sent me out overnight.'

'I've got an idea you'll soon be back.'

'Tell me more.'

'I can't. Here's Maria again.'

He handed over the phone and she looked serious as she talked to her husband.

When she hung up she turned to look at Powell.

'He's worried about talking to you.'

'It's OK, Maria. I promise.'

'He trusts you, you know.'

'There'll be no problem. How about you. Have you got any problems?'

'Only a missing husband.'

'I don't think he'll be away long.'

'I pray every day to St Anthony.'

'Who's he?'

'He looks after missing people and things.'

Powell smiled. 'Your old man's not missing, you dope.'

She walked down the garden path with him to the front gate, and she was still standing there, looking after him as he turned back to wave. She waved and blew him a kiss. There weren't many, three at the most, and Maria Anders was one of them. Girls he felt safe with. Warm and at home. But all of them were married. They were all pretty, but that wasn't their real attraction. They were safe girls. Girls who had chosen their man, were satisfied with their choice, and who created an ambience of love that was real enough and broad enough to encompass others too. It would be nice to be loved by a girl like that.

Vanessa was spending the weekend with her parents at a friend's flat in Eaton Place. They were having Lydia for the weekend and he had not been invited. He guessed that Ralph Gower was also going to be there. Not that that would be the only reason that he wasn't invited.

He had arranged to spend the Sunday with the Kenricks and Sammy, and Kenrick was to stay in the flat with him on the Sunday night so that he could catch the early flight to Berlin the following morning.

Powell met them off the train at Charing Cross Station and they took a taxi to the Zoo. Nothing was missed, they watched the lions being fed, and the sea-lions, but for the boy there had been one real delight. They had sat for over an hour in the children's zoo. One of the girls, seeing Sammy in his wheelchair, had brought a lamb for him to look at. She put it on his lap and it settled there as if it were a cat, its slender legs hanging limply each side of his, his arm holding it close to the warmth of his body. Sammy sat still, and the lamb's head drooped, its eyes closed, and from time to time its tail wriggled in its sleep. Not until the small creature eventually woke almost half an hour later, and bleated for its mother, did the small boy stir.

They all had tea at the flat and after they had seen Dolly and Sammy off on the train to Bexhill Powell and Kenrick went to see Woody Allen's *Manhattan*.

Back at the flat, after Kenrick had checked on the telephone that his family were safely home they had settled down for a drink. As Powell sat down he said, 'Has she agreed to see you?'

'Yes, but she hasn't agreed to talk.'

'I think you said that you'd met her before. Or was that somebody else?'

'It was me. I met her a couple of times when she lived with him in London.'

'That was after they were married?'

'Yes.'

'What was Philby doing then?'

'Editing some fascist news-sheet. I've forgotten what it was called.'

'And Litzi?'

'Getting drunk most of the time.'

'You understand what I want?'

'You want to know if she had any contact with him after she left him in 1936? Why did she meet him in Paris in 1939? And her general attitude to him now.'

'Yes. I'd be interested to know if she's seen him since he went to Moscow. And what happened to the man she was with, Honigmann.'

'What was the last you heard about Georg Honigmann?'

'Well, according to the records Litzi lived in Paris after she left Philby, and came back to London with her parents in 1939. Honigmann was openly Communist, so was she, and he worked for Extel's monitoring service during the war. I gather that he was well thought of by our people and they posted him after the war to Hamburg to help set up a German news agency.

'He was never seen again until somebody spotted him in East Berlin working on a newspaper. Litzi was with him. Then apparently they parted and she went to work for the East German film company, DEFA. And Honigmann was running some kind of cabaret.'

'How long can I spend on her?'

'As little as possible. A week at the very outside.'

'Can I give any hint as to why we want this information?'

'Absolutely not. If she asks, tell her that it's just for the record.'

'She's too shrewd to believe that we'd be doing that after all this time.'

'Of course. But she'll know we aren't going to give her any other answer.'

'She'll almost certainly pass it on to the KGB at Karls-horst that I've talked to her.'

'Not necessarily. Especially if you can make her feel that the questions are about her rather than Philby.'

Kenrick was back in three days. He had given a brief written report to Powell, and they met later in Powell's office.

'I gather she was unco-operative?'

'Not entirely. She just wasn't interested in what happened in those days. It was kind of strange. Our great interest in Philby and her indifference. To her he was just a man from way back, one more convert. OK, she married him. So what? She was young and foolish, and he was young and charming, and they were anti-Nazi before it was popular to be anti-Nazi. And she'd recruited a new convert to the cause.'

'Do you think she married him just to recruit him?'

'No. I think it was just a mixture of genuine affection and convenience. The affection waned on both sides and the politics were more important to both of them. Being married was convenient. It gave her protection because she was then a British citizen.'

'How does she think of him now?'

'She doesn't. He's just a man who was in her life over forty years ago. She isn't impressed by what he did for the Soviet Union. Thousands of people have done more was her attitude.'

'And she hasn't seen him recently?'

'No. She agreed that she probably met him in Paris in 1939 but she can't remember why. I'm sure it was genuine. She has lived a life that was constant meetings with fellow workers for Communism and Kim Philby was just one of them.'

'What conditions does she live under?'

'She's obviously done well. Good detached house, nicely furnished, and she's obviously devoted to her job at the film corporation. She's smartly dressed, doesn't look her age, interesting to talk to. Full of questions about Maggie Thatcher and Women's Lib.'

'Still a convinced Communist?'

'Absolutely.' He smiled. 'She started on me. Couldn't understand how anybody could be anything else.'

'Any problems getting over and back?'

'No. I don't know who you spoke to in Berlin but everything went smoothly.'

'Puts it in perspective anyway.'

'How do you mean?'

'We spend so much time thinking about Philby. Speculating on everything he ever did, and yet a woman who was married to him can barely remember those days.'

'I'm sorry that I didn't get more.'

'It was enough. It gave me what I wanted.'

Kenrick stood up, opened his mouth as if he were going to speak and then said nothing.

'What is it?' Powell's eyebrows were raised in query.

'Dotty said to say thank you for Sunday. We've got him a photograph of a lamb and he takes it with him everywhere.'

'I'm glad he enjoyed himself. Can I say something frank, and maybe unkind?'

'Say whatever you like.'

'Don't judge people by how they react to Sammy. You put him up for judgement and get hurt when the response is wrong. You torture yourselves. Take it for granted that everybody feels for him, and for you two. Nobody will be untouched, but not everybody can react in the way you hope. Take it for granted that everybody cares. Parents of children with no problems at all don't always find that their friends see their children as angelic. Remember what W.C. Fields once said – "A man who hates children can't be all bad".'

Kenrick didn't smile, but he nodded. 'There's a lot in what you say. I'll bear it in mind.'

# 25

Lynski had insisted that the meeting should be at Dzerzhinsky Square, not at the new place on the Moscow Ring Road. He was an old KGB hand, respected for past work but seldom consulted these days. But it cost nothing to humour him. Otherwise he would waste time reviling computers and teak office furniture.

The room was one that had been used in the old days for only the most important meetings. Lynski liked the old-fashioned, dark red, flock wallpaper and the heavy curtains at the tall windows.

The men who sat at the table were Vasilyev, Pelsche, Leonov, Paramonov and Lynski himself. They all knew one another well, but there was no love lost between any of them. Personal rivalries, inter-section rivalries, had left their scars over the years. But their acquaintance meant that the meeting could be frank and informal. And already a cloud of blue smoke hung over their heads.

Paramonov looked at his watch.

'Let's get started, comrades. He said if he wasn't here by three we should start. I have been instructed to inform you that there will be no minutes taken at this meeting. We want your frankest opinions.' He looked at Lynski.

'You go first, Alexei Ivanovich.'

Lynski looked around the table at the others. He had no idea of what their views were. Maybe Pelsche would go along with him out of departmental loyalty but it wasn't certain. He lit his cigarette with elaborate concentration and as he closed his lighter he looked at Paramonov.

'I was his contact in London from 1944. I was also his contact in Washington. I was one of the debriefing team in Kuibyshev when he came over. I've known him for many years. He provided useful information. He gave protection to Burgess and Maclean as far as he could. I never had cause to complain.'

Paramonov looked at the older man, half-smiling. 'An excellent summary, Alexei Ivanovich. But I wanted an opinion.'

'I'd like to hear the others' views first, colonel.'

Paramonov sighed and barely hid his irritation as he turned to Pelsche.

'Anatoli Ilyich?'

'I don't see it as possible. Firstly it is an insult to the Soviet Union. Secondly it would be a propaganda victory for the English. Thirdly his request makes me doubt his judgement. Not only today but in the past. I doubt his loyalty too.'

Paramonov nodded to Leonov. 'Nikolai Ivanovich. Your views.'

Leonov stubbed out his cigarette in the metal ashtray.

'There was a time when we had crystal ashtrays, not this sort of junk. A sign of the times I suppose.' He looked at the others, his lips pursed as if he found them wanting in some way. 'We're talking about a man who is sixty-eight in a few months' time. An old man. A man who has served us well for over forty years. He has not been concerned with anything secret, let alone top secret, since he came over the frontier. He has advised us on propaganda and has generally proved both correct in his analysis and successful in advising counter-measures.

'As for London gaining some propaganda victory out of this they haven't even said that they will have him back. If they do agree, they won't publicize it. They have nothing to gain. They looked fools in 1963 when he defected, they would look bigger fools now.' He looked at Pelsche. 'What do you imagine the headlines would be, Anatoli Ilyich? "British traitor comes home" or "The man who fooled us once does it again". It's ridiculous.

'Then to talk about doubting his past loyalty because of this is flying in the face of the facts. He gave us what we asked for. It was always accurate. It's sheer stupidity to talk of disloyalty to the USSR because he wants to die in his own country. He has asked for little enough over the years. Why do *we* exchange our captured agents for theirs? Why don't we just let our people rot in jail? They're no use to us when they're blown. They won't talk. So why the exchanges in Berlin and Helmstedt?'

'What if they put him on trial?' Paramonov raised his eyebrows as he asked the question.

'Can you imagine it, Viktor Viktorovich. A sixty-eight-year-old man comes home to die and they put him in the dock. They won't breathe a word that he's back. They'll insist that he goes back incognito.'

Paramonov looked away, towards Vasilyev. 'And what about you, Vladimir Nikolayevich?'

Vasilyev looked through the smoke curling from his cigarette. He spoke with a Georgian accent that reminded his enemies of Stalin.

'I've attended meetings once a year for the past fifteen years on the subject of Philby. Is he really ours, or is he maybe theirs? We've dug holes for him to fall in but he's never fallen in. If you like him you say, "There's the proof – he's ours." If you don't like him you say it just shows how clever he is. It's the same old syndrome. We Russians don't trust foreigners. No matter who they are. No matter what they do for us. Make them KGB colonels, award them the "Red Banner Order". Fine. But don't trust them.

'You've got no real problem, comrades. You've got two simple choices. Either say no right away, or wait to see what the British decide. If they'll have him back maybe you don't let him go. If they refuse, then make him a "Hero of the Soviet Union", a new, bigger *dacha*, and then forget him for God's sake. I'm sick of these stupid searchings for the truth. He'll be dead in a couple of years. Maybe you should help him on his way.'

Lynski leaned forward to glare at Vasilyev. 'You do me an injustice comrade. When he first approached me on this matter I was very negative towards it. But he makes a case all the same. He points out that he has asked for nothing. This is the only reward he has ever requested.'

'Alexei Ivanovich, you're getting old. Your memory's failing.' The sneer on Vasilyev's mouth was all too obvious. 'I had the three of them. Finding young boys for that drunken oaf Burgess. Getting him out of jail. His old friend Philby wouldn't even go to his funeral. And the drink problems with Maclean. Who had to deal with all that? Me. We waste our time with these interminable meetings. He's not that important for God's sake. I'm getting tired of hearing his name.'

Paramonov looked at Lynski. 'Who's his director these days?'

'Malik.'

Paramonov nodded and sighed. 'Comrades. I suggest we wait events. Let us see what happens and what Malik recommends. There's no hurry. I'm open-minded.'

Lynski at last plucked up his courage.

'I'm prepared to go on the record as recommending that he's allowed to go back. If that's what he wants, and they'll have him.'

In the elevator later, Vasilyev leaned back, an unlit cigarette in his mouth as he looked at Paramonov.

'I could solve the problem for you, Viktor Viktorovich. I wouldn't even ask for a single cartridge.'

Paramonov smiled. 'You'll never make head of department that way, my friend.'

Padmore had phoned him that evening just before he left the office. He was coming to London the next day. It would be nice to have a chat. He would see him at the Reform Club at twelve if that was convenient.

Powell looked at his watch. Vanessa wouldn't be back before nine. He walked down to Central Registry and filled in the chit for Kenrick's 'P' file. It was a thin file and he checked the cover. It was the third of three and he called for the other two and carried them back up to his office.

He sat at his desk reading the first page of file number one.

Kenrick had been recruited into MI6 direct from the merchant bank in 1939. He was then twenty. He had been recommended by a senior, permanent official at the Home Office and one of the partners at the bank. He had married in 1960 and there was a note in brackets referring to a page number in file 2. He read on a few more lines and then turned to the reference page in the second file. The entry was halfway down the page.

... T. J. Kenrick married Angela Stella Mortimer (USA), at Chelsea Registrar's Office, 3 July 1960. (For further details on wife see pages FI (14), F2 (35) and F3 (5).) A male mongol child was born 13 March 1970. The wife deserted Kenrick 29 September 1970 leaving the child with him, and returned to the United States. Kenrick formed a relationship in December 1970 with Dorothy Malins, spinster. She was then a member of a theatrical touring company performing in Hastings over the Christmas period. His wife, a Roman Catholic, has refused a divorce and Miss Malins adopted the name Kenrick and lives with him as his common-law wife. This appears to be a beneficial arrangement for Kenrick and should not be discouraged. (See medical report and consultant's report on Samuel Francis Kenrick. Appendix 34.) A monthly surveillance of his wife has been inaugurated through Special Branch (Insp. Sparrow). No subversive or problem associates noted. The usual regular checks have been made on Miss Malins. No significant indications. The personal situation of Kenrick has precluded several possible promotions as he has indicated that he is unwilling to serve outside the UK for longer periods than ten days. Discussions took place in 1973 with MI5 to consider Kenrick's transfer. They were agreeable to his transfer but the matter was left in abeyance. (See Home Office liaison file 72493 page 197.) There is virtually no possibility of rewarding Kenrick for his long service by promotion, but arrangements were made in 1971 for a supplementary payment of speciality increments under FO/1461/73194 COPSC. There is every indication that Kenrick appreciates the difficulties which the department...

Powell closed the file and looked into the darkness of the room beyond his reading lamp. There were times when his mind had wandered to marriage and a family. But the thought of responsibility for other lives frightened him. There had been tearful scenes with girls who had lived with him, and who had loved him in their own way. They were angry at having mistaken his caring and affection for an intention to marry them. He would be an ideal husband and father, they all said, despite their anger. They didn't recognize, and they couldn't be expected to, the inner fear he hid so well. Like the girls said, he was a loving and caring man, he understood the feelings and emotions of other people to an almost feminine degree, but he couldn't escape the carapace of insecurity that had been wrapped round him in the cardboard box that someone had left on the steps of Berwick Police Station. He could care deeply for those who needed help. And he could offer the help they needed. But he knew that he had to hold out his hand to the emotionally drowning from the bank of the river. If he dived in himself he knew that he would drown too. He sometimes wished that he had the courage to join them in the maelstrom but if you spend all your formative years in an orphanage your instinct for self-preservation is stronger than your instincts for sex, power, money or self-righteousness. He looked again at his watch. It was 9.30. She would be back by now.

But the flat was empty when he got back and it was almost eleven o'clock when he heard her key in the lock.

She was pale, her face tear-stained and her hand trembled as it reached for the drink he poured for her. He waited until she had sipped the whisky and then said, 'What's the matter, Van?'

She sighed deeply, and closed her eyes. 'A terrible, flaming row with the parents.'

'What about?'

'About us.'

'What about us?'

'Living in sin and all that crap.'

'What did you say?'

'The usual incoherent stuff, loosely translated, to mind their own business.'

'What did they suggest?'

'Said I should go back to Ralph. I pointed out that I was no longer in a position to go back. I'm not his wife, I'm his ex-wife. And *he* divorced me, not me him. They're labouring under the delusion that he wants me back.'

He said softly. 'They could be right, Van. I think he's very lonely.'

'What, with all those hunt balls, sitting on the bench doling out justice, the rolling acres to manage, and all those eligible, young, neighbours' daughters swarming round him.'

267

'Why not talk with him. He may have spoken to them and said how much he misses you.'

'All he misses is what I've got between my legs.'

He smiled. 'You could say that about most men you've known but not about Ralph.'

She looked at him. 'And what would *you* miss?'

'You. Us.'

He saw her lips tremble and tears edging down her cheeks. 'You wouldn't marry me would you, Johnny?'

He looked down at his empty glass and then back at her face.

'I don't think I'm the marrying kind, Van. There's a bit missing somewhere.'

'You'd be a nice husband and a smashing father.'

He smiled. 'I think I'm more of an uncle.'

She reached for her handbag, found a crumpled Kleenex and blew her nose. Then half-laughing, half-crying she stretched out her arm. 'Take me to bed.'

# 26

Powell was suddenly awake, his eyes wide open as he lay listening. Something had woken him and he wasn't sure what it was. He could feel the warmth of Vanessa's body beside him, he could hear her breathing, but there was no other sound in the room. He reached out a hand to the bedside table and turned on the alarm clock. The red digital display said 02:47.

He made his way quietly from the bed into the sitting room and through to the kitchen. He filled the kettle and pushed down the switch. Standing waiting he put into the mug the teaspoon of instant coffee and two spoonfuls of sugar. He was pouring in the boiling water when he remembered what had awoken him. It must have come up like a gas bubble from the mud of his subconscious as he slept. He knew now what 'harp' meant in the message on 'Milord's' pad.

Powell waited until McNay had made himself comfortable and then said, 'Tell me about Maclean.'

McNay looked surprised. 'Why Maclean? He's not involved for God's sake. It's Philby we're concerned with.'

'That's for me to decide, Mr McNay.'

McNay opened his mouth to speak, and then decided not to. He merely raised his eyebrows.

'What did you think of Maclean?' Powell asked.

'I had very little to do with him.'

'But you knew enough to have an opinion.'

'About what?'

'Let's say about his importance to the Russians.'

McNay shrugged. 'They all had some value to Moscow, all three of them.'

'Who was the more important to them?'

'Philby, I should think.'

'Why Philby?'

'I suppose you couldn't have a better situation than having one of the most senior officers of the enemy's counter-intelligence organization as your own man.'

'Wouldn't it depend on what he actually provided rather than what he could provide if he chose? A man in that position could decide to feed only what he chose. He could be a barrier in some ways.'

'In what way?'

'You wouldn't risk infiltrating anyone else into his area. There would be no point. But that also means that what he passes on to you is entirely his decision. If he chooses not to pass on something, then you never know what you are missing. You may get only what he thinks you deserve.'

McNay leaned back in his chair. 'What's all this about, Powell?'

'I think Mr Padmore is in favour of letting Philby back. I think Mr Walker is too. I know you are against it. So I wondered if you might reconsider your position if it turned out that Philby was not that important.'

'Nothing would make me change my view. You're wasting your time.'

Neither McNay's voice nor his look was convincing.

'But if I recommend that he is allowed back would you oppose it?'

Powell saw the hesitation before McNay replied and was sure that his suspicions were correct.

'I don't know, Powell. I'd have to think about that.'

Powell stood up. 'Thanks, Mr McNay.'

'Sit down. I want to talk to you.'

270

Powell sat down again, and guessed what was coming.

'You asked Mr Anders to translate a coded message in Polish, Powell?'

'Yes.'

'Why was it done so secretively?'

'It wasn't. It was done in the usual way.'

'Why wasn't it reported?'

'To whom?'

'To the committee.'

'I haven't been doing reports to the committee. You know that. I wasn't asked to, and it was implied that it was better to have as little as possible on the record.'

'Where is your copy of the message?'

'In my files in my office safe.'

'I'd like to have that copy, Mr Powell.'

'But you've got the original, Mr McNay.'

He saw the blood flush into McNay's face and heard the anger in his voice.

'Who told you that? Anders?'

'Why wasn't I told that you had the original page of the pad?'

'It's not relevant to your assignment.'

'Surely that's for me to decide. It was found in "Milord's" desk and he is very relevant.'

'In what way?'

'Because we know that he fingered Philby for the KGB.'

'He's dead. Out of the picture.'

Powell looked at McNay's face, watching carefully for his reaction.

'Not for me he isn't. I'm interested in who wiped him out.'

'You know who it was. The KGB.'

'I don't think so.'

For a moment McNay sat there, his knuckles white as his hands gripped the arms of the chair. Then he stood up abruptly.

271

'This is getting ridiculous, Powell. Maybe you need a rest.'

'That isn't what I need.'

'Oh. What is it you need?'

'I need the truth from all those people who are so busy trying to hide it.'

'I hope you're not referring to me, Mr Powell?'

'If the cap fits, McNay, you bloody well wear it. And I do mean you.'

And his anger wasn't simulated as he banged the door behind him as he left.


Padmore had avoided any talk of Philby as they ate their lunch. It was only when they were sitting in the two deep, corner armchairs that he came to the point.

'How's it going, Johnny?'

'I'm never quite sure, sir.'

'Any particular problem?'

'Always the same one. People don't level with me.'

Padmore's bushy eyebrows rose. 'You mean people are lying to you?'

'No. Just not telling me the whole truth.'

Padmore looked down, brushing some non-existent ash from his paunch.

'I gather you had a bit of a set-to with McNay. What was it all about?'

'Hasn't he told you?'

'I'd like to hear your version.'

'He complained that I hadn't reported a particular item to the committee. I pointed out that I'm not required to report anything except my final recommendation.'

'That's true. That's true. I understand that you suggested that Kim was not the villain he was painted.'

Powell noted the 'Kim'.

'He was a villain all right. I'm just not sure that he was the most dangerous one.'

272

Padmore shrugged his heavy shoulders. 'I don't know that we need to establish a running order for the three of them.'

'Why did SIS have "Milord" killed?'

He saw the surprise and consternation on Padmore's face. The older man held up his podgy hand as if to fend off a blow.

'What makes you think they did?'

'Everything. That's how McNay got the original of that message.'

Padmore's eyes watched his face intently.

'Let's get back to the real matter in hand. Have you made a decision yet?'

'Almost.'

'Which way . . .' Padmore rocked his hand in a see-saw motion. '. . . Which way are you inclined?'

'That we should leave him to rot.'

Padmore looked away towards the window and without turning his head he said softly, 'I wouldn't do that if I were you.'

'Why not?'

Padmore turned his head to look at Powell. His voice was barely audible.

'It would be a mistake, I assure you.'

'Why do we go through all this ritual of me investigating and making the decision. All of you except McNay want him back. Just say so and stop wasting my time.'

'Mr Powell. I think you're bordering on the impertinent.'

Powell looked at Padmore, his eyes angry and his voice harsh as he spoke.

'Padmore, I don't give a sod what you think. But you'll have to find some other stooge to play games with.'

He stood up, reaching for his briefcase from the empty chair between them.

'Sit down, Mr Powell. For heaven's sake don't make a scene in my club. And don't, whatever you do, lose your temper. I'm an old man. I apologize if I was short with you. Please . . .' He pointed at the chair. '. . . Please sit down.'

Powell tossed his briefcase back into the vacant chair and sat down. His face set and grim. Padmore leaned forward confidentially.

'Mr Powell, I want to give you a piece of advice. Advice that I'm not, in fact, entitled to give you. There were certain reasons why you were asked to handle this matter. But nobody had quite expected you to . . . er . . . to go into so much detail.' He held up his hand. 'Don't think for a moment that that is a criticism. Far from it. You are dealing with it as you think fit. And you are an experienced investigator. I'm sure that's why you were chosen. Unfortunately certain, er . . . factors, unexpected factors, have . . . complicated the issue beyond our expectations. Please, please carry on with your assignment.'

'Will you answer me one question truthfully?'

'Of course. If I can.'

'Is it a fact that you would all prefer Philby to come back? With the exception of McNay?'

Padmore sat there, his mouth opening and closing like a gaffed salmon, his right fist thumping on the arm of his chair as he looked at Powell. He brushed his hand across his brow, his fingers pressing his temple for a moment before his hand dropped to his lap.

'I can't answer that directly, Mr Powell. I beg of you to believe me. When all this is over I'll be able to explain. However, let me give you an indirect answer. There are old battles being fought behind the scenes. Useless battles, old prejudices, old rivalries have sprung up to bedevil us all.

'You were never party to those battles, they were long before your time. And that is precisely why you were chosen both as the executive arm of the "Milord" committee and for your present assignment. The only hope, the only chance, of putting those old rivalries to rest, is the assurance

274

to all concerned that you have not been influenced in your decision. Had it not been for this ... this internecine warfare, the matter would have been dealt with quite differently. A simple decision, yes or no to Philby's return.

'But who was to make the decision. Nobody who is senior enough to make the decision is not tainted by the past. Honest, loyal, and patriotic men distrust each others' judgement on this issue. If I should attempt to persuade you one way or another it would be unforgiven and unforgivable. Those concerned who are at the top agreed to accept your decision whatever it may be. That would be the end of it.'

'But you and others *have* tried to influence me. Not directly perhaps but by subtle indications.'

Padmore looked down at his big wrinkled hands, clasped between his plump legs, their backs covered with the tea-leaf stains of age. When he lifted his head he looked directly at Powell.

'That, Mr Powell, is because some of us know more than others and are not at liberty to divulge what we know.'

'Why?'

'Because, like you, we have all signed that bit of paper referring to the Official Secrets Act.'

'But between the intelligence services themselves surely it doesn't apply.'

Padmore sighed. 'In this case it does.'

'Is this the old fight about Philby between MI5 and SIS?'

'I must leave that for you to work out.'

'If there *is* something that could satisfy MI5's fears surely they could have been told way back.'

'There would have been security risks. And risks to a man's life. Perhaps to more than one man, if they had been told right at the start. And it would have been uncalled for. There was genuinely no reason why they should have been informed in those days, even if no risks had been involved.

It was not in their area by any stretch of the imagination. The need for them to know later on was entirely fortuitous, and impossible for even the wisest man to have foreseen. I assure you that this is so. I have attended dozens of small meetings to consider and reconsider the matter. Wise counsel from trusted, capable men always indicated that MI5 should not be told. Most of the clues are there, in the public domain. I have sometimes feared that you would uncover them. I still fear it.'

As Powell looked at Padmore he realized that the blue eyes might be watery but they were shrewd eyes, and, he would guess, honest eyes.

'I wish I'd known this before, Mr Padmore.'

'I've thought about you a lot, my boy, in these past weeks. It was like watching the re-run of some old film. The same plot, the same characters, and as so often happens with old films, out of their time you wonder how the damn things ever got made.'

'Can I ask you one more thing?'

'Of course.'

'If I knew what you know would it make my decision inevitable?'

Padmore closed his eyes. There was a long pause and then he said, 'Not inevitable. Let me correct that statement. It would make your decision morally inevitable. I put it no higher than that.'

'How could there be any other decision if there was a morally inevitable one?'

Padmore was nodding his head. 'You might well ask, Mr Powell. But you don't need me to point out that morality in normal civilized terms is not the only consideration in what *was* my kind of business and is still yours.'

'Can you give me any guidance?'

Padmore shook his head vigorously.

'I can't do that. I've explained why.'

'A signpost perhaps, in the general direction.'

The old man got clumsily to his feet and as he stood there he rocked very gently on his feet as he thought. Finally he turned to Powell.

'No. But I'll tell you this. I think you've got all the pieces of the jigsaw. You're just trying to press some of them into places where they don't belong.'

He held out his hand, and as Powell took it he felt warm towards him for the first time. He must have been a good father for his three children. And Powell set great store by good fathers.

He followed Patrick Walker into the elegant sitting room and Walker pointed to a chintzy armchair and walked over to the hi-fi on the broad white shelf below the book shelves. He stood waiting, with the lid of the record-player open. It was Gertie Lawrence and Jack Buchanan singing 'Fancy our meeting', and when it ended Walker lifted the arm and switched off the deck. As he turned he smiled and said, 'It's funny that for you that's just a song, but for me, and the others, it brings it all back.'

'What does it make you think of?'

Walker sat down, making himself comfortable, leaning back, his long legs outstretched.

'The whole period. Being young. Girls in white tennis dresses, long hot summers, white flannels with green stains on them, the Left Book Club, the *New Statesman*, Penguins and *Picture Post*. Harry Roy, Bert Ambrose, Jack Buchanan, and nice gentle songs with lyrics you could understand.' He waved his hand, his face softened by the pleasurable memories. 'It's hard to explain. It was the end of an era. The last romantic years.'

'And the war finished it?'

'Not really. The war emphasized it if anything. It was the war *ending* that finished it. It hardened everything up. One

277

still gets glimpses of those days. A distant view through the trees.'

'Tell me.'

'Oh, the last night of the Proms. That always warms me when I see it on television. All those young people, their enthusiasm, their faces so eager and innocent, so full of promise. We were like that in those days. My generation, Philby's generation. Then somebody somewhere pulled the curtain aside and showed us what it was really like. It spoilt it all.' He smiled and shrugged. 'The dream became a nightmare and we all reacted in our different ways.'

'What was the dream?'

Walker smiled and looked towards the window. It seemed a long time before he looked back at Powell.

'That it was possible for everyone to be happy. That the politicians would right the wrongs, or at least try to. That a glance from a certain girl at a tennis club dance could give you pleasure for a month. That doing good would actually *do* good.'

'And the nightmare?'

'Ex-soldiers, with one arm or one leg, selling matches in the streets. Nearly three million unemployed. Dole at 12/6 a week being cut. Coal miners starving on one hand, and people shivering because they had no coal on the other. All that brought total disillusionment.'

'With whom?'

'The whole damn set-up. The politicians whose only concern was staying in power. The feeling that the people who ran the country were there to ensure that capital and property were protected. The feeling that capitalists were merciless, and that workers were exploited. And day after day the realization that they weren't just fears, they were facts.'

'But why did it happen so suddenly?'

Walker shifted to make himself comfortable, as if he needed time to sort out his answer.

'I guess it was the Left Book Club and the *New Statesman* that did it. They took us behind the scenes. We discovered what it was really like. They told us the other side of the story. MPs who voted for rearmament who had shares in arms factories. Vested interests everywhere. And when we looked for ourselves we found that they were right. We wanted to put it right but we didn't know how to. Some saw Mosley as the answer, and some saw Moscow as the shining light. There wasn't much choice. None of the traditional political parties was worth a damn.'

'Why not the Labour Party?'

'They seemed just as divided and corrupt as the Tories. And when Ramsay MacDonald walked out on the Labour Party and headed a National government after Labour were routed at the election, that was it. And by that time the Nazis in Germany were polarizing opinion everywhere, particularly in this country. Half of Labour were totally pacifist and anti-war, and the other half were beginning to look to Moscow.'

'Which way did you look?'

Walker smiled and shrugged.

'I didn't join anything, because I'm not a joiner. But people whose views I respected saw Moscow as the only hope. I went along with that, but passively not actively. I was a bit like the believer who never goes to church.'

'What kind of people's opinions influenced you?'

'The Webbs, Shaw, Strachey, Kingsley Martin – there were dozens of them. Most of them changed their minds about the Soviet Union once they'd been there and seen what was going on, but that took time. We were all looking for life-belts. John Strachey, Harold Nicholson and Joad all joined Mosley's New Party first. But Joad ended up as a pacifist, and John Strachey became a leading Marxist.'

'Why did Cambridge become such a hot-bed of Communism?'

'Oh that was because there were hard-line, dedicated Communists there. Some of them openly so, others beavering away behind the scenes.'

'You think Philby was much the same as you?'

'He certainly was in the early days. He was academically much brighter than I was. He was right in amongst the Communists, but Kim Philby wasn't influenced much by people, he was influenced by facts. His circle was largely homosexual but I doubt if he was. He wasn't a joiner either, he was a loner. He was like his old man but a hell of a lot brighter.'

'So why did he stick with Moscow if he was that bright? Why didn't he change his mind like the others when he found out what was going on?'

'I can't be sure, but I'd say that he was influenced because the Russians were fighting the Nazis. He had no doubts about the Nazis, he'd seen them first-hand, at work in Vienna.'

'But you didn't need to be a traitor to support the Red Army.'

Walker smiled. 'You do if you're a romantic. And you justify it on the grounds that they were, after all, our allies. Fighting the same war against the same enemies.'

'You think those were the only reasons?'

'Of course not. That wouldn't explain the post-war treason.'

'So what do you think explains that?'

'The facts of life, my friend. The facts of life.'

'Tell me.'

'What do you imagine the response would have been if he had told his KGB control that now the war had ended he was opting out?' Walker shrugged. 'He was stuck. They'd got enough on Kim that they could leak back to SIS to land him in Wormwood Scrubs for thirty years. He wouldn't have had any choice but to go along with them. When you're riding on the tiger's back you don't get off.'

'Were Maclean and Burgess much the same?'

'Not really. They were both brighter than Kim intellectually, but much weaker characters. They couldn't stand the pressures that Kim had. The homosexuality and the drinking were typical. They were both arrogant men. Upper-class and snobby. The kind of men that Kim would normally have despised. But it was war time, there were wild parties; those were probably the only times that he met Burgess. But like many of their kind they had charm. And nobody could have believed that a man who behaved so outrageously in public as Burgess could possibly be a Soviet agent. He looked like just a perennial deb's delight gone to seed.'

'Do you feel sympathetic towards Philby?'

'Yes. I do. I suppose I say to myself, "There but for the grace of God go I etcetera". And a good many others from SIS will think much the same.'

'Despite the treachery?'

'I couldn't justify it, Johnny. I wouldn't *try* to justify what he did. It was unforgivable. But it's a bit like the prodigal son. I could push the treachery into the back of my mind. If he's guilty then I share at least part of his guilt.'

'In what way?'

'I thought much the same thoughts as he did. I shared his views but I didn't have the guts to do anything about it. I played safe.'

'Maybe you weren't as arrogant as he was. Deciding yourself that other men should die because it suited Soviet ends.'

Walker smiled. 'That's what I sometimes tell myself when I think about it all. But it ain't the whole answer. It still took guts to do what he did. It won't look like that to outsiders. To them it's all blacks and whites, I see it differently.'

'Despite what the Soviet Union has turned out to be?'

'Yes. Despite that. That's hindsight. You've got to judge him on the times as they were. He could have been caught.' He shrugged. 'Rosie's put out some lunch for us if you'd like a bite.

'Thanks.'

'You're finding this a great problem, aren't you?'

'Yes. I am.'

'I told Padmore you were the wrong man for this job right at the start.'

'Why did you think that?'

Walker smiled. 'Don't look so put down. It was a compliment. You've got great perception, my boy. That's why you've got on so well in SIS. You've got that rare ability to look into the other man's mind. You'd make a good judge. But what we needed on this was somebody ambitious, open to influence. Somebody who could read the signs with promotion in mind. Somebody who would see when he was being guided and pressured towards a certain decision. And who'd go along with what his elders and betters desired. Instead of which we landed ourselves with a sea-green incorruptible who took us at our public word instead of reading between the lines.'

Powell half-smiled. 'I suppose you could always take me off the assignment.'

Walker stood up. 'I'm afraid not. It's gone too far for that. You're the last hope of the anti-Philby squad.'

'They could be right.'

Walker nodded. 'That's the rub. They could. Let's go and eat.'

He looked around the restaurant. It reminded him of the Café Royal. But it wasn't the Café Royal, it was the restaurant of the Hotel Ukraine. It was beautiful, dignified and peaceful. And he loathed it.

It wasn't that he disliked Slatkin or Malik or even that the

282

conversation bored him. The food was magnificent, Georgi Malik would have seen to that. He just wanted to get away and sort out his thoughts.

Malik reached across the table and offered him one of his Havana cigars. He took it, smiling, but he wanted to scream.

It was an hour before Malik dropped him in Red Square. The wind was cold as he stood there in the April sunshine. The long, high, outer walls of the Kremlin were bathed in a golden light that made them look like a gigantic stage set for some new ballet by Glière. He took a deep breath because it was the only thing he could think of doing to stop himself weeping. And why he should want to weep on a sunny April day he had no idea.

He walked slowly to the far side of the Square. Slowly, because he was tired. He knew where he was going.

They were cutting the grass on the lawns as he got there. It must be the first cut of the year. And there was a barrow with pot plants to put along the top of the granite blocks. The blocks contained soil from the six Russian cities that were battered by the Nazis. Beyond them was the stone pathway and the sunken grave. The flame was burning vigorously, orange-red in the early afternoon light. Inside the grave were the remains of a young man who had died defending Moscow in the war.

On the far side was a wooden bench and he walked to it, turning up his coat collar against the wind. He sat there for nearly two hours in the sunshine and only left when the shadows from the trees made him colder than he could bear.

It had started with the girl at the party. She had touched his face gently with her long fingers and said that he looked sad. Sad, she said, like Marcello Mastroianni in *Una giornata particolare*. When he asked her what the film was about she had kissed him gently without passion and said it was about a man who was an anti-Fascist. It took place on a day in Rome when Hitler was visiting Mussolini. The man was ill at ease amongst so much Fascist display. And, she added, he was a queer, but a very handsome queer.

For those two hours on the bench by the grave of the Soviet Unknown Soldier he thought long and hard but to no purpose. The purpose only came when he stood up, and for one fleeting, electrifying moment he thought that he was in St James's Park and he turned to go back to Ryder Street.

Very few men can sit down and realistically consider their lives. Weigh the worth in the balance of their actions and reactions. Men are mercifully not given to such introspection unless it is part of their framework as philosophers, psychiatrists, priests or poets. And Kim Philby was none of those. But his malaise had been with him for almost a year. Not the heavy cloud of a deep depression. More a black dog that followed behind him, haunting his footsteps, ready to run whenever he turned angrily, but always slinking back to fall in a few yards behind him.

Nothing he had done all those years since the thirties had been irrational. His life had had the central discipline and dedication that he had committed himself to those long years ago. He had seemed to succeed beyond his wildest dreams. But somehow, some part of his mind would no longer accept the facts, the success, or even the dreams. What other people said, what he said out loud himself, had become like one of those biographies that look at a man's life-work but not at his life.

He had always accepted his father's precept that you had to be independent of all other people. And he had recognized right from the start that that meant sacrificing people. They had to be abandoned and deceived for a greater good. But when, in the last few months, his mind had gone over the long list of the sacrifices it seemed somehow a sad and tatty list. They had been easy targets, virtually defenceless, their only weapon the withdrawal of their affection and love. Only a few had utterly succumbed to the pain and the anguish, most of them had put a brave face on it. The terrible, ice-cold thought had recently crept into his mind that he too had put a brave face on it. And might still be putting a brave face on it.

Sometimes he woke sweating and crying out from a dream. It was always the same dream. He was standing in a clearing in a wood where two paths crossed. And the children were walking away from him. Always he called after them but they never heard, and he would run to them on leaden feet, never closing the gap between them. And then their screaming as he came out of his dream, and never knowing what had happened or why they had screamed.

Awake he could rationalize. He had seldom seen his own father but he had still loved him. And surely he had been right to make the sacrifice and leave the children in a stable background. They were friendly and caring on their brief visits now they were older, but was that just their own goodness? Was it even pity rather than love.

All he had ever wanted to do was make things better in England. To save it from predators, to give the hopeless some hope, and the helpless some protection. To do that he had had to do other things. Until the Nazi evil had been smashed history had to stand still. And it was Maclean who had said the dreadful words late one night. He had said that they had tried to put the clock back, to stop the world while things were rearranged. And they had failed, because it couldn't be done. They had both agreed that they would never regret the attempt. He still didn't regret it. There was a phrase from the Bible that always came into his mind – 'and Christ ascended into heaven'. That was what he would like to do. Not die. Just ascend into heaven.

He sometimes remembered a comment of Aileen's when they had spent a week in Vermont. She had said it was just like England; he had been irritated, and said that maybe it was the other way round. And why did everywhere have to be compared with England. But he had done it only the day before himself, in Sokolniki Park: walking with Malik, he'd said it was like a cross between Hyde Park and Battersea Park and the words had gone on ringing in his ears for hours.

He knew that he wanted to go back. But why? What did he want so much? The things that came to his mind were so small. After all that he had risked and done his dream was no higher than a cottage and roses. Bookshops and news-papers, daisies and dandelions. And if that was all he wanted he could have them a few miles out of Moscow. But he knew in his heart what he wanted. Donald Maclean had known. He wanted to put the clock back. Not to do things differently or to tread a different path. He just wanted to go back to square one. To be young, not old. To be hopeful, not cynical. To be undecided, not despairing. To care, but not know.

It wouldn't work. It couldn't work. But what he had now didn't work either. Maybe nothing would ever work for him again. He'd just have to go on with the same old act until they put the kopeks on his eye-lids. He wished very much he had a father. Or even a friend.

# 27

McNay's home was in Tunbridge Wells, in the centre of the town, but in a row of similar Georgian houses that swept in a sheltered curve around one corner of a park. There was a barred gate to the private road that stood open on that Sunday morning.

They were all elegant houses but some were less well looked after than McNay's, which gleamed white, its iron-work unchipped, its windows sparkling in the morning sunlight.

Until he had read through McNay's 'P' file he hadn't realized that McNay was married, with a son who was a barrister and a daughter who was a freelance journalist.

McNay himself answered the door and led him through the hall to a sitting room that gave on to a conservatory. Covering the glass roof was an old, well-established vine, heavy with bunches of green grapes, its broad green leaves giving shade to the rows of house plants that were ranged on the slatted staging. Two bamboo chairs with flowered cushions had been placed side by side by a white, wrought-iron garden table, set out with all the paraphernalia of coffee-making and drinking.

The man himself seemed entirely different in his home setting. Not only more relaxed, but charming and amiable, and attentive. He was casually dressed in a check shirt, slacks and sandals without socks.

'Maggie's away in Canterbury with one of her theatre groups, and the children are both away. James is on some golfing thing of the Law Society, and Fleur's interviewing

287

some fading pop star in Paris. I'll have to do my best for us. Sugar?'

'Please.'

'One or two?'

Powell laughed. 'Three if I may.'

Powell wondered if Padmore had had a word in McNay's ear warning him not to be too obstreperous. McNay wasn't going to like a lot of what he had to say so he was determined not to inhale the hospitality too deeply. When McNay sat down with his own coffee he turned to Powell.

'I'm sorry to have dragged you down here, but I thought when you said you wanted to talk to me that it might be better if we talked away from the office and London in general.'

'I'm glad you did. It's much pleasanter to talk down here and I think you could help me.'

'Good. Now tell me how I can help.'

'Almost everybody I've spoken to about Philby has had mixed feelings about him. They felt that maybe he had been badly treated or that there was some mysterious explanation for his treason. You are the only one who has been categorical in his criticism. For you he is a traitor, and that's the end of the matter. When I started this assignment I had a completely open mind.

'After I had read the files my view was much the same as yours. He was a traitor and the evidence was there. Otto John, Volkov, Albania, and Maclean and Burgess. Apart from that he had boasted in public at a press conference in Moscow that he had been a Soviet agent for years. He also wrote an autobiography that said the same things.

'But after I had talked to a lot of people I began to have doubts. Not about whether he had done these things, he clearly had. But there was obviously insufficient evidence to put him on trial and be certain of convicting because he had

288

been careful to cover his tracks. And the people who knew him, who worked with him, were still reluctant to condemn him. They weren't just romantics, or too susceptible to charm, they were experienced men, men who know what's going on behind the scenes. And then always that final mystery. Why did SIS, after all that was known and suspected, still get him on to the *Economist* and *Observer*, use him themselves, and keep contact with him in Beirut? Not for a short time but for years. Just over six years in fact. If he was suspect why was he used, and if he had done half of what it appeared he had done, why wasn't he found dead in some backstreet?

'So I've done the full circle and I've only found two people who are cast-iron in the views on Philby. One is an American, ex-CIA, and the other is you. Now on my analysis I feel that the American knows too little of the whole picture to judge, but in your case that doesn't apply. You were around when it all happened. You saw him at work, you met him daily. So why are you the one exception?'

McNay scratched the side of his face and then reached out and moved a pot with a blue cineraria a few inches to the right before he spoke.

'I think you've already answered it, Johnny. He did those things and that's enough for me. And as you say, he's a self-confessed traitor boasting that he was a KGB officer right from the start.'

Powell took a deep breath. 'Mr McNay, I'm sorry to have to say this, but I don't believe you.'

McNay half-smiled. 'You don't have to agree with me Johnny.'

'I didn't say that I don't *agree* with you. I said I don't *believe* you.'

'What does that mean?'

'It means I think you're not telling me the truth.'

McNay shrugged and smiled. 'That's your privilege, Johnny.'

'Why did you send Anders to Hong Kong?'

'There was work for him to do there.'

'Why didn't you inform me about the message on "Milord's" pad?'

'I understand that you already had the details.'

'Not true, Mr McNay. You didn't know that until Anders told you that he'd translated the same message for me.'

'Well, you had the information, and that's all that matters.'

'Do you remember the message, Mr McNay?'

'The gist of it, not the exact words.'

Powell reached in his pocket, pulled out a sheet of paper and unfolded it.

'. . . no possible doubt we came second to harp stop at least two years late stop . . .'

He looked up at McNay as he folded the paper and slid it back in his jacket pocket. 'What was it all about?'

'I've no idea.'

'What does "harp" mean?'

McNay gave a short laugh. 'This sounds a bit like an interrogation rather than a chat.'

'You know what "harp" means, McNay.'

'What makes you think that?'

'Because *I* know what "harp" means. So I know that you know.'

'Are you claiming to be psychic too?'

'No. But when Anders wrote out the translation for you you put a capital aitch on "harp". That's why I know you know.'

'What's the significance?'

'Because "Harp" is Philby. They're his initials. Harold Adrian Russell Philby.'

290

McNay looked back at Powell, his face still and impassive, and he said very quietly, 'I'm not going to be able to assist you any further, Mr Powell.'

'You recruited Philby didn't you?'

McNay smiled. 'If you read his "P" file carefully you'll find that it was Guy Burgess who recommended Philby to Section D. Burgess was already in Section D.'

'I'm not talking about that recruitment.'

'If you want to go further back than that I imagine you would have to go back to "Milord".'

'No, I'd go back two years before "Milord", to when you recruited him and planned the rest of the scenario.'

'If that was the case then why have we been wasting our time on "Milord" all these years? Were we all wrong, including you?'

'No. "Milord" only looked him over for the Soviets after he got a tip-off from the Communists in Vienna.'

'So?'

'And you had recruited him for *us* two years before that. You wanted him to penetrate the Soviet intelligence service. You put him out as bait and the Soviets took it.'

'More coffee, Johnny?'

Powell sighed. 'Please don't let us go on playing games, Mr McNay.'

McNay looked at him and said softly, 'How can I help you?'

'Tell me what happened right from the start.'

McNay looked along the rows of potted plants, reaching out his hand, slowly pulling a yellow leaf from a geranium, slightly turning the chipped saucer that held a cyclamen in a pot. Powell sat quietly, almost afraid to breathe, knowing that in the next few moments it would all be decided. If McNay talked, that would be the end of the matter. He would know what to do. If McNay refused to talk, or maintained his old charade, that would equally be the end. A different ending but certainly the end. He wondered what thoughts, what memories were going through McNay's mind. What would make him decide whether to talk or stay silent. It was no longer than a couple of minutes before McNay turned his head to look at Powell, but it seemed like a life-time. In some ways it was.

'You're right,' he said softly. 'I recruited Kim Philby long before the Russians got to him. Communism was rampant at Cambridge and we needed to know what was going on. That's all it was meant to be when we started. He was sympathetically disposed to them but he wasn't in any way convinced or committed. We had chats. He kept me informed. It worked so well that we gave him some basic training and staked him out in the hope that the Russians would see him as suitable material for what was then the NKVD. It worked, as you know. He was noticed in Vienna and was contacted immediately he got back here by Harpenden and others. We advised him on every move. The rest you know.'

'Do you mean that he's still ours?'

'I've no idea. Neither has anybody else. That's the problem. We put him into the Soviet network deliberately. Some of what he passed to them was on our instructions. A lot of it wasn't. He undoubtedly gave away vital secrets but he gave us information about them too. Damaging stuff and definitely not planted. We set traps to try and find out. He didn't fall into them. By 1943 we didn't know whether he was ours or theirs.'

'Or maybe both.'

'Exactly.'

'When did you decide who he belonged to?'

'We never did. There was no way of finding out. We could have proved that he was passing information to the Soviets. Even well enough to satisfy a court. But that was what he was there for. We had trained him to do it. We supplied the information. That would have been his defence, and it would have been a perfectly good one. What he did beyond that, we couldn't prove. Still can't. As you know we sent out Walker to Beirut to see if we could nail him one way or another. It was the same old scenario. He was working for us – on minor things only. And we knew he was working for the KGB as well – and on minor things only.'

'So why did he skip?'

'We put too much pressure on him. The interviews with Milmo, the sacking, putting Walker on to him. And then Walker finally confronting him with the information that Dolnytsin gave us when he defected in Helsinki in 1961. Once Dolnytsin's information had enabled us to arrest George Blake Kim must have known he was going to be connected. So he was left in the position that we were not only suspicious but might be ready to grab him. The Russians were mildly suspicious about his relationship with us but not pressing. So he had to decide. He didn't really have much choice. He chose Moscow. And then he was committed.'

'Did he ever get in touch with SIS after he went to Moscow?'

'Yes. Twice.'

'What happened?'

'The first contact was through an old friend of his, a Labour MP. Just a message to indicate that there was no reason why the old arrangement shouldn't go on.'

'How did we respond to that?'

'It was ignored, and he then gave the press conference in Moscow. The second contact was a letter from him, posted in England, postmarked Sheffield. It was bitter and angry at the lack of response to the first message and claimed that we had sold him down the river. He accused me specifically.'

'Had we?'

'God knows, Johnny. How could we tell? He was an

officer in SIS, he had been set up for the Soviets and they took him on. He was working for both sides. And both sides knew it. But for years both services thought that their bit was the real bit. They both thought he was loyal to them. When he bolted to Moscow it looked as if he had decided the issue once and for all. But they wouldn't have caused all that upheaval when they kidnapped Otto John and interrogated him about Philby if they really trusted him. Neither side trusts him now. And yet . . .'

'Yet what?'

'He says he wants to come back. He's sixty-eight. He can't do any damage. Why should he want to come back after all this time if he's totally guilty. We took a young man with strong socialist feelings. Told him to play games with the Russians. Gave him an OBE for his genuine services. Then he's exposed by old Lipton in the House. The Foreign Secretary exonerates him publicly. He's sacked, given a tin handshake and left to rot by the Russians and ourselves for two years. I heard that the poor bastard was selling toothpaste at one time. We eventually find him a job in Beirut. Partly out of guilt on our side. Pay him a retainer, and then send out Walker to corner him. He must have wondered himself which side he was on. Finally he gives up the ghost and does a bolt. Who can blame him?'

'So why were you always against him coming back. So angry about him?'

'I had to. I had to appear totally against him. Because I started it all off. I got him into it. The Russians must have wondered why we exposed him, then cleared him, then dropped him, then used him, and finally let him get away. They must have wondered a hundred times if we hadn't just been terribly cunning and planted him on them again. There was so much covering up for him in public, and so many people still willing to keep contact with him that Moscow must inevitably have wondered what the hell was going on. I

294

did my best to show that there were people here in the know who saw him as an out and out traitor. I had to do that with you too. The KGB could have been contriving this whole damn thing just to have one last go to find out if he really was our man.'

'Has any thought been given to what would happen if he came back?'

'Yes. A lot. We should want an undertaking that he comes back incognito. New name, new background, no contacts with anybody. A small pension and, if necessary, some plastic surgery. A cottage has already been unofficially bought for him in Wales.'

'I've no doubt he'll agree to any conditions that we lay down. And once he's back he'll know that even one false step would be his last.'

'It'll have to be your decision. You know the old rivalry. MI5 never wavered. To them he was always suspect. They assumed that SIS protected and defended him just because he was SIS. They didn't know the facts.'

'Will they be told now?'

'That's for Sir Ian to decide.'

'And the Prime Minister.'

'Who suggested that for God's sake?'

'I forget, somebody said it at one of the early committee meetings.'

'That was probably to keep you happy. Let's not pretend. Sir Ian will not, repeat not, inform MI5 or anyone else. The only people who will know are you, me, Padmore and Walker. The papers will be destroyed.'

'And if anything goes wrong the whole saga will start all over again.'

McNay looked at him. 'We had in mind you would write a report to Sir Ian. Top copy only. We'll put it in a bank locker. You and he can have the keys. No record anywhere else. When one of you dies the other destroys the only copy.

295

If Philby dies first, which is almost certain, the copy is destroyed with both parties as witnesses.'

'It's a pity I couldn't have been told this at the beginning.'

'We couldn't, Johnny. Almost certainly the KGB has some idea of what's going on. They know your name, that you've been in contact with him in Moscow. You've probably been watched and ...' He shrugged '... there are still Soviet stooges in the establishment. It's maybe a matter of life or death to Philby that they see him the right way.'

'The Russians may feel that they lose face this way.'

'I don't think so, Johnny. They'll not want any mention of it, no more than we do.'

'Why has it all been such a problem?'

'Because the three of them were exceptions. It won't ever happen again. It isn't possible. The times will never be like those times again.'

Powell looked at him quizzically. 'That can't be true. You and I know better than that. They've got their stooges still, at all levels. We both know their names. We've both seen the evidence.'

McNay shook his head. 'They're not the same, Johnny. Not by a long chalk. The present lot want to destroy the whole of our society. They want to bring us to our knees. They want a Bolshevik Britain and they don't mind how they do it. They want power for themselves in the new deal. Those three never wanted that, or anything like it. They just wanted their own idea of fair play. And the whole scene has changed since then. Unions and workers are no longer downtrodden and begging for work. They put in for pay rises that they know will cause lay-offs and redundancies. They want huge pay rises without working harder, and if it's necessary they'll do what they did last winter. Leave the dead unburied and the critically ill to die. Last winter was the end of an era. We saw the unacceptable face of union power when trades-union leaders told the government how they would govern, until even that complaisant government had had enough. And the country decided it had had too much. It wasn't just the Tories who said enough, it was the workers themselves. Most young men in the thirties felt like Philby and the other two did. I did myself. Fortunately, most young men weren't in a position to do what those three did. It all looked so clear-cut in those days. It looks very different today. The Sakharovs, the Solzhenitsyns have evened the balance. Those three weren't looking for power for themselves, or money, or any material reward. They didn't get it anyway. But the bastards who are doing the same thing today are after personal power and money.'

'Were you ever tempted?'

McNay smiled. 'No. You need a kind of special arrogance to do what they did. They wanted to play God and put the world right. They didn't succeed, of course. Nobody ever will.'

'Why not?'

McNay shrugged. 'Because people will go on being people. Refusing to do what they don't want to do, no matter how many times they're shown that it's better for them some other way. It isn't hydrogen bombs that will break up the Soviet Union.'

'What will it be?'

McNay smiled. 'Georgians and Kazakstanis who hate Russians. Poles and Czechs who hate all of them, and peasants who grow a few potatoes and flowers in some corner of a collective farm and sell them in the cities. Ezra Pound got it right, he said something about "Governments – Communists, Republicans and Democrats couldn't make a hen-coop. Only men can do that".'

'Why do the Soviets tolerate him discussing coming back?'

McNay shrugged. 'Heaven alone knows. So long as it's not publicized in any way they're probably glad to see the back of him. Maclean's no problem. Burgess is dead. Philby's just an old man. He's no use to them now, he's completely out of touch after all this time.'

'How much *did* he matter?'

'Not much. You were right. Maclean was the one who mattered. That's why they were prepared to sacrifice Kim's cover to get Maclean out. They weren't expecting Burgess to tag along with him.'

'Did "Milord" recruit Maclean too?'

'No. That was someone else.'

'Who?'

McNay shook his head. 'Keep out of it, Johnny. Leave it alone.'

'Somebody still alive?'

'Very much so.'

'Why don't we pull him in?'

'No proof. Same as "Milord".'

'Why don't we knock him off?'

'The good Lord's doing the job. He's dying of cancer.'

'I'll have to put something on paper to justify what I'm doing and to give me the authority to do it.'

'You could duck the responsibility by calling a last meeting of the "Milord" committee, submitting your recommendation, and asking for the committee's approval.'

'If I did that we'd be back to square one. The three of you would be left carrying the can.'

'Does that matter?'

'If that had been the best solution then you could have all just told me to go and bring him back right at the start. The three of you could still be accused of covering up for him again. And you still wouldn't be able to tell them the truth of why you're willing to let him come back.'

McNay said softly, 'Why do you think that we are willing to let him come back?'

'Because you set him up to do something in good faith.

Probably good faith on his part as well as yours. At some point it went beyond what you intended. He was like some actor who gets rave notices for playing some character and in the end the character takes over. You told him to play "footsie" with Moscow and he did. You took for granted that he was under your control. But your horse bolted with the bit between his teeth and everybody thought he was still play-acting. So in moral terms you've never been able to apportion how much guilt was his and how much was yours.'

McNay half-smiled. 'Despite the mixed metaphors that's about it. Were we just fools or guilty fools? None of us knows.'

'I don't think Philby knows either.'

'And you can probably include the KGB in that too.'

'I don't think that the KGB lose much sleep about guilt.'

'Maybe not. So what are you going to do?'

'I'll go and fetch him back. I'll need one of you to get me genuine documents under another name for him. One of you will take him over from me and that will be that. I won't know where he is or what he's doing. It will be up to the three of you.'

'What about Sir Ian?'

'I'll do a report justifying my decision. There'll be only one copy. It's up to the four of you what you do with it.'

'You'll be dependent on Kim's goodwill with the KGB.'

'I assume I can trade bodies with them if necessary.'

'With some reservations, yes. But they may just give a flat "Nyet".'

'If they do it may take a bit longer but I'll get him out one way or another. We've got a team . . .'

McNay held up his hand. 'Don't tell me, Johnny. I don't want to know.'

'Why didn't SIS remember that he was married to a Communist?'

'We did remember of course. It fitted our scenario perfectly

299

so far as the Soviets were concerned. When the press got on to it later we just had to keep our mouths shut. We couldn't give away the fact that we put him out for the Russians deliberately and therefore being married to Litzi was a plus not a minus. We had to grin and bear it for Kim's sake.'

'Why was he taken back and sent to Beirut when you knew he was guilty of treason?'

'Two reasons. First of all you've got to realize that Kim was in fact only sacked because of his friendship with Guy Burgess who had done a bolt. Milmo's interrogation was later, and it was inconclusive. When Sir John Sinclair became the new "C" he felt that Philby had been treated very badly. And he knew nothing of the real background. He saw Philby as a victim of a vendetta by MI5 and the press. He gave the instructions for Kim to be found something in the Middle East that wasn't sensitive but would earn him a living.'

'Why did it take so long to uncover him once Burgess and Maclean had confessed in Moscow?'

'They never did confess. The record shows that. It's a myth that they confessed. They defected in 1951; they didn't give the press conference until 1956. They didn't answer questions, they just circulated a statement. And they and the Russians claimed that neither of them had ever been spies. Just honest officials who despaired of British policy. And remember, it took the KGB twenty-three years to uncover Penkovsky. The same old inter-service rivalry. He was GRU and they saw it as a ploy against them by the KGB. They defended him for years.'

Powell stood up. 'I'd better get on my way then.'

'Can I phone Padmore and Walker?'

Powell smiled. 'If you think your phones are secure?'

'Where's your car?'

'Just down the crescent. I can see myself out.'

McNay stood looking at him. 'I've thought about the day I first persuaded him into all this and it still haunts me. He

300

*did* care about what was happening. And I've a terrible feeling that I abused another man's mind, and maybe his soul.'

Powell said softly, 'Maybe my trip will square the accounts in the end.'

McNay half-smiled. 'The omens were not that good on that day.'

'Why not?'

'We'd walked from Trinity up to St John's and we stopped on the bridge over the river. We must have stood there, talking, for almost an hour. And it was there that he finally agreed to go along with what we wanted. It wasn't until I was back in London that I remembered the name of that bridge.'

'It's St John's Bridge isn't it?'

'No. That's the next one up the river. The bridge we were on is called "The Bridge of Sighs".'

'I wonder if he remembers. I'll ask him.'

As they walked to the outer door McNay said, 'I'm relieved that it's settled at long last. It was a bad business in every way and I've always regretted the part I played in it.'

'Were you surprised that he wanted to come back?'

'No. Not at all. But I'm surprised that the KGB will let him.'

'That part worries me too.'

'Why?'

'The decoded message from "Milord" that told them that we had got to him first. Assuming that it was actually transmitted or passed on, it can only increase their suspicion as to whose side he was on.'

'I suspect that they'll be as divided as we have been down the years. Totally unfair of course on both sides.'

'Why?'

'Well, the truth is that he served both sides remarkably well. His work against the Nazis can't be ignored. We benefited from that. Moscow had their pound of flesh. And

301

yet instead of both sides valuing him for the good he did them they both chose to concentrate on what they didn't get. Most unfair.'

Powell stood at the doorway anxious to leave but aware of McNay's need to talk.

'I'll let you know when I'm leaving. It will probably be Tuesday.'

'Best of luck, Johnny. I'm sorry about all the deception but I guess you understand.'

For a moment Powell was tempted but he bit back the words. 'Of course.'

# 28

*Eyes only Sir Ian Pouley, K.C.B.*

Sir,

I have now completed my investigation into the advantages and disadvantages of agreeing to H.A.R. Philby's personal request to be allowed to return to the UK.

At an early stage the members of the 'Milord' committee made clear that whilst they were available for comment or advice the decision and recommendation would be mine alone.

It will be obvious from my age that I played no part in any of the events in the past relating to this affair. I had never met the subject of this investigation prior to my two recent meetings with him in Moscow.

No positive and irrefutable conclusion was possible because the historical facts provided could support either of the two extreme views held about Mr Philby. That has been my main difficulty throughout the investigation.

The facts and the opinions could justify any of the following theories:

(a) H.A.R. Philby was a traitor from start to finish.

(b) That he was a double-agent working for both sides.

(c) That he was a triple-agent.

The only criterion I could positively apply was to investigate the probability of theory (a). The weight of evidence is strongly against this, either as a possibility or a probability.

On theory (b) there are some grounds for considering favourably Mr Philby's request.

On theory (c) there is little doubt that Mr Philby should be allowed to return.

When considering the question of return I have taken for granted that Mr Philby would have certain conditions applied concerning incognito, place of abode, no publicity of any kind etc. etc. I have no doubt that he will accept and abide by any conditions stipulated.

There is now no doubt in my mind that H.A.R. Philby was recruited first by SIS and was ordered to make himself available to agents of the Soviet NKVD. He did this succesfully and was fed with classified information by officers of SIS to pass to his NKVD contacts. At some point he began passing additional unauthorized information to the Soviets. This arose because of his own political leanings of which SIS were aware when he was recruited. This basic misjudgement was the root of the whole situation. But there was no way for SIS to withdraw from its position. Nothing to justify any negative action could be proved. Other events, including the defection of Burgess and Maclean, intervened and the situation continued to deteriorate. From the point of the B & M defection the operation was out of control. Neither the SIS, the Soviets nor even Philby himself, knew positively their several relationships.

In the light of the above, all three parties concerned had doubts about the situation. SIS valued Philby's work and had no formal grounds for taking more than the tentative actions forced on them by the questions in the House. Their indecisiveness did no further damage beyond that point, but their pursuit of Philby in Beirut was undoubtedly the cause of his defection to Moscow. He had previously shown no signs of intending to do this despite the danger of action against him by SIS. His defection, which I consider both forced and unwilling on his part, appeared to confirm his long-term treason. The basic fact of his recruitment to penetrate the NKVD was known only to two or three SIS officers and could not be disclosed for a variety of security reasons, including Philby's own security once he was in Moscow.

The Soviets had not initiated his defection. It had no advantages for them but they accepted the situation and used it for propaganda purposes. His autobiography and the press conferences were merely his payment to the people who then controlled his life and his fate.

I conclude that though Philby has much to answer for, the most substantial responsibility lies with SIS. Even in this area it has to be said that what now appears to be a fatal misjudgement, the recruitment of a known Communist sympathizer to penetrate the NKVD, was, at the time when it was made, almost a brilliant inspiration. The proof is that it worked. Unfortunately it worked too well.

On the grounds that actions taken over forty years ago can only be judged in the framework of those times there would be no justification for refusing Mr Philby's return to the UK nor censuring those who took those actions.

I am proceeding to Moscow to negotiate Mr Philby's return and will report to you in person when I return.

J. Powell

# 29

As he handed his passport to the immigration officer he looked around for Philby, but he couldn't see him. Maybe he had been delayed. He turned back to the immigration desk. The man was using the telephone. He said something brief in Russian, listened for a moment, said '*Da, tovarich*' and hung up. He looked at Powell, still holding the passport.

'You come with me.'

He led Powell down a short corridor, knocked on a door and opened it, waving Powell inside.

A man sat at a metal table smoking a cigar. He stood up.

'Mr Powell?'

'Yes.'

'Colonel Philby sent me to pick you up. I will drive you to his apartment.'

'I need my luggage.'

The man half-smiled. 'Is in my car already.'

The man was well dressed. The light blue suit was either London or New York, and the shoes looked Italian. And he was handsome in an Italian sort of way. Brown eyes and a lot of clean white teeth when he smiled. He opened the door and waited for Powell to walk back into the corridor.

He followed the man to a side entrance where a big black Zil was parked. The man opened the passenger door, smiling.

'My name is Georgi Michailovich. Please make yourself comfortable.'

The man chatted about the Olympic games and the preparations. The weather in Moscow and London. And Margaret Thatcher. He spoke excellent English, almost without an accent, and he was obviously well-informed.

They pulled up outside Philby's apartment and the man got out, lifted out Powell's bag from the back seat, and took his arm as they moved towards the steps at the entrance to the building.

As always, the guard snapped to attention and saluted them smartly. The lift gates were already open. The Russian let himself into the apartment as if he knew it well. There was no sign of Philby.

Georgi Michailovich smiled. 'Let us have a little talk while we're waiting.'

He sat down in one of Philby's leather chairs and pointed to another. Powell sat down. And the Russian smiled his dazzling smile.

'What message do you bring for our friend?'

'I don't bring any message.'

The Russian smiled. One of those charming, Viennese operetta smiles.

'Mr Powell. I shall enjoy talking to you but there is no point in us wasting time or playing games. We know why you are here.'

'So why ask me the question?'

The Russian shrugged. 'Those are my orders.'

'From Kim?'

'Of course not. From my superiors.'

'I can't help you.'

'Your previous discussions in this room are all on tape, my friend.'

'Did Kim know that?'

Again a shrug. 'Who knows? Maybe not. But he knows how these things go.'

'When is he coming back?'

'When you and I have finished our little talk.'

The Russian slowly unknotted his white silk tie as he looked at Powell.

'You have grown fonder of our friend, yes?'

'What does that mean?'

'On the tapes you were always a bit formal. Philby or even Mr Philby. But now you speak of Kim.'

'It's of no significance, I assure you.'

'What have your people decided?'

'About what?'

'Are they willing to let him go back?'

'Why should he want to go back?'

'Who knows. Maybe to claim his reward.'

'What reward?'

'The reward for all his good work.'

'The record says that his good work was for your people.'

The Russian's eyes were hard. 'You know better than that, my friend. He was an officer of SIS.'

'That was his job. But it was a cover for working for you. He was also an officer of the KGB. He committed treason for you.'

'Oh no. Never.' And he made a cutting movement with his hand. 'Maybe he helped us but he did nothing to damage your interests.'

'Not true.'

'So tell me. Give me one example. Just one.'

'When Otto John saw him in Lisbon. He didn't report the offer. It could have shortened the war.'

'Do you know how many Russians were killed in the war?'

'No, but I know it was a lot.'

'Twenty million. Put the populations of London, Birmingham, Manchester and Glasgow together, and then imagine them dead. All of them. Men, women and children. You and the Americans would have left us fighting alone. You would have done a deal with the Germans.'

'That was highly unlikely. In any case that was for others to decide, not Philby.'

'True. But it should have been decided by those others who were doing the actual fighting. Us.'

'There were more people killed in the following nine months than in the whole war before that. Those deaths could probably have been avoided.'

The Russian shook his head. 'In your war maybe. In the real war, no. More Russians were killed than all the Americans and British forces who were ever called up for any kind of service.'

'But the treason wasn't just confined to war time.'

The Russian smiled. 'So we had the bomb a little earlier. We would have had it anyway. You spied on us, we spied on you. We still do. Both of us.'

'But you call yours traitors too.'

'Traitors to mankind.'

'You don't believe that, Georgi Michailovich. No more than I do. When you can get your hands on the dissidents you kill them. Or get the Czechs or Bulgarians to do your dirty work for you.'

'You go too far, my friend.'

'So let's wait until Philby comes.'

'You know I am KGB major?'

'No. But I assumed you were KGB.'

'Maybe you know me better from your files as Malik. Georgi Malik.'

The Russian smiled as he saw the recognition in Powell's eyes. As Philby's director in Moscow he knew that he would certainly be on the files somewhere in SIS.

'You know that name, Mr Powell?'

'Yes.'

'Are you willing to talk now?'

'No.'

309

'So maybe is best I take you back to Sheremetyevo and you go home. Nice and comfortable.'

'Are you threatening me?'

'Of course not. But you say the word and I drive you back now.'

Powell stood up. 'OK. Let's go.'

He walked to where his bag leaned against the bookshelves near the door.

As he stood up he saw the Russian's angry face. The top lip flat against his teeth like a snarling dog, and his hand reaching forward. Powell's hand clamped round the KGB man's wrist. 'Don't do that, Malik, or I'll have to hurt you.'

'My men are outside.'

'Makes no difference. I'll break your arm before they even get inside the door. And it isn't necessary.'

The Russian's arm was trembling with his effort to move it, but it might as well have been set in concrete.

'What is it you want?' Powell's voice was quiet and not aggressive.

'We wish to know about Philby.'

'What?'

'Is he yours or ours?'

'Maybe we'd like to know too.'

He released the Russian's wrist and walked back to the chair. Malik followed slowly, rubbing his wrist to bring back the circulation. He looked angry and resentful as he sat down opposite Powell.

'That was very stupid, Mr Powell.'

'It's stupid to bluff, Major. If you didn't want me to leave you shouldn't have pretended that I am free to leave.'

'That's not important.'

'What is it exactly that you want to know?'

'I told you. We want to know if he is ours or yours.'

'Why do you think he might be ours?'

'Why did you leave him in Beirut for so many years if he was a traitor?'

'Why did *you* leave him there? He was working for you as well.'

'We wanted to find out. To decide.'

'You must have decided or you wouldn't have let him go to Moscow.'

'We never decided. Your people made us take him. You pressured him.'

'How?'

'You kept contact with him. You played cat and mouse. He was not important to us but you made him important.'

'In what way?'

'You knew by then what he had done but you left him free.'

'Because we couldn't prove it.'

'Why should you prove it? You could have had him killed.'

'So could you.'

'I told you, we wanted to know. If he was still yours everything would have to be evaluated again that he had passed to us. Everything would be suspect as a plant. We *had* to know.'

'And once you had him back. What then?'

'The usual procedure. We debriefed him for almost two years. Going over every point a hundred times.'

'And?'

'And we were almost sure he was ours. But there were some. Experienced people. They still had doubts.'

'Was that why you kidnapped Otto John?'

'Of course.'

'Otto John was an anti-Nazi. One of the plotters against Hitler. You ruined his career and his life.'

'What is one man?'

311

'But you made Philby a colonel in the KGB. A Hero of the Soviet Union. A man with great privileges.'

Malik shrugged. 'A scenario.'

'But you used him as an adviser.'

'We kept him occupied. Nothing more.'

'Why do you think that he wants to go back to England?'

'We heard him say so on the tapes.'

'I didn't mean that. I mean that if he does really want to go back, what do you think are his reasons?'

'There are two views on this. Those who are on his side say he is like an elephant going back to the elephant's dying ground. Those who suspect him say that he is going back to be the returning hero. To expose us. To denounce us.'

'Nobody would believe it. He betrayed us. He said so in public, he wrote it in his book.'

'Your propaganda machine could still use it.'

'What propaganda machine?'

'The press, TV, radio, everything.'

Powell smiled. 'You know better than that, Malik. You aren't a Soviet stooge. You know what it's really like in the West.'

'There are important people who don't know. Or maybe don't choose to accept the position.'

'And which side are you on?'

Malik shook his head. 'I don't know. I really don't know. I want you to tell me.'

'You won't believe me.'

'I will. I will. Either way I shall believe you.'

'And if he was ours?'

'Then he cannot go back.'

'And if he was yours?'

'God knows. If he was ours why should he want to go back? And why would you let him go back?'

'Why have you let him go so far? You could have stopped him right at the beginning.'

'Because we needed to know the truth.'

Powell looked at the handsome face. It seemed out of place. As unreal as their conversation.

'You won't ever know, Malik.'

'They will not allow you to go back until you tell us.'

Powell snorted. 'What's it going to be? Heavy doses of pentathol. Electric clips on my testicles, or the water treatment. What had you got in mind?'

'I am not joking, Mr Powell.'

'Neither am I. I'm in the business. I've seen enough of your defectors' reports to know how you interrogate in the Lubyanka.'

'You think we will not do that?'

'I'm sure you won't.'

'Why do you think that?'

'You're not stupid, Malik. Your superiors are not stupid. If I knew the answer to your question I shouldn't be here in Moscow. If we knew he was yours we should let him rot. If we knew for certain that he was ours there would have been no discussions with him in Moscow. We should have got him back. He would have been debriefed to treble-check if you were playing games, but he would have been back weeks ago.'

'What does that mean?'

'It means that we don't know either. Neither does Philby. You can put him in the Lubyanka and give him the treatment. He won't be able to answer you because he doesn't know.'

'I can't believe that.'

'You can. You do believe it. You already know it. But you're all bureaucrats, you want tidy answers to tidy questions. Yes or no.'

'What did your people say?'

Powell hesitated for a moment, then, 'We were prepared to have him back.'

'Why?'

'A lot of people thought he had been badly treated. He wasn't really that important. He wasn't a master-spy. It was Maclean who mattered, wasn't it?'

Malik nodded. 'For us it was Maclean. We had no doubts about Maclean. He was ours right from the start.'

'What about Burgess?'

Malik smiled. 'Can you imagine what it was like with Burgess in Moscow?'

Powell smiled. 'It must have been quite a performance.'

The KGB man lit a cigar and blew out the match. As he tossed the used match into the glass ashtray he looked up at Powell's face.

'I'll have to talk with my people, you realize that?' He looked at the cigar. 'Would he be prosecuted if he returned?'

'It's very unlikely. Let's not kid ourselves, Malik. We're letting him come back to die. Nothing more. He may deserve it, he may not. We're just giving him the benefit of the doubt. There will be no announcement and no publicity. He'll come back incognito and stay that way.'

'I'll have to ask you to sleep here tonight.'

'Where is Philby?'

'At his *dacha*.'

'Does he know that I'm here?'

'Yes. But he had no choice. He was sent out of Moscow until this is settled.'

'Am I free to go out?'

'No. I'm afraid not. There is a special security squad on the building.'

'How long will you take?'

'One day. No more. We need to clear it up once and for all. It's becoming an obsession.' He stood up, straightened his jacket. 'There's food in the refrigerator. I'll see you

314

tomorrow. Probably in the afternoon. The telephone is not working.'

The Russian walked slowly to the door as if he were thinking. He stopped and turned.

'If you want a girl for tonight there's no problem.' He half-smiled. 'There are no hidden cameras.'

Powell smiled. 'Girls aren't blackmail material anymore, Georgi. But thanks. I'll survive on my own.'

'*Da svedanya.*'

'*Da svedanya.*'

In the small kitchen he cut himself a slice or two of salami and a piece of black bread. It seemed strange to be alone in Philby's flat. He walked out into the sitting room, a cup of coffee in his hand from the flask.

He stood looking at the books on the shelves. Many of them were in Russian, and most of the English titles were textbooks on Soviet affairs, history and biographies. There were paperback copies of P. G. Wodehouse, a few anthologies of English poetry, Dos Passos's *USA*, books about Philby himself in several languages, and half a dozen foreign language dictionaries. There was an old copy of Wisden, several cricketers' autobiographies, two bound copies of *Punch* for 1928 and 1939, Roget's *Thesaurus*, and out-of-date Fodor guides to the USA and England. And on a pile of magazines was a copy of Richard Deacon's banned *The British Connection.* He picked it up and glanced slowly through the pages. There were notes and comments scrawled in the margins.

He set his small travel alarm clock for eight o'clock and went into the bedroom. He was in bed when his curiosity overcame him and he walked silently to the outer door and slowly turned the big brass knob. It was locked.

It was nearly nine o'clock when he was shaken awake. Not

315

roughly, but urgently. It was Malik, his face drawn and haggard as if he had been up all night.

'Pack your bag, Mr Powell. And I take you to the airport.'

'What's going on, Malik. What's the hurry?'

The Russian shook his head, angrily.

'I cannot discuss. Just get dressed please, quickly.'

'What about Philby?'

'I have orders, comrade. I cannot discuss.'

Powell dressed and washed his face, but the Russian insisted that there was no time for him to shave. He stood watching, impatient and tense.

There were four or five uniformed men in the corridor and more in the foyer. There was a Red Army driver in the car.

Malik sat silent all the way to the airport, his eyes closed, his mouth grim. He too was unshaven.

At the airport the KGB man carried his bag and escorted him to an office marked 'Administrator'. It was empty, but there was an envelope on the desk. The Russian glanced at it and tore it open. He checked the documents carefully and then handed them to Powell.

'Your tickets. Aeroflot to Amsterdam. Then you fly KLM to Heathrow.'

Powell took the tickets and Malik said, 'I take you direct to the aircraft.'

As they walked across the tarmac Powell said, 'What's going on, Georgi?'

Malik sighed and shrugged. 'I can't say. I did not succeed.'

The Russian saw him to his seat in the aircraft. The plane was half empty, and as he left Malik spoke to the steward, then turned and nodded briefly to Powell before he headed towards the open door and the trolley steps.

It was a slow flight to Amsterdam and his flight to Heathrow was not until eight o'clock in the evening.

He hired one of the small rest rooms and shaved and changed his shirt. He checked the British Embassy number in The Hague, and an Answerphone suggested that if his business was urgent he should contact the consulate. It was Saturday afternoon. The public telephones would be insecure.

He bought a paperback from the bookstall, a kilo of the best Dutch asparagus and a small bottle of Madame Rochas for Vanessa. Fifteen minutes later he was asleep on the small bed, and he slept until just after five. He ate in the airport restaurant and just over an hour after he had finished his coffee his flight was called. He started working out in his mind the best way of getting Philby out of Moscow. It would have to be through Berlin or Warsaw. Or maybe somewhere on the Baltic coast.

They had been airborne for ten minutes when the pilot announced that owing to landing problems at Heathrow the plane would be landing at Gatwick where rail transport to London would be available and at the airline's expense.

At Gatwick he phoned the flat. There was no answer so he went straight to the train.

It was raining by the time he left the station at Victoria but he stopped at the side entrance and bought the final editions of both evening papers. The flat was too near to waste time queuing for a taxi so he walked.

It was 10.15, but the relief of being back in London after the grimness of Moscow had smoothed away his tiredness.

There was no light on upstairs in the flat windows and he walked up the stairs and let himself in. She was probably with her parents.

He walked through to their bedroom, dumped his bag and went back into the sitting room. He took off his jacket, then went back into the bedroom and picked up the two evening papers. As he tossed the *Evening News* on to the coffee table he saw an envelope and a small parcel.

317

The envelope was addressed to him and he opened it. It was in Vanessa's big scrawl. He read it very slowly.

Dearest Johnny,

When I had done something stupid and was beating round the bush to tell you, you used to interrupt me and smile and say, 'Get to the part where you've sold the grand-piano'. So that's what I'm doing now.

I've gone back to Ralph to try and make a 'go' of it again. I've seen him a couple of times with Lydia and we talked about it. I think we've both learned some of the lessons. I know you'll understand if I say I am happy. To have a home, a family again, and to see Lydia every day is so wonderful I can't really believe it yet.

Ralph said you would understand. He seems to have taken a shine to you. He's ordered a special rod for you from Hardy's. You should get it in about two weeks' time.

I think this is the only letter that I've ever written to you, and what I've written isn't really what I want to say. And what I want to say I don't know how to write.

I suppose I shouldn't say any more that I love you, but I do. I think of you when I'm with Lydia. It feels somehow right, what I've done, but despite that I know it's not fair. You cared for me when I was down and out, and somehow I wish it was OK for you to live with us. I know that's not possible and silly, but I do think it.

Please understand dear Johnny, and thanks for all you've done for me.
      Van.

He sat for a few moments, perfectly still, and then he stood up and walked slowly into the kitchen. He made himself a cup of coffee and went back to his chair. He picked up the parcel and tore off the wrapping paper. It was a leather-bound copy of Palgrave's *Golden Treasury*. On the fly-leaf was written – 'To dearest Johnny, with love, Van.' He put